Pretend it's Forever

THE CAGE FAMILY
BOOK FIVE

CARRIE ANN RYAN

the cage family

Pretend It's Forever

CARRIE ANN
RYAN

NEW YORK TIMES BESTSELLING AUTHOR

Pretend it's Forever

Pretend it's Forever
A Cage Family Prequel
By: Carrie Ann Ryan

Cover Arts by Sweet N Spicy Designs and Wildheart Designs.

All content warnings are listed on the book page for this book on my website.

Praise for Carrie Ann Ryan

"Count on Carrie Ann Ryan for emotional, sexy, character driven stories that capture your heart!" – Carly Phillips, NY Times bestselling author

"Carrie Ann Ryan's romances are my newest addiction! The emotion in her books captures me from the very beginning. The hope and healing hold me close until the end. These love stories will simply sweep you away." ~ NYT Bestselling Author Deveny Perry

"Carrie Ann Ryan writes the perfect balance of sweet and heat ensuring every story feeds the soul." - Audrey Carlan, #1 New York Times Bestselling Author

"Carrie Ann Ryan never fails to draw readers in with passion, raw sensuality, and characters that pop off the page. Any book by Carrie Ann is an absolute treat." – New York Times Bestselling Author J. Kenner

"Carrie Ann Ryan knows how to pull your heartstrings and make your pulse pound! Her wonderful Redwood Pack series will draw you in and keep you reading long into the night. I can't wait to see what comes next with the new generation, the Talons. Keep them coming, Carrie Ann!" –Lara Adrian, New York Times bestselling author of CRAVE THE NIGHT

"With snarky humor, sizzling love scenes, and brilliant, imaginative worldbuilding, The Dante's Circle series reads as if Carrie Ann Ryan peeked at my personal wish list!" – NYT Bestselling Author, Larissa Ione

"Carrie Ann Ryan writes sexy shifters in a world full of passionate happily-ever-afters." – *New York Times* Bestselling Author Vivian Arend

"Carrie Ann's books are sexy with characters you can't help but love from page one. They are heat and heart blended to perfection." *New York Times* Bestselling Author Jayne Rylon

Carrie Ann Ryan's books are wickedly funny and deliciously hot, with plenty of twists to keep you guessing. They'll keep you up all night!" USA Today Bestselling Author Cari Quinn

"Once again, Carrie Ann Ryan knocks the Dante's Circle series out of the park. The queen of hot, sexy, enthralling paranormal romance, Carrie Ann is an author not to miss!" *New York Times* bestselling Author Marie Harte

For those who fought.
For those who are fighting.
You are worth more than they told you.
You are worth everything.
I see you.
We see you.

The Cages

The Denver Cages:

Aston

Flynn (t)

Hudson (t)

Dorian

James

Theo

Ford

The Colorado Springs Cages:

Isabella

Sophia

Kyler

Emily

Phoebe

The Cages in Age Order:

Aston

Flynn

Hudson

Dorian

Isabella

James

Theo

Sophia

Kyler

Ford

Emily

Phoebe

Prologue

SOPHIA

LEG EXTENDED, I LEANED INTO THE STRETCH, MY joints aching for more than one reason today. But the world didn't need to know why. I let out a breath and sank deeper into the stretch, before moving out of the angle and deepening my breath so I could continue my movement.

It had been a long day of classes, the twins needing a thousand things, and just exhaustion in the head. School had just finished, and that meant that everybody's priorities were shifting. Oh, many students would come back for their favorite classes, and continue on during the summer, but others wouldn't return until the fall semester.

Some of my middle schoolers would begin the path toward advanced classes, and even private tutoring. While

I was no longer a principal ballet dancer for the Denver Ballet, I still danced to my heart's content as much as possible.

So I didn't have as much time as I once had.

But that made sense. I was a mom of two, owned my own business, and was doing my best to make my marriage work.

I rubbed my temples, telling myself that it *was* working.

Yes I made a few mistakes here and there, but those couldn't be helped. I wasn't the sweet, affable Sophia that Cale had married so few years ago. I was no longer dancing full time, or in the same shape I had once been. I had let myself go when the babies had come, and was working on strengthening everything that I could. It's what Cale needed from me. He worked long hours and went on countless business trips to provide for our family.

When we had gotten together, I'd had a decent savings from my time dancing, but it wasn't until my father's will had been read that I'd been able to be financially solvent enough to find balance in everything that we'd wanted.

But that was okay. We were learning this new life of ours.

I did a few of the moves, letting the music sing its way through my bones. I loved dancing. Ever since I had been a little girl, I had tried to stand on my toes, plié, and jeté. I wanted to be the graceful dancer in a skirt and tutu, gliding and flying over the dance floor as if I could walk on air.

I had been blessed in my career and had gone out on top. I still danced with a local troupe, one filled with retired dancers who no longer wanted to dance professionally but still had the bug.

I couldn't join often these days, not with the twins at home and a husband who needed to be looked after, but I did my best. Besides my family, dance was the one thing that could truly be mine.

I smiled at myself, letting one final move take me, before bending down for my towel to dry off the sweat.

I needed to shower, get presentable, and then head home so I could feed the girls and get ready for dinner. Cale had been out of town for the past week. He'd had a tough trip, with his bags being lost on the way there and having to change hotel rooms halfway through, so I knew he would be excited to get home and see me and the twins.

My lips curved into a smile as I thought about our babies.

I never thought I would be a mom. It wasn't that it had been a definite no, it was that my priorities had shifted. I had only worked towards being a dancer. My sister Isabella, as well as my mother, had done everything they could to ensure that I had the childhood I needed in order to find balance. I had been competitive and determined. Much like my brother Kyler, we had gone into the arts and never turned back. Kyler was still out on a world tour, and had just won yet another Grammy, because of course he did. I couldn't wait until my little brother came back to visit, but until then, I would be the artist at home. Even if I didn't do it professionally anymore.

Violet and Hazel, however, had changed my life. They were my babies, my darlings, and were somehow, over two years old. They were little people now, rather than infants, who were developing their tiny personalities. And they were changing day by day.

I knew Cale missed spending as much time with them as he wanted to. He was always on the road, doing what he could for his companies, and that meant he missed out on a few firsts.

I rubbed my shoulder, an odd pain that I pushed back. But he would see other firsts, and as soon as we finished with the next step of my father's will, Cale said he would pause and take more time to be with the family. After all, we would have more money now, thanks to my philanderer of a father.

I pressed my lips together, doing my best not to think about that. I had loved my father as a little girl. He had doted on me and called me his little princess. And then he had ignored me so he could focus on his business, and his other family.

I hadn't neglected naming him in my thoughts when I had imagined who had helped me push myself to where I was today. My father's ambitions might not mirror my own, but he had similar determination. And that had been pretty much the only similar things about us.

But he was dead, his secrets long buried, and now thanks to my brothers and sisters who actually knew what they were doing when it came to business, Cale and I would be far more comfortable in our financial standings, and we would be able to breathe more.

Cale wouldn't have to work as hard, and I would be able to spend more time at home with the girls, just like he wanted me to.

I rolled my shoulders back and headed to the small shower area that I'd had added to the office space above my dance studio.

I did not like traveling covered in sweat, and Cale hated when I came home looking like I had drenched myself in a pool. So it was best all around if I did my hair and makeup and got ready for the evening while still at the office. I checked my watch and winced. I had danced on my own a little bit too long, and the sixteen-year-old girl I was privately tutoring had been on such a roll, that we had gone overtime. Her parents had been thrilled, but now I was a little behind.

I showered as quickly as I could and thanked the goddess that Kyler had gotten me this fancy blow-dryer for Christmas. My thick hair could sometimes take nearly an hour to dry, even with the best blow dryers out there, so I was grateful that now it wouldn't take as long.

Minutes later, I was as ready as I was going to be, but I still put my hair back in a low ponytail.

I dabbed some concealer over the bruise on my jaw and ignored the ache.

I had hit my face on the floor when I had fallen, but it was a hazard of the job.

I met my gaze once more, the shadows there no longer surprising me. No, I was fine. Everything was fine.

I grabbed my things and headed out to my car after locking up. If I hurried, I would make it home to relieve the nanny before Cale got there. Neither one of us liked having a nanny, even part-time, but the girls were too big for me to wear them both while at the dance studio. And it wasn't like Cale could bring them into a business meeting. He was a very important person in his job.

A small part of me wondered exactly where those voices had come from. Or why I was even saying them. It didn't sound like me.

But I pushed those away because the more I dug into them, the harder it would be for everyone. If I just gave in a little bit, it would be easier. And soon we would both be home more, and it wouldn't be like this.

Everything was just fine and working how it should. My hands fisted on the steering wheel as I turned into my driveway and pulled into the garage.

Everything had to be fine.

I turned off the engine and grabbed my bag.

When I walked in, the sound of little girls screaming hit my ears, and I paused, realizing Cale's luggage was in the front foyer, and I had failed to realize that the nanny's car hadn't been parked in front of the house.

It was late.

This wasn't going to be good.

No, it was going to be just fine. Cale would understand. He always did.

I set my bag down next to his and walked into the living room. Cale stood in the kitchen, facing the window, a glass of whiskey in his hands. Both Violet and Hazel were in their playtime pen, their heads thrown back as they screamed. Their little faces were red, their hands fisted at their sides, and I moved quickly towards them, heart thudding.

"What's wrong, little girls? Your daddy's home. You should be happy."

Hazel launched herself at me, and I caught her before reaching down and pulling Violet into my arms. I kissed the tops of both of their heads and swayed back and forth.

"They're crying because their mother wasn't here like she promised."

I swallowed hard, rocking my baby girls as they quieted down.

"I must have lost track of time. But it's so good to see you home."

I turned, so focused on the babies I had missed him moving closer.

The blow caught me off guard, the back of his hand slamming into my cheek. I staggered back, one step, two, until I was falling. Horror rocked through me as I tried to maneuver so I would fall on my back, or even on my side, doing anything to protect my babies.

Hazel and Violet had both quieted down, but were now screaming in my ears, and yet everything moved so slow.

My butt hit the ground first, and the momentum pushed me back, the back of my head slamming into our hardwood floor.

Stars shot from beneath my eyelids and blood coated my mouth. I had bitten my tongue, and tears stung my eyes.

I sat up quickly, ignoring the nausea, as I looked down at my baby girls.

"Mommy okay??"

"Mommy tripped, girls."

Cale moved forward, as if to reach for them, and I turned, moving so they were both behind me.

"I've got it. Don't touch them," I snapped.

My voice chilled, and Cale just looked at me, tilting his

head. One blond lock fell over his gaze, and he smirked at me.

"Excuse me?"

"Don't touch them. I didn't fall." Words tumbled out of my mouth, and I realized if I didn't say them, I wouldn't ever.

Who was this person? The one who had cowered, and would have most likely leaned into the idea that I had tripped.

But he had nearly hurt my babies. And I would never allow that to happen.

I ignored the thoughts that whispered to me that I had already done so by staying. By trying.

"Don't be so melodramatic."

The girls crawled behind me, and I stood up, still woozy.

"Don't touch me. Or my girls."

"*Our* girls. You forget that I'm the father, don't you? Or were you spreading your legs for someone else."

I blinked, wondering exactly how many drinks he'd had before this. And when exactly had I allowed his venom to pierce me.

"Get out. Just get out."

"Why? Why should I leave when it's my house? Oh wait, it's not. Your family money helped us with the down payment, didn't it? I'm the useless one who has to sleep with his wife in order to gain anything. Is that what your family thinks? Why they allow me to be in their presence? The beautiful and brilliant and billionaire Cages. They don't care who they step on to get where they are. You're nothing. You're the left behind Cage that's getting the scraps. Why the fuck do you think I've stayed this long? Because those scraps are worth far more than you. And they'll be mine soon. So don't find your damn spine now. You know you'll fall at my feet whenever you remember exactly what I can do to you, or exactly what I would do to take your kids. Because those girls are half mine. Remember?"

"Get out." I knew there was more I needed to say to stand up for myself. But it was all I could do to try to put any distance between him and the girls.

I had known that Cale was changing. That the shadows that had coated him had long since fallen away. My family hadn't found out, and I'd done my best not to let them see too closely, but I was failing.

I had failed my babies, failed my girls. And I wasn't going to let it happen again.

Hazel moved forward, past my legs, and towards him, and when Cale smirked, reaching for her, I pushed out, slamming my palms into his chest.

"Don't touch her."

"You think you can hurt me?" Cale snapped out before he fisted his hand and punched me in the face.

I fell back, both girls screamed their little hearts out, and Cale hovered over me.

"You're going to clean up this mess, put the girls to bed, and make dinner. And then you're going to remember that you're my wife. The only Cage we need is the one that will help us sustain where we need to be in society. But you are *mine*. Remember that. You might not have taken my name because you wanted to show that you were a part of your precious fractured family, but I'm the one that let you do that. I *own* you. Just like I own these little girls. I'm tired of pretending to be the weak one in your family so they feel better about themselves. Remember *exactly* who I am."

I tried to crawl away, to cover both girls with my body, but Cale just sighed, grabbed my ankle, and pulled.

A scream ripped out of my throat as I scrambled to get away from him, but I had forgotten how strong Cale was.

"Are you really going to make me do this the hard way?" With a sigh, he leaned down and punched me again.

Darkness welled over me, and I tried to shift. Everything moved as if I was in a fog. I reached out, trying to grasp anything, but it was too late. Everything was just too late.

There were a few whispers, and the babies crying, but I couldn't do a damn thing.

"Come on, girls. You're coming with me."

I tried to scream, tried to wake up, but there was nothing.

Hot breath coated my face, and my eyes were forced open.

"You're spending too much time away. You don't remember your place. So I'm going to have to ensure you always remember."

My eyes widened, clarity sliding through me as I looked for my babies but couldn't find them.

And then Cale was in front of me again, the baseball bat that was always in the front closet in his hand.

I screamed, trying to scramble away, but I was too slow. The first break made my eyes roll to the back of my head as nausea swept over me.

And then he hit me a second time, and I knew I would never dance again.

Unconsciousness took me under once more, and all I could think about were my babies.

"Please don't take my babies."

"Sophia? Oh my God."

"What the fuck do you think you're doing?"

The first voice had been familiar, but I didn't know the second.

One of my eyes was swollen, but I still could crack open the other.

My brother. Flynn was here. Horror etched on his face as he touched my cheek, but I had to warn him.

"Cale," I rasped.

"It's okay. The cops are on their way."

"Babies. Girls." Why couldn't I talk? Why couldn't I say what I needed to?

"Carson took care of Flynn. And he's getting the girls. The girls are safe. You're going to be okay," Flynn whispered, though his voice cracked.

I didn't know who this Carson was, and I didn't trust him with my babies. I didn't trust anyone.

But then Flynn was holding me, and a man with dark hair moved forward, both of my girls in his arms.

And they weren't crying.

He had his hands underneath them and was whispering something about not looking.

And I was grateful.

My babies were safe.

But Cale would take them.

"Cale's not going to take them. He's tied up. And the cops are right here. Stay with me, Sophia. Stay with me."

I tried to fight. Tried to stay awake for Hazel and Violet.

And I met the gaze of that stranger, those green eyes piercing.

"Stay awake," the stranger ordered, and tears slid out of my single working eye.

"I'm going to go let the cops in. I'll be right back,"

Flynn said, and then he was moving, and nothing made sense.

I couldn't breathe, could barely think.

But my girls were safe, and not crying while they sat in a stranger's arms.

And I wasn't sure what else there was to say.

"I'M GOING TO KILL HIM," ASTON SNAPPED. "KILL him."

"Aston, be quiet."

"Funny you're saying that, Isabella, when you're the one that shouted earlier and nearly got us all kicked out," Aston growled.

They were speaking so quickly, and it was hard to catch up, but this wasn't the first time that I had been awake since coming to the hospital.

"I'm okay," I said after a moment, and everyone stopped speaking and shouting at each other to stare at me.

"Sophia," Isabella whispered, and I swallowed the lump in my throat.

"The girls?" I asked.

"Blakely has them."

"Okay. Okay." Tears threatened again.

"Cale's in custody. We'll make sure he stays there,"

Flynn warned, his gaze intense. Flynn was always the smiling brother, the laughing one. I'd never seen him so serious. But then again sometimes it felt like I was just getting to know my brothers.

And I didn't want them to know me like this.

"I'm sorry," I whispered.

"It's okay, don't be sorry. Everything's going to be okay." Isabella reached out as if to cup my cheek, and I flinched.

I wanted to crawl in a hole and die at the pitying look on her face. But I wouldn't. I had already failed Violet and Hazel before, and I wouldn't do it again.

Unconsciousness swept over me once more. By the time I woke up, there was only one man in the room, and for an instant I thought it was Cale. But I recognized those green eyes.

"Who are you?" I asked, my voice hoarse.

The stranger moved forward, grabbed the pitcher of water, and poured a glass. When he gestured for me to take it from his hands, I forced myself to sit up slightly, and nodded in thanks, ignoring the pain in my head.

"I heard you say you were sorry earlier. You don't get to say that again. You understand me?"

I frowned, ignoring the tug of the stitches on my forehead.

"I know you don't know me from Adam, and that's fine. But your family's going to be back in here hovering, because that's what they do. So you're going to let them because I have a feeling that's what you do. And maybe that's what you need. But don't apologize. I'm the one that needs to apologize."

"I don't even know you."

His lips quirked into a smile that didn't reach his eyes. "No, you wouldn't. That's fine."

"Then why are you apologizing?"

"Because I didn't kill the bastard when I had a chance. Get well, Sophia Cage. Those little girls are too cute for words. And they're going to need their mom."

And with that, he walked out, leaving me just as confused as ever.

But he was right.

My little girls did need their mom.

And that meant I needed to figure out exactly who Sophia Cage was. Broken, lost, and shattered as she was.

Chapter One

SOPHIA

ONE YEAR LATER.

Tiny dancers swirled along the floor, the glossy wood shining underneath the soft steps of the little slippered feet. Giggles filled the room and I smiled, watching my past blend with my present, knowing there couldn't be a future.

With a frown, I pushed those thoughts from my mind. Today was about *joy*. Today was about teaching.

Today wasn't about what could have been. Those thoughts had no place here within the soft laughter and eager learning.

To pretend otherwise would be to forever lie within misery, wondering when one could find peace. And I wasn't about to find that kind of peace.

"Ms. Cage! Ms. Cage! Do you like my dress?" Meredith asked as she twirled towards me, nearly tripping over her own ballerina shoes.

I moved forward quickly and held her shoulder, keeping her upright. She had more energy than a few children put together, and I adored her.

I knelt down to be at eye level, ignoring the twinge in my knee and sharp pain in my hip. The reminders of that evening would forever be within my body, scarred on my soul, but I wouldn't let these children know. "I love your dress. You look beautiful."

"Thank you." She preened. "You're always beautiful. Will you dance for us later?" the eight-year-old asked, and I heard a few of the parents whisper beneath their breath, and I ignored them.

Instead, I looked over at my eager students and nodded. "If we have time, I will at the end, something small. Only because you have all done such a good job today. If we can't today, I will make sure it's scheduled for next time. Now, let's work on our turns, because our recital is coming up."

"I'm nervous," another student said as she came forward, and a few others nodded, their eyes wide.

This would be their first ballet recital as a class, as we had started a new year, and I was nervous right along with them. However, nerves were how I succeeded in my life. Or at least, how I had once succeeded in my job.

As long as I lived, breathed, and knew my soul could withstand the truth, I would always be a dancer. No matter how long it took for me to stretch these days, or the idea that I couldn't put all my weight on the same leg as I once had, or the fact that I was no longer a principal dancer at the Denver Ballet, I would continue to be a dancer at heart. Just like many of these little girls were.

My other classes had a mixture of boys and girls within the class, but this particular one just happened to be filled with only little girls. I hoped that soon, more boys would sign up and attend and had great hopes that they would.

Everybody was welcome to dance here, and between myself and the two instructors I had hired, the studio went from toddler age all the way to high school. I had a few college-age students as well, ones that were more one-on-one to prepare them for auditions, and other things, but for the moment I didn't have anything beyond that. I once had. I once had been sought after even at my age.

But those dreams had been crushed along with so many other parts of my body.

I swallowed hard, rolled my shoulders back, and reminded myself that I was Sophia Cage. And I could do anything. I might not have been born a Cage precisely, but I had taken the name of my family when the worst had happened.

"Okay, girls, plie."

I began the next section of the dance. And corrected when needed, praised when warranted—and since I wasn't the cool teacher that I'd once had, or even the far more strict ones, there were always ways to find praise.

By the end of class, I was grateful that we had run over, but I ignored the guilt from that. "Next time. Next time I promise I will show you a little bit of your performance on my own. I promise," I reiterated. The girls clapped, while some of the parents gave each other knowing looks. I ignored that.

After the *incident*, I had lost a few of my favorite students. They had needed an instructor who could perform right alongside them, and someone who hadn't lost the strength that I had in my dominant leg.

It had taken me a year to get to this point in my life, where I could put on tights and do small parts around the studio, but I would never be again.

Not after I had trusted the wrong person.

"Oh, Sophia," Margaret Sayer, one of the moms shouted as she came forward, hand out-stretched. She'd pulled her strawberry blonde curls into a cute bun and looked far more put together than I felt. "I wanted to talk to you a few moments before you head to your next class. Do you mind?" she asked, her eyes boring holes into me. My leg ached, and my wrist wasn't doing any better, and all I wanted to do was sit down and drink some water before I had to do my next class, but I wasn't about to show any form of weakness in front of these people.

Not all dance moms were overbearing and pushy—my mother certainly hadn't been. But my mother came with all of her own issues. Hence why I was trying to change the narrative when it came to my daughters, and how I taught.

"Of course, Margaret. How can I help you?"

"We're just curious about a few things." She smiled as she said it, and I tried my best not to stiffen, knowing it was probably something I wouldn't like.

Three other moms had joined her in not saying a thing. Margaret was the ringleader after all.

"Of course."

"I know when you named the studio a few years ago with the name Cage attached, it had to do with the family dynamics and the fact that Cages do sell. After all, the family is a billion-dollar business."

They smiled so hard, my resulting look made the back of my teeth felt like they were grinding together. "I figured having too many names on the door front would cost too much for all of the detailing. So I went with the shortest name." I looked off to the side as I said it, knowing that it was a lie.

I went with Cage for many reasons, but they didn't need to know about all of them. A few years ago, my world had altered completely. I held back an internal sigh at that. My world had been irrevocably changed multiple times over the past few years, but I didn't owe those reasons to anyone else but myself.

"So you're keeping the name Cage?" one of the other moms asked, and for the life of me, I could not think of her name. Her daughter Molly was adorable but didn't want to be in class. She would rather be on the ice rink, full pads, and trying to be a left wing in hockey like her brother. But Molly's mother wanted nothing to do with that. I knew of someone who still played for the NHL, as well as another person that played for the PWHL, so I already had a plan concocted to bring them in to talk with a few of my classes and the parents. It might be a little sneaky, but I didn't want to squash anybody's dreams.

I had been lucky enough to live mine for as long as I had.

"You mean Cage on the business? Of course. You do know the Cages. We tend to put our name on everything."

"So you're sticking with the name Cage as your last name. That's what I meant," the woman answered. Eliza. Elizabeth? What the hell was her name?

"Excuse me?" I asked, blinking, a little confused.

"You changed your name. And I hear you also changed your little girls' names. That was pretty quick for the courts, don't you think?"

I stiffened visibly at that, and I saw the gleam in their eyes. They had wanted my reaction, and they weren't going to get all of it. Because part of me wanted to lash out, to show them exactly what had been left behind in the ashes of my marriage and my dreams, but then I would end up in jail where Cale wasn't, and my little girls would be without me.

"I am a Cage. And I always have been. And if that's all, I need to get ready for my next class."

As they hadn't gotten what they wanted, they made a few excuses and walked away, as if they hadn't just tried to break me.

I would never understand women like that. We lived in a world where it wasn't easy to breathe as a woman. I had my privileges beyond most, so many of them, but I still had to deal with not being in a seemingly woman led field, and never being enough for anyone.

I didn't know any of those women's backstories. For all I knew, they were going through their own hells and lashing out because it was easier than breathing and facing it, but I wasn't going to be one of them. I didn't need to push them down just because I was hurting.

I rubbed my leg, grateful I had another half hour before my class.

I made my way to my office and sat down, resting my leg up on the chair next to me.

The sound of relief that escaped me probably should have been embarrassing, but thankfully I was alone for the time being, as my other instructors were off for the day.

It hadn't always been like this. The dance studio had been a pinnacle of my dreams, something I put my heart and soul into. I had painted most of the walls, with my family helping finish what I couldn't. Soft colors in some rooms, and bold in others. I didn't want to wash out the imagination and emotions that came with dance. I wanted to bleed into it in body and soul, and I had put everything into this place.

And Cale had tried to take it away.

I sighed and rubbed my temples.

The divorce hadn't been easy.

As I had never filed a police report, never thinking I'd need one, the single attack in which Cale had broken my leg, ensuring I would never dance again, and beat me to the point that I still didn't remember most of the next week, had been his only flaw according to his lawyer. I had enraged him, cheated on him, and he'd snapped. It was a moment of weakness, he had said.

And the male judge, and the male lawyers, and everyone else around them that perpetuated that lie, had given Cale a slap on the wrist.

He had gone to anger management classes but hadn't been able to contest the divorce fully.

Paperwork had been pushed through, and I was no longer married to that man.

Cale had tried to take some of the Cage money along

the way, but my brothers and lawyers were stronger than the attorney.

He had tried to take my business, and I'd nearly given it all to him. He'd taken half of the building, half of my savings, and half of my life—anything in order to keep custody of my baby girls—the twins he didn't love because they were not boys, and were too needy for him.

But my brothers and sisters had helped there too, using the family name and money to keep Cale away.

The courts had failed us though. Just like they failed so many people.

I had a measly restraining order, as if a piece of paper could keep Cale far from me and my family. I had a divorce, and was able to change my name to Cage, as well as my little girls' names. But that was it.

Cale was able to visit once a month if he wanted. Could take them for a whole weekend, and he could continue to fight for custody.

He didn't get jail time. Probation and anger management. That was it. As if nearly killing me—and it *had* been attempted murder—wasn't enough to justify time behind bars.

And Cale would continue to fight for custody, not because he wanted the girls, not because he wanted my business, but because he wanted to see me fail.

He had married me because he had wanted the Cage money—something that had been new to me at the time

—and hadn't touched it. He'd taken half of my life, but not the Cage family dynasty. That was the difference.

I had been a principal dancer for the Denver Ballet for long enough, and had made enough investments, that I'd been well off on my own without touching the Cage money. But Cale had wanted more. And he tried to break me open as if I could give him anything more than what I had within my soul.

I let out a breath, tried to push him from my mind.

He didn't matter now. My girls were with their nanny, and would be with my mother after that. I needed to work to keep this place open, and to ensure my girls had a future.

And I couldn't focus on what their father wanted.

I hadn't been born a Cage. Not truly. Cage had been my middle name, as it was for the rest of my full siblings.

Our father had been in and out of our house, seemingly on work trips, but we hadn't known that he hadn't truly been married to our mother. Hadn't known that he'd had a secret family.

Suddenly, my family of five children was a family of twelve. Twelve children over two families, with two women. Two women who had known and had covered up his secrets and mistakes so they could have some part of him.

I knew my brothers' mother, Melanie, had stayed with him for money—at least that's what they'd told me. But my mother, Constance Cage Dixon, had stayed for love. A twisted love that I would never understand and wanted no part of.

And after my father had died, and we found out at the will reading that we weren't alone, the Cages had grown in notoriety, but connections had solidified in strength.

Our father had wanted us to fight with one another, clawing for the inheritance. The will and his greed even forced us to have meals together once a month in a show of theatre. Instead, it had brought us closer together, and sometimes I forgot that I hadn't grown up with the majority of my brothers.

So when I wanted to change my name after the divorce, I had taken away the strings that had tied me to a past I wanted no part of. And I wanted my girls to have a true family.

Dixon was my mother's name, and while I was slowly finding common ground with my mother, I would never understand her choices, and while I didn't respect or even like my father, may God rest his soul, I loved and respected the others with the Cage name.

So I was now fully a Cage, as were my girls, and since my family tended to slap their names on everything, including the small town they owned, me having a dance studio with the same name just made sense.

I once again did my best to ignore all of the trappings of the complications of my past, and went to my next dance class, this one with twelve- to thirteen-year-olds. I couldn't help but smile at their glee and the concentration on their faces.

I ignored the pain in my leg and went back to dancing.

I knew my mother was worried about me, as were my sisters and brothers. I had been ignoring their texts all day, as all they did was check on me and ensure that I wasn't working too hard.

I scrunched my nose, played with the new septum ring there, and smiled. Ballerina princesses did not have tattoos and septum rings, but I did. I wanted them, and I wanted more.

I was trying to figure out who I was now, as a single mom, and one who had dance in her heart, but wasn't able to dance a whole song without falling in pain.

By the end of class, I was a sweaty mess, and the kids were ecstatic. We were getting ready for our next ballet, and I was so excited. It was summer, and that meant no Nutcracker around here.

I went to my office bathroom and quickly washed up, knowing I needed to be ready after lunch. The harder classes would be then, and I honestly couldn't wait.

"Knock, knock," a familiar voice said from the doorway, and I whirled and put my hand on my chest, grateful I hadn't screamed. I could feel the blood slowly sliding from my face, and Flynn cursed under his breath before moving towards me slowly.

"I'm sorry, Sophia. I didn't mean to scare you. Fuck. Are you okay?"

I smiled, blinking and hating the nerves that constantly ran through me these days. I was not weak. I wasn't going to be jumping around every corner. "I was just startled. It's good to see you, Flynn."

Flynn was technically my half-brother, and one of my favorite people in the world. He and his twin Hudson were the second oldest of the twelve while I was technically the eighth oldest. Which was ridiculous in retrospect, because I was technically the second oldest in my half of the family. But suddenly I had far too many older brothers, and two younger ones, and the over protectiveness was getting a little ridiculous. But I stupidly loved it.

"I'm really okay, Flynn. I didn't know you were stopping by." I tried not to sound annoyed with him, but nearly every day a different Cage family member or friend stopped by just to check on me.

Flynn however, frowned. "It's on the calendar. We have lunch today. Remember?"

I blinked, and then pulled out my phone, scrolling through my files.

"Oh. You're right. I'm sorry." I cringed, looking down at my clothes. "Let me put on jeans real quick, and this sort of works as an outfit."

I was in full dance gear, and since it was summer, a cute double-layered tank top and jeans would work for an outfit. “Unless we’re going somewhere fancy, and then I’m sorry, I’m a failure.”

“You’re not a failure,” Flynn bit out, before he closed his eyes, and let out a deep breath. “I should have texted before I came over, but apparently you’re dodging texts.”

He raised a brow, and I shook my head. “Flynn.”

“No, I’m not going to say anything. The others will do that enough. But we *are* going for lunch, and we can just go to the cafe down the street. I do love a good sandwich.”

“And for some reason I’m craving soup,” I said, even though it was way too hot outside.

“Soup on a hot day sounds ridiculous, but now I’m craving it too. You good for taking lunch though?”

I looked through my calendar again and nodded. “Yes. I do have time. I scheduled the day like this for a reason and wasn’t paying attention. Let me put on some jeans and then text the nanny to check on the girls.”

“Tell them that their favorite uncle says hello,” he said with a soft smile.

There was something in his eyes that told me he was once again hiding something, but that was the Cages, living up to their name being cagey at best.

He looked down at his phone and cursed, before gesturing towards me. “I need to answer this,” he said, his voice slightly cooler. “You could dress, call the girls, and we’ll head to lunch. It won’t take that long. Promise.”

"Flynn?" I asked, and he shook his head before answering in hushed tones.

Flynn was the vice president of Cage Enterprises, and while I knew it was a very important job, and he had become best friends with our younger sister Emily, I didn't know that much about Flynn's day-to-day life. His twin was happy and in a relationship, and many of our siblings were married, having kids, and finding their ways, but Flynn always kept things close to the vest.

I shook my head, knowing he wouldn't want me focusing on him while I was trying to do the same for others. After all, I hated when people worried about me.

I quickly pulled on jeans and added a touch of makeup. I didn't need to look like the complete ghost I felt like.

I called the girls, and they were happily playing in water-based paints with their nanny, and I was grateful that I wouldn't have to clean up after them this time.

It hurt my heart to think about my baby girls. I loved them so freaking much. Violet and Hazel were my everything, my reason for being.

There was nothing more that I needed.

I met Flynn in the front of the studio, then locked up behind me. "I'm all alone today, so I don't need to leave it open."

Something ticked in Flynn's jaw. "Your security camera's going well then?"

I nodded, knowing why he was asking. The tension in my shoulders crept in again, but I was used to it by now. "Yes. I'm not usually alone."

"Maybe we need to put someone on the door." He frowned.

"For a small studio? No. We don't need to."

"But you have a lot of minors in there, and you're on your own without a full team to help. You're amazing, but outnumbered."

"And their parents are there too." I sighed. "I don't think a person at the door will be very soothing to the kids, but we can look through the security system again. I know Ford worked really hard on it."

My other half-brother owned a security company and installed systems. If anybody could keep my students safe, it would be him. He installed the one at my new place as well and checked on it frequently.

"Okay. We'll talk with Ford. He'll know what to do."

I smiled at that, because Ford was one of the youngest of us, and yet, seemed the steadiest.

We turned the corner, and I ran smack into a large body. I nearly said I was sorry, fear creeping up my spine, as I looked up into oddly familiar, piercing green eyes, and then everything went blank. I barely heard the scream or felt the touch on the base of my spine as I fell into darkness.

Chapter Two

CARSON

I reached out instinctively and gripped Sophia in my arms, careful with her so she wouldn't hit the ground. She was too damn light. Yes, she'd been a professional dancer, but she'd lost muscle in the past year—understandably. Someone needed to take care of her and make sure she was fed. She had far too many siblings for her to be this *damn light*.

Her eyes began to flutter, and I realized she hadn't passed out completely, but what the hell? One look at me and suddenly I was too fucking scary to take the next breath? As if the sheer idea of me caused people to pass out in fear or worry.

I was a damn menace, but I hadn't thought I'd crossed that many lines.

"Sophia?" Flynn Cage said as he came forward and tried

to take his sister from my arms. The worry on his face held so many layers. I knew the man wasn't only thinking about the night we'd found Sophia and her girls on the floor. No… there were other memories layered beneath in which I knew he'd do anything to keep others from finding out about.

I pulled back, feeling oddly protective, glaring at the man. "Hold on, let's make sure she's okay." The last thing I wanted was for Sophia to feel like I couldn't stand the touch of her. No, that wasn't the problem. In fact, with her pressed against me like this, it was the exact opposite problem. I wanted to keep her safe. To keep her near. And that's how I knew I needed to hand her over. Quickly.

"You can let go of her. I've got her. She's my sister," Flynn snapped, worry in his tone, and a little confusion etched in. After all, I was territorial over most things—my job, my fights, my property, and anything that my gaze landed on like I was Mufasa in the Pride Lands. No, perhaps that was more Scar.

But I wasn't territorial over Sophia. I didn't even know her.

And from everything that I had heard about her, I did *not* want to know her. I was messy enough. I didn't need whatever this Cage provided.

Her eyelashes fluttered once more, and she opened her eyes, before freezing in my grasp, as if realizing how close to the predator the prey had become.

I snorted at that, wondering how long I was going to be on this *Lion King* kick in my own mind. I didn't hurt women. I didn't stick with them either. I knew what happened when you gave yourself to someone and tried to form a so-called relationship. You failed at it. It didn't matter how pretty she was, how honest her eyes looked, you would fail each other.

My parents had. And as evident with the Cage family news, the Cages knew it as well.

"What? Who are you?" Sophia asked, the fear in her tone annoying me. I hadn't meant to put it there. She'd been through hell, and I had seen it firsthand, and I wasn't about to add to it.

Flynn eventually got tired of me and pulled his sister from my arms.

"Sophia? Are you okay?" He glared at me over her head, as if asking me what the fuck was happening or what the fuck was my problem. Considering I didn't know, I couldn't blame him for that reaction.

I did not know why I had just held onto Sophia for dear life, or why I hadn't wanted to let go.

That had been the problem the year before.

I'd seen her on the ground, blood pooling beneath her, her body shattered. She looked as if she'd been a marionette, dropped on the floor carelessly, her limbs in the wrong directions. That she had been trying to crawl towards her children, trying to protect them from the monster lurking in the light rather than the darkness.

I'd meant what I had said to her that day in the hospital. My regret was that I hadn't killed him right then and there. It would've been justified.

The anger in my veins, and the darkness in my heart didn't mean that I wouldn't feel guilt over murdering a man who dared to do that to a woman.

I had failed in that aspect twice in my life now. Once with my father, and the other with Sophia's husband.

The former had been a mistake, then again, I hadn't realized what I'd been walking in on at the time. The latter? It had been a bit of betrayal to all of us that I had let that bastard continue to breathe afterward.

"You. It's you?" Sophia said softly as she straightened, pulling away from Flynn. She brushed off her clothes, as if she were covered in dirt or lint, and I knew it wasn't because I had touched her. No, she was embarrassed. That much I got. I could read people better than they thought.

At least most days.

"Me," I said after a moment, my voice low. I slid my hands into my suit pockets and tilted my head, studying her.

I knew Sophia Cage. Even amongst all her names.

My sister loved the ballet, so I had seen Sophia on the stage more than once. And I'd been drawn to her not knowing why. And then I had become friends with many of the male members of the Cage family. And as any good Woods family member, I studied them.

Including the woman in front of me.

Those blue eyes felt as if they could see far beyond your soul, into your darkest secrets, and to every sin you had ever thought of. Her dark hair fell beneath her shoulders and had a slight wave to it as if it had been in a bun on top of her head earlier. She had cut it before but seemed to have grown it out again. The newest addition to her though, was that septum ring. A tiny little gold hoop that looked sexy as fuck.

I had grown up being told that women with tattoos and piercings were whores and delinquents who deserved whatever they had coming.

I had never gone out of my way to date only women with tattoos and piercings—no, I dated whoever the fuck I pleased. But Sophia Cage with a septum ring? Damn, maybe my knees were the ones about to go weak.

"Sophia, are you sure you're okay?"

"I'm fine, I must have tripped," she said, her gaze not leaving mine.

I would let the lie pass, even though the three of us knew there were reasons for her words.

After all, the only two times she had ever met me, she had been bleeding out, or in a hospital bed. And both times I had threatened to kill her now ex-husband. But I wasn't quite sure she had been conscious enough to remember the first time.

Pity.

"Sophia, this is Carson. He's working on a few developments with the company."

I raised a brow at that, my jaw clenching. If that's how Flynn wanted to introduce me, that was fine. A business associate. Not the man who knew more Cage secrets than most. Or the one who taught them how to box or helped them relieve whatever tension they had. After all, getting in a ring and trying to beat the shit out of your opponent usually helped with things like that.

"I would say nice to meet you, but I suppose we've already met."

Another kick to the gut. I hadn't wanted her to remember me and yet I'd known that was a lie. I *needed* her to remember me. To think of me. And that was why I was damned to hell. "I would say it's good to see you standing, but you did just swoon in my arms."

Her gaze narrowed and I couldn't wait to find out what she was thinking.

Flynn cursed under his breath. "Really, Carson?"

I didn't bother looking at him when I answered. "What? She did."

"I did not swoon. I tripped." She raised her head, her eyes still on mine.

"Whatever you say, Princess."

"Don't call me princess."

"Didn't you play one on stage once?" I hadn't meant to say that, and when her eyes widened, and Flynn cursed once again, I realized I might've played my hand. Though I wasn't sure which at that point.

"Let me take you home, Sophia."

She held up her hands and frowned.

"No. I'm fine. Really. Let's go get lunch, and then I need to head back to the studio. Thank you, Carson."

I didn't know how I felt about hearing my name falling from those luscious lips that I craved and dreamed about.

No, I didn't like it at all.

"You don't need to thank me at all. Just like you never need to apologize."

Her eyes widened, and I knew she remembered that entire conversation now. Good.

"Flynn, good to see you, even in the unexpected. I'll be at the meeting tomorrow."

"Okay. Sophia? Are you sure?"

"I'm fine, Flynn. You don't need to keep worrying about me."

But as she took a step away from him, her leg gave out slightly. I reached forward, gripping her arm without thinking. She stiffened and looked down where my large hand covered her small forearm, and she let out a sigh. Then she lifted her chin and met my gaze.

"Thank you. I'm fine though."

"If you're sure."

That bastard had really done a number on her. I'd seen the bat, the blood on the floor. He had shattered her dancing leg and broken a few ribs...let alone other things. I didn't know all the details, mostly because I hadn't looked. If I had, I would have found that man and ended him long before now.

I'd yet to give in to my temptation to murder men who hurt women, but Cale Whatever the Fuck his Last Name Was deserved it.

"How are the girls?" I asked, wondering where the hell those words came from.

Flynn looked at me like I had lost my mind, and maybe I had.

But Sophia's eyes warmed. "They're good. I still can't believe they let you hold them. Without screaming."

As soon as she said the words, I realized she'd had flashbacks, and I cursed under my breath. "I probably bribed them with candy. I don't remember. Good to see you, Flynn. Sophia." Again, her name came softly under my breath, and I shook my head before moving past them, grateful that I had let her go. Flynn could take care of his sister, as could the multitudes of Cages that were out there. I would get to my family and forget Sophia Cage.

Even if she haunted my dreams like no other.

I turned the corner and walked up to The Teal Door. Ironically, another Cage owned it. Theo Cage wasn't working that day, since I had been texting him earlier, but I knew Luke Hodges, his best friend and co-owner would be in the kitchen. I would go and see him later, but first, I was meeting the person I loved the most in the world.

Cora stood up, her dark hair pulled back from her face, her smile wide. Her eyes were puffy though, and her lips wobbled after a moment, and I knew today was going to be a hard fucking day.

I pulled my sister into my arms and kissed the top of her head. She wrapped herself around me and sighed deeply. She didn't shudder, she didn't cry, no, the Woods family did not cry in public. But we stood there for a moment, ignoring the host and waiter hovering nearby. This was a fancy restaurant, with white tablecloths and mood lighting, and you needed a reservation to come for even lunch, however, they knew me here, and I was going to hold my sister until she needed me to let go.

She finally did and patted my cheek.

"You need to shave," she said with a smile, before I pulled her seat back and gestured for her to sit. She did so, and I took the other seat, taking the menu from the grateful host.

"I already ordered some sparkling water. Did you want iced tea or anything?" Cora asked.

"Water will be fine." Though I had a feeling I could use a drink a little bit harder after this conversation.

The waiter came by, again, with all the specials, and we ordered our lunch. Of course, anything at The Teal Door would be fantastic. The Cages knew what they were doing. Hence why I worked with them and was becoming friends with them.

"Thank you for meeting me for lunch, I know you have so many things to do during the day."

I reached forward and gripped her hand. "You're my number one priority. Always."

There was a ten-year age gap between us, and she had always been my *baby* sister. I had taken her from the nanny more than once to hold her, to show her around the house and backyard. Then our parents would pluck her from my arms, and I would deal with the consequences for not listening to the nanny.

But Cora was my light. The reason that I didn't fall into the abyss. One of the few reasons why our father still breathed.

"Why did you want to meet? And why have you been crying?"

"Mom and Dad sent back their RSVP for the wedding." A heavy pause that would never lead to anything good. "They're not coming."

A lead weight settled in my stomach, though the news wasn't a surprise. Hell, it wasn't a surprise to Cora either.

She should have known our parents wouldn't be coming to the wedding.

After all, Cora and I had never once done anything that made our parents proud. So why would they display praise by showing up to some of the most important parts of our lives?

"Fuck them," I said and held back a wince when the waiter came by. I might be uncouth sometimes, but I did know my manners.

"I apologize," I said.

"I happened to hear part of the conversation ahead of time, so don't bother apologizing. I agree." The waiter winked at Cora, before dropping off our food, explaining a few things, and giving us privacy.

My sister gave me a watery smile, and I just shook my head.

"See? Even strangers are on our side."

"There shouldn't be sides. They should come to my wedding. It's because I'm not marrying the person that they want me to marry."

"They decided exactly who we would marry when we were toddlers. And neither one of us is doing that."

I had said no because I wanted nothing to do with that family or lifestyle, and Cora would have never married the man that they had chosen for her. Not in a million years.

"What does Juliet have to say about it?" I asked, speaking of Cora's fiancée.

"That I shouldn't have even bothered to ask. Because they've never once actually cared about what I do. She wanted to go over there and strangle them, but I told her sadly that our parents had better lawyers."

"I'm sure if I opened the door for her, and she happened to trip inside and accidentally strangle them, then, it wouldn't be that bad," I surmised.

"That sounds very premeditated to me," Cora said with a soft smile, before she dug into her Caprese salad.

"Good. You need to eat more," I ordered, grumpy as ever when it came to my baby sister not taking care of herself.

"I'm eating. I promise. Juliet won't let me starve. I'm just so pissed off."

"Good. Be angry. Don't be sad." I set down my fork, ignoring the delicious food, and shook my head. "I hate when you're sad."

"You are just a big marshmallow sometimes, aren't you, big brother?"

I snorted. "Not even a little bit, little sister."

"Well, you are. Our parents suck, Carson."

I nodded, took another bite of lunch. "Yes. They do. They don't deserve you. They never have."

"They don't deserve you."

Little did she know... I might not be the monsters they

were, but I wasn't a good person. Not when I took what I wanted because if I didn't, no one would believe I'd earned it. I protected people when no one else would and that meant sometimes, I walked away with darkness on my soul, etched within my bones. "I'm not on their radar anymore."

"You are, you know it." She snorted. "You're in the media all the time for your company, any move you make, and anyone that happens to be on your arm. So yes, because you can do something for them, even if you don't want to, they're going to pay attention to you."

"Look at you, getting snarky and perceptive when it comes to the cruelty of our parents."

"You've taught me well." She cleared her throat, and I tilted my head, studying her.

"What else? Is something wrong?"

"Other than dealing with wedding plans and the fact that our parents suck? No. But I do have a big ask of you, and I'm not sure what you'll say about it."

"Anything. You can tell me anything, Cora. You know that."

"Will you give me away?" she asked, her eyes filling with tears again, but she blinked them away. "I want you to walk me down the aisle and give me away to the love of my life. Our parents won't be there, but you will be. And you are my family."

I swallowed hard, hating the way my throat tightened.

"I don't need to give you away, Cora. You're your own person."

She rolled her eyes. "Yes, and you're not giving away a virgin either."

I growled. "Really?"

"What? I'm just saying. I'm not meaning the whole give your child away because she doesn't have any possessions of her own and she's just a sad little woman thing. No, I would like you to walk me down the aisle so I can see my future wife and know that my family has now grown. I want to dance with my brother to a ridiculous song and just be. So what do you say, big brother? Will you give me away?"

I pulled back from the table and moved around so I could stand next to her. She wrapped her arms around me, and I kissed the top of her head once again.

"Of course. You are my baby sister, my family. My everything. Of course I'll give you away. I mean, if Juliet's going to be the one to actually deal with you, it only makes sense."

She slapped my chest, and I threw my head back and laughed, ignoring some of the other patrons. Maybe I was far more uncouth than I gave myself credit for.

And as I sat back at the table and finished my lunch, I listened as my sister spoke of happiness and her future, and I was grateful for her. So fucking happy to see that she was healing, and a whole person. Fuck whatever my parents thought.

And if Cora wanted to believe in love, maybe she had found it with Juliet. But she was one of the few people I knew who would ever have that. That much I knew.

Chapter Three

SOPHIA

THE PATRIARCH OF THE CAGE FAMILY HAD BEEN dead for five years now. Five years in which Loren Cage was no longer a physical menace in our lives. His presence would always be felt in the ramifications of his lies and treachery, but he no longer lurked in the shadows, ready to take so much away from those he professed to care about.

He would never be a grandfather, never be the one the next generation would look up to.

He'd gone to ash and bone and remained deep within his secrets until death.

When we were growing up, my section of the family had rarely seen my dad. It had been Isabella, then myself, then the lone boy in our family—or so I thought—with Kyler, and then Emily, and finally, Phoebe.

The five of us had been a close-knit family and had run our mother to exhaustion sometimes with all our extracurriculars.

That was probably why Isabella had stepped up at a far too young age to fill in wherever she could.

I'd had years of ballet, dance, gymnastics, and countless other classes in order to be a dancer. I had finished high school in a special program because I needed to dance full-time and didn't have time to be in school all day. Scholarships had helped pay for it, or so I'd thought.

It turned out that my father had paid for it out of guilt when Mom had forced him into it. But he hadn't wanted his children on this side of the family to know he had any money. Because then someone would start to ask questions.

The Cage family was well-known, but thanks to his friends, and other people connected within the higher-ups in Cage Enterprises, he'd been able to keep his identity a secret. And we had been none the wiser until he was gone.

He'd lived with us and yet hadn't. He had been on the road for so long, and our mother had covered for him. I remember once he had come to a recital when I'd been in high school. I cried in happiness that he had shown up and had been so proud of me.

Isabella had scowled at him, and Emily and Phoebe had soaked in his attention, so happy that he was there. Kyler had been in his emo phase, his hair dyed dark black and over his eyes, and had just glared at our father, before storming away. Kyler still wouldn't tell me why he hated our father so much back then, because I knew it had to be for some reason beyond his neglect.

Or maybe I was just seeing what I needed to, because Kyler wasn't in town often.

While the rest of us lived in the state, either in the Denver Metro area, or within Cage Lake—a town that the Cages owned a majority of—Kyler technically didn't.

He was in a band called Caged and Reckless, the lead singer and lead guitarist, and amazing. He performed in sold-out stadiums and had just finished a tour in Europe. He had a house in Denver, near me thankfully so he could see the girls, but he was rarely home.

Tonight, however, he was home.

And all of us were at our big brother Aston's mansion, enjoying a family dinner.

Because in those five years since dear old Father had died, we had become a family of our own. All twelve siblings, creating connections that I don't think he would have ever thought of.

Part of me had wondered if perhaps maybe he wanted us to get closer. To find out who we were together. That had to be a pipe dream. Because our father was not nice like that. He wouldn't want us to be happy or to find any sense of solace in his passing. Because that would let the power slip through his hands—even if he was dead.

I had always thought that he had stipulated in the will that we needed to have dinner once a month, with five members of the family meeting, a blend of each section, so we would fail. Because we were different than the other Cages.

The other seven were all boys and had grown up in privilege. They had made something for themselves outside of who Loren Cage was. But their childhood had been far different.

I didn't resent them, and I knew my sisters didn't either. I didn't think Kyler did, but he kept his secrets so close to the vest, I couldn't tell.

Either way, we had defied our father's wishes and had actually become a family. I saw Flynn with his short dark hair and kind eyes, often, and Dorian, with his longer hair, bright eyes, and perpetual smirk, practically kidnap the twins just to be the best uncle. With a regal grace that screamed royalty rather than businessman in his suit, Aston stood beside Isabella most days as the new patriarch and was the big brother that anyone could ever want. Aston's dark hair was always perfectly done unless he was around his wife Blakely, and then it looked as if one of them ran their hand through it often.

When I went to Cage Lake, Hudson with his scowl and long, messy hair, would be there, and he would keep us close and make sure that we were always taken care of.

James, Theo, and Ford constantly checked in on us,

had family dinners, or invited us out with them. Ford had a husband and a wife, and a beautiful baby boy, who was cousins with my girls. And they would all grow up together, along with Aston's son, Stone.

We had countless group chats with a mixture of each other, and it was no longer the main siblings versus the bonus siblings. And it depended on which Cage you were speaking to as to which group was called the other.

Our father wanted us to fail. He wanted the company that he had put his blood, sweat, and tears in to perish without him, because he thought he was the linchpin. He wanted the town to go under and hate the Cages.

And he had failed.

Because now, here we all were, with our families, laughing at a catered dinner and enjoying ourselves.

"You know, I could have cooked, but really, there's just too many of you," Blakely, Aston's wife, said. She'd let her long curly hair grow out so it lay in deep layers. She'd done her light eyes up in a dark shadow and her smile brightened like no other.

"And you're getting better at cooking every day," Isabella teased. She pushed her short brown hair from her face and grinned.

Isabella and Blakely had been friends for years. Longer than Blakely and Aston had even been together. That had been a point of contention, of course, but they had overcome it, and now Blakely was another sister.

Phoebe giggled at something her husband, Kane, said, and I smiled at my baby sister, grateful that she found happiness in a man who was honorable, and was worth everything.

She smiled at me, and yet I saw the way that she studied my face, and the worry there. I ignored it, and tried to brush it off, just like I did with everyone else.

I loved my family, but they worried about me. They were waiting for me to break, for me to scream into the void at the unjustness of it all. But I wouldn't. I had married a man just like my father apparently, in the cruel ways of irony. And I had made a terrible choice.

Part of me thought maybe I had married him in the first place because I'd been missing my father, but I didn't want to think I had those kinds of father issues.

But Cale had preyed on me, and now I needed to deal with the consequences.

"When are you getting down to Cage Lake again?" Hudson asked, his arm around his wife, Scarlett.

Scarlett was the manager of the Cage Resort, an honest to God ski resort up in town that, once again, the family businesses owned. I had a small stake in Cage Enterprises because Aston had made sure each of us did. But I sold mine before I had gotten married, wanting to use the money to work towards my dance practice. I was grateful that I had done that, because it had closed another avenue that Cale would've had into the family finances. And when the divorce was over, and the paperwork settled as far as it could be in this moment, Aston had forced me to take another slice of the company. He had wanted all of us to be part of it.

Even Ford, the youngest on that branch, had bought back into the family business.

He owned the security company that kept my home and my business safe now, and he had walked away from the family long before all of the secrets had come to light.

Considering our father had been a bigot and an asshole—some things we hadn't realized until too late—it made sense.

Ford was a bisexual man in a poly relationship, and damn happy about it.

Of course, nearly every single one of my siblings was either bi or pansexual, so it was no wonder that our father had wanted us to fail.

We were everything he hated.

And most of us were finding happiness.

"You're not eating," Weston whispered, and I looked over at my brother-in-law, and smiled. He and Bella had been married for a little while now, and alternated between living in Denver and Cage Lake, depending on which business they were working on in the moment. With Weston's adult siblings in Denver now, they were visiting for a while.

And it was like having yet another big brother when I already had far too many of them.

"I am. I ate all of my soup and a second helping," I said.

He gave me a look, and Isabella tapped him on the shoulder and whispered in his ear.

I glared at her, knowing that she was only wanting to keep me healthy, but everybody was so worried about me that it enraged me to no end.

The conversation grew louder, as everybody began speaking to one another, and I continued my perusal of the group.

Theo and Flynn were in an animated conversation with Emily, and I smiled at the three of them. Emily, I knew, was in the middle of changing careers, figuring out what she wanted, and I was grateful that she had the time and space to do so. Our father had pushed her into one area and hadn't let her do anything else. Now, she had time to grow and was working hard at it.

I was surprised Theo and Kyler were here though, considering Theo owned two high-end restaurants, and Kyler had just gotten back from tour.

But my entire family was now here, and I was just taking it all in, knowing that days like this were rare.

"The kids are upstairs, right?" James asked from across the table, and I nodded, doing my best not to pay attention to the person at my right. In fact, I had done my best not to think about that person all night.

James was one of the quieter Cages of the family. I was grateful that everyone else seemed to be in their own little bubbles, speaking amongst themselves, so he could get a word in.

However, a little part of me was annoyed about his guest.

The guest that sat right next to me.

"I was surprised I hadn't seen the twins," Carson drawled beside me, and I stiffened.

Why the hell had James invited Carson to our family dinner? It made no sense. Only spouses and significant others came to dinners like this. Not friends or associates.

Then I looked between Carson and James, and something clicked. Oh. Maybe they were significant others, and I was just behind on the times. For some reason, that let me relax slightly, and my shoulders eased.

"They had a long day. They will probably be up before the others though, and they'll be little terrors. But that's why I love them." I smiled at Carson then, grateful that I had figured it out.

There was no need to be nervous around this man now, or the fact that he had seen me at my weakest, because he and James had to be together. And that meant I was happy and didn't need to worry about a thing.

Carson gave me an odd look, but then I turned to

Dorian and Harper, who had asked me a question about an upcoming birthday, since Harper was a baker, and I immediately forgot all about the man at my side.

Or at least I tried.

Sometimes, it was hard to get every single one of my family names and connections correct, but in the end, we were all family.

Ford had his wife and husband near him, Phoebe had her husband, and all of the kids were upstairs, sleeping since it was a little late.

When dinner was over, we broke apart in our natural groups, some of us bouncing from one to another, and it just felt right. A large family dinner that had nothing to do with the holiday, and everything to do with the fact that we just wanted to be together. Some days, when the screaming in my soul was far too loud for me to take a breath, I knew that I needed these moments.

Then as I looked at the couples, and the way they leaned into one another with such trust, my chest tightened. I ran my hand over my heart absently and squeezed Flynn's hand before walking away to stand out on one of the many balconies of Aston and Blakely's home.

Though it was summer, the air was cool tonight, and I put my hands on the stone railing, before sucking in a deep breath. I closed my eyes and counted to five.

"Do I want to know what's wrong?" that deep voice asked, and I stiffened, annoyed that he would follow me out here. Especially since James was still inside speaking with Hudson and Scarlett.

"I'm just taking in some air before I check on the girls," I said stiffly.

"I see. You know what's funny?" he asked.

I didn't turn to look at him, though his cedar scent swirled around me, soaking into my skin.

Did he bathe in the stuff or was it just his natural scent?

"I really don't know what you're talking about."

"There were at least fifteen conversations going on at once, and I did my best to keep up with every single one of them, and I know you did the same, and yet, I think you only said maybe six sentences the entire time."

I turned to him then, just a tilt of my head, and studied the strong lines of his face. He had dark reddish-blonde hair that looked even darker underneath the moonlight, and he'd shaved his beard since I had last seen him. But I had a feeling it grew quickly, because you could already see the stubble beneath. Beneath the moonlight, however, those piercing green eyes were just as bright as ever. His strong jaw was squared off with high cheekbones, and that rugged look that should scare me, honestly, just confused me. His nose had a bump in it, as if it had been broken a time or two, and I realized then he had tiny silver hoops in his ears.

The CEO and owner of a major corporation, that

worked in billion-dollar businesses with the Cages, had silver hoops in his ears.

Interesting.

"Is there a reason you were studying how many words I said during dinner? Is there a quota?"

"I was just wondering. You don't need to get worried about it."

"Maybe I do." I paused. "Did Isabella ask you to watch me like she's been asking everyone else? If so, you should just tell her I'm fine. I don't need her to measure my words like she's measuring my food intake and physical therapy." The words came out much more clipped than I had intended, but there was no taking them back.

He tilted his head and studied my face. "Such a large family, and so many eyes on you. They must be worried about you after everything that happened. But no, Isabella didn't ask me to watch you. I couldn't help but want to."

I froze, staring at him. "You shouldn't say things like that. Especially since you're here with James. It's rude."

He blinked a few moments, perplexed, before he threw his head back and laughed. It was a deep laugh, one that made my fingers curl around the stone and my cheeks heat. "I'm not here with James, Princess. Although your brother is attractive, he's not my type."

He gave me a pointed look that told me exactly who his type was, and I took an involuntary step back.

"Well. I didn't realize we were bringing business associates to family dinners then."

"I was at the office and Blakely invited me. I was going to wave it off, but I was hungry and she said it would be catered by your brother's restaurant. And since I love Theo's food, I went with it. I'm not here to check on you. I promise you, Princess. I already told you what I wanted to do to make things better, but as that's a felony, I won't offer it again."

Why did him offering to make my ex-husband go away permanently turn me on slightly?

No, that was just those conflicted feelings that told me I needed a nap. Or a large drink.

Or to dance again.

As if on cue, my knee buckled, and my femur felt as if it was on fire. A squeak escaped me, and then Carson was there, holding my elbow to keep me on my feet.

"Sophia?"

"I'm fine. Please just go."

He studied my face, the warring of emotions carved into his eyes worried me, and yet I couldn't let go. I didn't want him to let go.

"Not until you're settled. You don't have to be whole. You don't have to be okay, Sophia. I'm not going to let you fall out here on the terrace."

Tears pricked the back of my eyes, and I had to wonder exactly who this man was.

"Carson—"

"Mommy?"

I whirled, ignoring all pain because of that little voice, to see Violet and Hazel standing in the doorway, hands clasped, looking at me oddly. It was Hazel who had spoken, and then I was moving towards her, away from Carson and his hold.

"Girls, you're not supposed to be on the terrace alone." Images of countless accidents filled my brain, and my mouth went dry.

"Their toes haven't touched the tile," Carson corrected, and while he was right, I still turned to scowl at him.

"Thank you very much, Mr. Woods."

He raised a brow at that but didn't move away.

I reached down to pick up my daughters, but my legs were too shaky, and tears threatened again. I should be able to hold my daughters without pain, without falling, and I would. I just needed a deep breath.

"We missed you," Violet whispered, and this time a single tear did fall.

Before I could say anything, Carson was kneeling beside me, arm outstretched.

"How about I help your mom here and take one of you? I'm Carson, your mom's friend."

I nearly snorted at that, but I didn't want my girls to just walk away with a stranger, and frankly, I wasn't sure I could even stand up with the girls in my arms at the moment. I had never hated my injury more than in this moment.

"Uncle *Flynn's* friend," Hazel added and beamed.

That made Carson grin, and I just shook my head, a smile threatening. He picked up Hazel without a second thought and stood, his hand on my elbow at the same time. That let me lean on him as I lifted Violet and set her on my good hip, then kissed her forehead.

"Thank you, Mr. Woods."

"Carson. I'm Carson."

"Thank you, Mr. Carson," I rasped.

Violet buried herself into my neck, as Hazel spoke a mile a minute to Carson as if they were old friends, and he listened intently. I stood there, confused as to how I had gotten in this place, in this moment, but I couldn't move, not without Carson doing it first.

And once again, I was out of my element, and a new kind of pain settled in.

Chapter Four

CARSON

The fist to the jaw shouldn't have been a surprise. However, I hadn't expected Flynn to be the one to make the connection.

Lights dancing behind my eyes, I cursed under my breath and then moved to counter that fucking jab. Sweat slick, slightly bruised, and with only one drop of blood so far, practice wasn't going too badly.

I set my feet into a readying position, and when Flynn tried to move again, I jabbed. The straight punch must have surprised the other man, because his head knocked back, and I was grateful I had only used a light probing shot, instead of something far more powerful. I didn't want to break my friend's face. I wasn't that much of an asshole. Especially since I had business with him, James, and Aston later that day.

Flynn shook off the hit much like I had, and then we were moving again.

An overhand, a single leg takedown. I hit the ground, rolled back up, and used my round kick to pivot towards the other man. When Flynn grinned back at me, I knew the fight was almost over, and we were just having fun.

I wasn't in the mood to get on the ground, to sprawl, or to pin the guy, so instead, we bruised ourselves just a little bit more, the tape long since digging into my skin, and by the time we each decided to bow out, we were sweaty, and I had a feeling that I'd end up with a black eye, and Flynn with a bloody lip.

"Are the two of you done? I thought this was supposed to be a light practice," James complained from the side. He wore joggers, and a tight black t-shirt, as he hadn't come to fight, or train, but rather, just get on the treadmill and run out his demons.

I had tried to do that earlier, and then I had lifted for twenty minutes, until Flynn had shown up at my gym with a scowl, tight shoulders, and gym clothes. Then it had been on.

I loved working with the Cages. They were brilliant at business, took no prisoners, and didn't get down with shady shit. They made sure whoever they were working with knew who was in charge.

Of course, when it came to our two companies working together, the play-by-play of who was in charge looked much like our bout just then. Bloody, taking turns, and nobody truly the leader. And I was just fine with the byplay. If it had been any other group, I'd have balked at the idea, but not the Cages

Unlike working with other companies, I trusted the Cages. And considering what their company had been when their old man had been alive and in charge, that was saying something.

I took out my mouth guard and winked at James. "What? You don't like a little blood between friends."

"I don't have anything to say to that," James said dryly as he glared at his brother. "You do realize we have a meeting tomorrow. And you're going to end up with a fat lip, and we have to deal with another country and all their fucking bylaws. They're going to think you're an idiot."

Flynn shrugged, without saying a word, and moved forward to fist bump my hand. I did the same, knowing there were no hard feelings. This was just a fight, and not even a real one. Just us blowing off steam and trying not to beat the shit out of each other. Before, when we did things like this, I had to hold back completely. All of them had been new at fighting, and I wasn't about to be the one that would break a Cage.

I had respected them too much because of what they had to deal with over their late father, to try to hurt them business-wise or physically. But since the shooting, when Flynn had ended up coming back with more than a few scars, the other man hadn't held back. He'd trained harder and was getting downright dangerous.

Maybe not to other people, but for himself if he wasn't careful.

Flynn went to get a drink from his water bottle, and I met James's gaze. I didn't have to say a thing, because then James gave me a chin lift, and I realized that he would deal with it.

That was the Cage brothers. They took care of each other.

Then again, it wasn't truly the Cage brothers anymore. I had been working with them for long enough now, that I had been witness to the monstrosity that was the patriarch's will. Even my investigators hadn't truly figured out the scope of the betrayal of that old man.

When I had first come to work with the Cages, I had known that Loren, their father, had numerous affairs. And not just with Constance Cage Dixon. And from what I could tell, Melanie Cage—Flynn and James's mother—hadn't cared in the least.

It was no skin off my nose if that's how the family ran, but the concept of a secret family? That had escaped our notice. I had known about Kyler Cage, the rockstar who growled more than I did, and had thought he was a single love child. I hadn't realized he'd been full siblings with the rest of his sisters.

Silly me, I thought that Loren Cage and Constance

had had a simple affair, and he'd only had one extramarital child. It turns out he had five of them. Twelve kids. The man had been busy. Sophia was one of those children. She sure as hell wasn't a child anymore.

I swallowed hard and did my best not to think about her. Considering I wore small-ish gym shorts so there was less for Flynn to grab onto when we fought, there wouldn't be much to leave to the imagination if I kept that woman on my mind for too long.

I cleared my throat, thought about baseball and financials, and went over to James.

"In the mood for a quick bout?" I asked.

The other man just snorted. "Hell no. You look to be in a mood, and I don't want to end up bloody before our meetings. Thanks though, for letting us work out here. I liked our old gym, and I enjoy the one in our building, but this one just feels more private."

I shrugged, knowing it was the truth. I owned the building, as well as most of the sponsorships for any fighters here who went amateur, or pro in one case. I liked to make sure I was the one in control when it came to my life and my choices.

The Cages probably had more money than I did and could build a gym like this of their own, but they hadn't yet. It was a large warehouse, converted into something slightly industrial, but not so much that the sound echoed. I hated when restaurants and buildings went for the industrial look. It meant bare ceilings, pipes everywhere, and the noise would turn into a cacophony with only two sets of people there. Having floors and walls and ceilings that dampened the sound made sure I didn't end up with a headache after a workout. It was a private place, and you couldn't just pay your way in. Some of my competitors had wanted to join the gym just to say that they had, but I'd denied them. They could build anything that they wanted on their own, but I knew that they wanted to be here to trade secrets, or to try to figure out the Woods and now the Cages.

Those people could just fuck right off.

We weren't out on the golf course, shooting the shit and having to listen to men degrade their women and pretend they weren't terrible people.

That's not who I was, and that's not who this generation of Cages had turned out to be.

No, that was all left for my father, and their late one.

"I'm going to hit the showers," Flynn said as he strode towards the locker rooms, and I frowned.

"What's up with him?" I asked, confused.

James ran his hand over the back of his neck and frowned. "I have no idea. I tried to get Hudson to get it out of him when we were at the family dinner, since he and Scarlett rarely come down to the city these days, but I still don't know."

"Did he talk to anybody after the shooting?" James's

eyes widened, and I snorted. It wasn't like me to bring shit like this up, but I also wasn't going to turn into my father. I'd made enough promises to myself along the way to whatever person I'd become that the idea of speaking to a professional wasn't as scary as it should have been. "Yes, I am talking about therapy. My sister forced me to go a while back, and she still goes often. Talking it out helps. So does punching things. And while I don't mind getting in the ring or on the mat with him, his kicks are getting a little more pointed." I rubbed my jaw, and James winced.

"I don't know if he's talked to anyone professionally about the shooting. It was scary as fuck, and well, between that and what happened with Sophia? It's been good to have some quiet over the past year." James cursed under his breath. "I can't believe I just said the Q word. That's like asking for trouble. And considering we're still dealing with the paperwork over that asshat, I shouldn't have said it at all."

I stiffened, a thousand different worst case scenarios filling my brain. "Which asshole? The ones that came after your family? Or that loser ex-husband of hers that I should have killed when I had a chance?"

There were other people in the gym, and while James and I were trying to be as quiet as possible, that didn't mean others couldn't overhear. So I inched toward him, aware that I would find a way to end that rotted vegetable's life. Anybody who did what he had done to a woman, didn't deserve to breathe.

"Scarlett and Hudson are fine. Yes, they went through hell, but they're good together. I was more talking about Sophia's ex." The other man gritted his teeth, his jaw tightening, and I moved closer.

"What the fuck did he do now?"

"He's suing for custody again. He's not going to get it. We're not going to let him. Sophia is finally letting us use the family name to try to keep that asshole away from them, but he's pissed off that the courts let her change the kids' names to Cage. And the man wanted money to begin with, and he's not stepping back. He might be able to get additional weekends, however, because the laws like reunification more than they like keeping kids safe, but then again, I'm in a piss poor mood and not thinking about when things actually work. Instead it's just about the paperwork of keeping that asshole in power."

"Why isn't that asshole in jail? I know what Flynn and I walked in on. He would've killed her. Killed her and taken those kids and found a way to make it all about him in which he ended up the poor widower or some shit."

"He knows people. And the courts don't listen to women."

"They had my testimony. I'm a fucking man. Why didn't they listen to me?" I shook my head. "They should have listened to her. I should say that first."

"I know what you meant." James's lips tilted into a smile, though it didn't reach his eyes. "They gave him anger management, and I don't know who the fuck is signing off on it, because passive aggressiveness is even worse. Now he's spewing all over socials and in the community about her dance studio, and I think he hired a PR team to work its way to Kyler's socials too."

I frowned. "What the fuck do you mean?"

James ran his hand through his hair as we made our way to the locker room. "Just stupid bots that are saying crap about the family and tagging Kyler's socials. I know for a fact that my brother doesn't run them, but Emily sees them."

"Emily's your youngest sister, right?" I knew each of the names of the Cages of course, and had met them all, but it still wasn't easy to keep them all in my head.

"One of them. And she's the one most connected to social media and things like that. We're trying to keep it away from Sophia, because she doesn't need any more issues."

I shook my head as I stripped off my shorts and gloves and got into the shower. "Keeping secrets from your sister is just going to backfire. She deserves to know everything that man is doing or could be doing. And are you sure it's Cale hiring that firm for the bots and shit? Kyler is a celebrity that speaks out against issues and is damn popular. People are going to want to tear him down. Let alone the connection to your family."

"Company's looking into it."

"I can do the same if you want." It wasn't an offer I made lightly. The Cages had their connections, including a cybersecurity business within the family. But I knew shadier people, and my company could find most things. And since we hadn't found all the secrets of the Cages the first go around, we were even more hard-pressed to dig deep when it came to people who could hurt my family.

"I can't ask you to do that," James put in.

"You're not asking. I am offering. I don't like when weak-willed men take advantage. And he didn't get enough pain from what I can see."

"I should have killed him right alongside you," Flynn said as he came forward, towel wrapped around his waist.

I turned off the water and reached for my own towel.

"We could have figured out where to hide the body," I said with a shrug.

James looked between us and sighed. "Sometimes I don't know if you two are being serious or not."

"I'm not joking," I said simultaneously with Flynn. We met each other's gazes, and Flynn grinned, looking like the happier man that I had once met.

James was right, something was going on with his brother, and while part of me wanted to dig in and figure out what it was, I didn't think doing so would be good.

Whatever was going on with Flynn didn't have to do with the company, or his connection to my family. So I let him have his privacy. For now.

"You two need to take it down a notch. Cale isn't going to get custody, and he's not going to get money. If anything, he's going to get another restraining order and find someone else to prey on." James sighed. "Which makes me sound like a terrible person, but I just want Sophia and those kids to be safe."

"Ford was at the studio yesterday, adding additional security, so there's at least that."

"Ford's the best at what he does, that's good."

I'd even let Ford and his company run the security in my house, and that was saying something. They were also working on my sister's condo and would build an entire system for her house with her future wife, once they settled on the down payment. Cora didn't exactly know that was happening, but it was a wedding present, and she would just have to deal with my overprotectiveness.

"Okay, we have to head back to the office, but you'll be there later?" Flynn asked, as if we hadn't just discussed killing a man.

"I'll be there. I want to make sure we get this deal set, because I have a few more ideas."

"No wonder Aston loves you," James said, a full smile on his face now. "I should warn you though, Blakely and

Isabella might want to set you up with someone next time you come to dinner."

I froze, turning slightly as I looked at the other man. "What?"

Flynn held up both hands. "They have a friend, and they promised not to set up any of their siblings with anyone, but you're seemingly fair game."

"I'm not fair game," I said stiffly, images of Sophia filling my mind. Which was ludicrous because she wasn't mine, and I didn't want her.

Liar.

"I'll let them know, but they do have a friend, and apparently, they think you two would fit. They wouldn't force a setup, but they might test the waters."

"They sound like my sister," I said dryly.

"Your sister's wedding's coming up, right?" Flynn asked as we finished getting dressed.

"Yes, and I'm walking her down the aisle." My jaw tensed and I tried to force myself to relax slightly. It didn't work.

Flynn grimaced. "Your parents are still assholes then I take it," he said simply. The two of them as well as most of the Cages who worked with Cage Enterprises knew that my parents were evil incarnate. Their business ran alongside the Cages', and as soon as the Cages figured out exactly how terrible my parents were, they cut business ties with them.

It hadn't made my father happy, but I had taken that place. While I hadn't meant to steal all of my father's contracts, it was a benefit of not being a bigoted asshole.

"It'll be good that they're not there though, without that dark cloud," James added. "Your sister is a nice person, at least for the two seconds that I saw her that one time. She deserves a happy wedding."

"Yeah, she does," I said after a moment, and tried to find solace in the fact that I would at least be there. It didn't sound like much.

We finished getting ready, and said our goodbyes, and I headed towards a local cafe to pick up lunch. I wasn't in the mood for a salad or whatever else my assistant would have for me, and frankly, taking as much time as I had in the middle of the day wasn't like me. But I had needed the push, and so had the Cages.

I walked into the small cafe, the gleaming sage green walls soothing, and immediately stiffened at the sound of a familiar voice.

"Okay girls, what do you say?"

"Thank you," little voices sing-songed together, and I couldn't help the smile on my face.

I did not understand children, and I wasn't even sure I liked them, but those little girls were adorable as all get out.

Sophia looked up from the counter, as she moved towards the closest booth, and nearly tripped over her feet.

"Carson."

"Sophia."

She'd pulled her hair back from her face again, a simple bun that I knew she wore mostly when she danced, but part of me wanted to let her hair fall loose and see it brush her shoulders.

I was ridiculous.

Instead of saying anything along those lines though, I looked down at the mini replicas of Sophia at her side and knelt in front of them.

"Hello girls."

"Hi," one of the little girls said as she skipped towards me, and threw her arms around me. I froze and looked up wide-eyed at Sophia. I wasn't good with kids—hell I didn't know any—so I had no idea what the hell I was supposed to do right now. Sure, I'd burn the world down in order to protect these two, but I didn't know what to do when they tried to hug me like this.

The other little one hid behind Sophia's legs but waved shyly at me.

"Girls, this is Mr. Carson."

"I know, Mama," the littlest said and kissed me on my cheek, surprising the hell out of me.

"You must be Violet," I guessed, trying to remember the difference between the two. She beamed, and then little Hazel skipped towards me and hugged me just as tightly. "And you're Hazel." Without thinking, I stood, lifting them both in my arms and sitting them on my hips. Sophia reached out as if to stop me, or help, I wasn't sure, and I had no idea what the hell I was doing.

I had met these girls a couple of times now, and the first time had been in the most horrific circumstances. I hoped to hell they didn't remember me from that time. I didn't understand kids ages or what they could remember or forget, I just hoped they remembered sunshine, and rainbows, and all that other shit.

"I didn't realize you were so good with children," Sophia said after a moment.

The surprise in her voice should have insulted me but considering how my thoughts had been along the same lines, I couldn't fault her. However, I wasn't about to let her know that. "I'm not. But they're like little monkeys that cling, so it can't be that hard."

Both girls made monkey sounds, and I chuckled roughly, before gesturing towards the booth closest to the window.

"Take a seat, I'll follow."

"You don't have to carry them, Carson. We were just getting a little snack."

"Snack, snack, snack, snack," both girls said at the same time, and I continued to laugh.

I followed Sophia, since she had no other choice, before setting the girls down in the booth.

Nobody was paying attention to us, and for that I was

thankful. I knew Sophia didn't like to be the spectacle, not anymore. Not that she had ever wanted to be, but as a dancer, being the center of attention was one thing, and this would be another.

"It's good to see you," she said, and I wasn't sure she meant it. I wasn't sure I wanted to see her either, but here we were, standing awkwardly near each other once again, her daughters nearby.

"I'm just here to get lunch, I was with your brothers earlier."

"Which ones? Apparently I have forty."

I laughed then, grateful she could tease about such a complicated story.

"Flynn and James."

"So you're the one with the gym." She reached up and brushed her fingers along my jaw. I wasn't sure she realized she had done it until we both stiffened. She let her arm fall, and I immediately missed her touch. "You're going to end up with a bruise there."

"Flynn's going to end up with a few bruises as well. James wasn't happy with us."

"I can't believe he fights." There was a bite to her tone, her face pale, and I wanted to curse, but the girls were staring at us.

"We take it easy, I promise. It's nothing like—"

She held up her hand. "I know. I know. Anyway, I should go pick up our order from the counter."

"I can do it for you. Sit with the girls."

"I don't need you to. But thank you."

"Thank you, Mr. Carson," Violet said, and then Hazel echoed the words. They patted my arm, and I reached down to tug on each of their pigtails.

"You're very welcome. Now tell your mother to sit down."

"Carson—"

I ignored her, and then went to pick up their food, ignoring the odd look from the person behind the counter.

As I set down their pastries and chocolate milk and latte, Sophia gave a dramatic sigh.

"You're just like my brothers, never listening to me when I say I can handle things."

"And you're just like the women in my life who don't understand that it's okay to be offered help. This way you didn't have to leave the girls behind," I whispered under my breath.

She sighed and nodded. "Thank you. Seriously. And thank you for being nice to the girls."

I rolled my eyes. "You don't have to thank me for that. Though maybe you could thank me by asking your sister and sister-in-law to not set me up on a date."

Sophia's eyes widened. "What?"

I explained what James and Flynn had said, and she shook her head. "I'll explain. I'm sorry. You know happily married people. They want everyone else to be happy and married as well."

I didn't ask if she had ever done the same. Because part of me thought that wouldn't be the case. How happy had her marriage been after all?

We stared at each other for a moment, her latte getting cold, before I nodded my goodbyes and waved at the girls.

Sophia Cage was one of the most beautiful women I'd ever met in my life.

A fragile soul underneath a hard shell of resolve and tension.

Gentle, but broken.

And the granite and coal that made up my soul couldn't piece shattered porcelain together.

And it was well time that I reminded myself of that.

Chapter Five

CARSON

"You only need to sign a few more things, and then we're nearly done."

I looked up at the Cage admin and nodded. "I have signed a few contracts before in my life, give me a moment." I took the papers and thumbed through them, realizing that I had already gone through these electronically at least eight times. I might trust the Cages with my life, but my business was another thing. Which sounded as if I might have control issues that bordered other harsher ones, but that meant I was just a damn good businessman.

"Going through line by line again?" Aston Cage asked as he strolled into the decently grand guest office, his gray suit bespoke, and his hair pushed back from his face.

For a man who wore an expensive suit and could wheel and deal like nobody's business—while being trusting at the same time—his hair looked like somebody's hands had run through it. I let out a breath since the man's lips were slightly swollen.

My lips quirked upwards without thought. "Should I ask where Blakely is?"

Aston just narrowed his eyes and then took the seat across from me. "I would've expected your entire team to be here honestly."

I shrugged. "They were here, and we went through everything already. They'll be back after lunch. I just wanted some time with the contract."

"Should I leave you alone then with the paperwork?" he drawled. He leaned back in his chair, looking as if he hadn't a care in the world when I knew for a fact it was the opposite. As the eldest of his siblings and president of the company, he had countless worries and responsibilities, but he was still a good man—something I was learning and appreciating.

I snorted. "No, not that type of time. I'm always like this with contracts. I need to go over them once more on my own to make sure there were no additional changes, and frankly, to get a feel for it."

"I would question you on that, but I'm the same way. Our father instilled in us certain aspects, and not all of them grand."

I leaned back in the chair, mimicking Aston, and nodded tightly. "I'd like to think mine isn't as bad as yours was but comparing them feels like an exercise in misery."

"I never liked working with your father," Aston said point-blank. "He was an asshole, didn't like women in the building unless they were serving him coffee, and refused to work with any of our higher-ups."

"It's not like your father had many, if any, women in the echelons of the company," I pointed out.

"That is true. But he had slowly begun to hire people other than white men over time, probably because he couldn't keep his hands on all facets of the business when James, Flynn, and I moved our way in."

"You have people from all walks of life working here. People from different backgrounds who are all the best at what they do. It's a good place." I tried to make my business along the same lines. It wasn't easy when some recruiters and other old school businessmen tried to take over, but I pushed them out. Old school was just another name for asshole bigot in my book, and I didn't deal with them. I bought them out and made their businesses better.

Aston's smile looked real and I was grateful for that. While I'd known Flynn longer as we shared secrets no one else needed to know, I'd slowly become friends with many of the Cages—Aston and James the closest. "We're trying. I was glad when you broke off from your father's business and started your own. We can build good economically and environmentally-sound businesses together and ensure that we annoy your father. I feel like it's a win-win."

My lips twitched. "It does sound like a win, doesn't it? My father's an asshole. He's not a good person. And he's going to do everything in his power to stop this partial merger, but I don't care. He doesn't have the wherewithal nor the standing in whatever society he thinks he needs to make it any higher than he is. He's failing. The judges he used to bribe are dead or retired, and he hasn't found enough new ones like I have."

"As if you would bribe someone."

"I would do all manner of things to protect my family, Aston. You know that more than anyone."

The other man met my gaze and nodded. "That is true. I hear you've been spending a lot of time with my siblings."

For a moment I thought he meant Sophia, but that wouldn't make any sense. The only time they would've known we were in the same room or near each other would've been on the street with Flynn, at that family dinner where everyone had been there, and when I had found her the first time.

No, it wasn't Sophia.

"Should I apologize for Flynn's busted lip?"

"No, he probably deserved it. I've seen you fight, Carson. You're not accidental in any of your moves, and you're ensuring that my brothers are the same way. Meaning they're doing something that they want to do, albeit safely. You might have to deal with my wife later on though."

"What will I have to deal with?" Blakely asked as she walked into the room, her gorgeous blonde hair flowing past her shoulders, and wearing a similar gray pantsuit.

She looked like a million bucks, but I would never say anything like that. I was allowed to think that my friend's wife was hot, I wasn't allowed to act like an idiot. There was no need. Because there was only one woman on my mind these days, and that bothered me to no end.

"I'm teaching your brothers how to fight MMA style. And box, and kick ass. We're having fun."

Blakely gave a dramatic sigh. "Boys."

"I think the word you're looking for is men," I teased.

"Stop hitting on my wife, Woods."

"If I was hitting on your wife, you would know it."

"Oh, that's a good line," Blakely teased. "Do you use that on all the women that stroll around you and swoon?"

"Maybe. The swooning gets tiresome though. Constantly having to catch them before they hit the ground. Nobody wants a concussion."

She grinned, and Aston rolled his eyes dramatically.

"Read your contracts, and we'll go over everything electronically before you head out. I hear you're meeting Dorian later?" he asked. "Catching up with every Cage?"

Not the Cage that I wanted, I thought, but I didn't say that out loud.

"He just opened that new club last week, and I haven't been by. I'm too old for dance clubs with loud music and lights that blind you, but this one has whiskey, cigars, and a little bit of dancing."

"It's really nice." Blakely leaned forward and organized the papers on the table better. "Dorian knows what he's doing, and the place will do well, I think."

"Considering you're the one that helped with the business side of it, I know it'll do well," Aston said proudly.

I grinned up at Blakely. "Thank you for working on this deal by the way," I said. "I know you have too many things on your plate, but I wanted the best."

I wasn't trying to suck up to her at all, not because she was friends with Sophia, or even Aston's wife. She was a brilliant business manager who specialized in strengthening ties, and finding ways to keep people in their job, without bleeding the company dry. And while Isabella Cage was a forensic accountant who excelled at so many other things that were helpful, I knew I was in good hands with the Cages and always had been.

"My pleasure. I like a company that is honest. You don't find that often these days. Have fun tonight, and maybe try not to break any of my brothers-in-laws' noses. They're kind of cute."

"I thought I was the cute one," Aston said with a growl.

"You're the cutest." She leaned down, kissed his cheek, and waved before heading out to her office.

I shook my head and tapped my pen on the table. "What's it like working with your family, your wife, your brothers, sisters?"

"I've always worked with my family. We've just added more over the years."

"Have you ever looked to see if you have any other half-siblings?" I asked softly.

Aston nodded. "We did. Couldn't find any. And frankly, if our dad did have other kids, he probably would've put them in the will to try to break all of us. I don't think there're any more surprises."

Aston leaned forward and knocked on the mahogany table. "Just in case I put that out in the universe. We don't need to jinx ourselves."

"Damn straight," I said after a moment.

We went over the contracts one more time, before my team came back, then we signed everything electronically. By the time we were done, we had a good partnership going. Another step to the Cage and Woods legacy, one where I would ensure that my sister and her family—the one that she made over time—would have a secure financial life. My sister might not work for my company, but I would never let her go for wanting. Her wife took care of her, they both took care of each other, and were damn brilliant at their jobs. But I was going to make sure that she was even more secure. That way our father couldn't be the one to try to break her.

After our meeting, I sent a quick text off to my sister, knowing I would see her soon, and went to my house to change.

I could have probably shown up in the same suit for the club, but I didn't feel like wearing a tie tonight.

Instead of the black suit I had worn, I changed into a slightly more casual stone gray one, sans tie, and used my driver to get to the club. I wanted a couple of drinks, and I wasn't about to get behind the wheel.

My phone buzzed as we made our way downtown, and I answered, hating myself for doing so.

"It's about time you answer your phone."

"Father."

My usual driver looked up at the rearview mirror, and I shook my head.

No, I didn't need to pull over or pretend we were going in a tunnel. I would deal with this.

"I've been busy. You know how it is."

"Busy poaching clients."

I held back a smirk at that. My father loved playing the victim but he never was one. "It's what you were good at. I learned from the best."

"Stop being such a fucking recluse and do what you're

told. I hear that you are letting this wedding continue. It's a monstrosity is what it is."

I leaned forward, trying to collect my temper. "You don't have a leg to stand on when it comes to her. We both know this."

"I gave in when she decided to be a lesbian."

"You don't decide to be a lesbian, you asshole. But we both know this."

"I gave in. But why does she need to make it legal? To flaunt it in front of our society."

I didn't want to get into the logistics of finding someone that you loved and wanted to spend your life with. While I had never done that, the fact that my sister could was a triumph considering how we were raised. Our father didn't love our mother. But their families had wanted a merger that went beyond paperwork, and they had been perfect for each other in that evil, corrupt way.

I didn't want to get into the concept of marriage, and the fact that my sister being legally able to marry when it was still newly lawful these days. He would never understand who my sister was, or what she deserved. Because she deserved the world.

"You do not have a say in it. Frankly, I'm glad that you said you wouldn't be coming."

"Of course we aren't. We're not going to allow this to happen."

"Stay away from her. Stay away from her fiancée. And

stay away from me. We're not your family anymore. You made your choices, and now you have to deal with the consequences. You don't have a line. You don't have a legacy. You just have hatred. If you come near her again, I will end you. If you try to hurt this wedding, I will end you. And believe me, I have enough anger within me to make it happen permanently."

My father was silent for long enough that I was afraid the call had ended, but instead, he growled.

"You're a disgrace."

"If you're calling me that, it tells me that I have made progress. So why don't you fuck off?"

I ended the call and nearly threw my phone. Instead, I calmed down and let out a deep breath.

"Still want to head to Progress?" Andy, my driver asked.

"Yes. I could use a drink. And since you had to deal with that phone call, you could probably use the night off."

"Don't worry, sir. I'll pick you up. Maybe I'll go punch something at your gym while I wait."

"That sounds like a plan. I don't know how long I'll be."

Andy pulled up to the three-story building in downtown Denver, and I smiled at the line already forming. "Dorian sure knows how to build an audience."

"Yes, he does."

"Have you been inside?"

"I don't think it's my kind of place."

"You know it is, Andy. You like the finer things. And Dorian will let you in. He knows you."

"Oh yeah?"

"Yes. If you want to, bring a friend. Maybe that guy who I know you've been seeing for a while now."

"I don't know if that's going to last," Andy said before I could get out of the car.

"I'm sorry about that. He seemed nice from what you mentioned."

Andy shrugged. "I don't think he understands that I like being a driver, and sometimes bodyguard."

"You protect my sister when you drive her around, that's worth all types of salary. If your friend doesn't understand that, then he doesn't deserve you."

"Thanks for that, Carson."

"It's just the truth."

I nodded my goodbye and got out of the car.

I liked Andy and had known him for most of my life. His father had been one of the staff at my house growing up, and Andy had been in and out, helping where he could. When I had moved out, and moved on, I brought Andy with me. I'd offered him any place that he wanted in my company, but he liked driving around, and being the bodyguard for, my sister and other team members who needed it. It gave him time to read, and to catch up with different classes online. He had gotten his bachelor's degree, mostly because I had forced him into going to college. The guy liked to learn and had wanted a degree but never thought he could afford it. Now, he took other classes to learn history and arts. Anything he could soak up. And in his current job, he was able to do that. It was a win-win for everybody.

I just hoped he found the person he wanted. Because some people deserved happiness.

Like my sister and her fiancée.

I nodded at the doorman, who let me in past the line, and didn't bother to look over. They knew me here, because I knew Dorian, and I didn't need to lord it over those who waited to get in. Dorian was particular who got into his clubs, but it wasn't who knew who all the time. It was about fire codes and making sure people were safe.

Another reason why I liked the Cages.

Dorian stood by the bar, his arm around a cute brunette, and I realized that he had his wife with him.

I liked Harper, though I didn't know her well. They were newly married, much like many of the Cages, and seemed happy.

What must that feel like?

Dorian grinned at me as he caught my eye and murmured something to the person he was talking with before he came over.

"You showed."

"I said I would."

I looked around at the dark walls and gleaming wood fixtures, and nodded. "Nice."

"I was going for comfortable elegance."

"At least there aren't any sparkled, gilded cages around."

"You just don't like the name of the other place," he teased his wife.

Harper looked up at me and smiled wide.

"It's good to see you, Carson."

"Lovely to see you, Harper." I leaned forward, took her hand, brushing my lips against her knuckles.

She laughed as Dorian scowled.

"Seriously?"

"Flirting with my friends' wives is safe. Because you know I won't do anything, and I don't need to promise anything."

"The typical bachelor line. I like it," Harper said with a laugh.

"I'll show you what you like," Dorian snarled, then he whispered something that must have been salacious as Harper's eyes widened, her cheeks pinkening.

"Should I ask?"

"No. Go dance, find a woman. And not mine."

"Whatever you say," I said with a soft laugh, before I said my goodbyes, and nodded at a few other people that I knew.

I got my bourbon and stood in the corner, watching as people milled about the seating areas, and then turned towards the dance floor.

Even in an elegant place like this, Dorian would want dancing. That was just how the man was, and it worked here.

Countless bodies thrummed against one another, not as if at a rave, but gentler dancing that mostly came in pairs. I rolled my shoulders back and realized that it had been a little too long since I'd had a woman. If I was continually thinking about Sophia as I had been this past week, I needed to find someone. So I sipped my drink, then set it down, nodded at the wait staff nearby—they would make sure nothing happened to it—and headed out to the floor.

With one look, the woman next to me opened her arms, and I grinned.

"Hello there."

"Hi, I'm Melissa."

"Carson."

Then I wrapped my arm around her waist, and we danced.

After Melissa there was Lacey, and then Dylan, and Megan. And then two more women whose names I couldn't remember. It didn't matter. I just needed a night that had nothing to do with her.

And as if I had dreamed her up, a familiar layered

scent washed over me, and I turned to see Sophia dancing in the corner with Harper, her dark hair flowing down her back, and a small smile on her face. She had a slight limp as she moved to the side, and I knew she had to be tired. What had Dorian and the others said to pull her out of her house at night? Because I knew she never left. But the fact that she was even out, considering everything that had happened, I was so fucking proud of her.

As the song ended, I said my goodbye to the other woman, and knew it was time to go.

My cock was threatening to push against my zipper, and that meant I needed to leave.

Because it was Sophia that did that to me. One look at her and I couldn't fucking breathe.

I moved down the hallway, needing a breath, and realized I hadn't been the only one to make that choice.

Sophia looked up at me then, and her face paled.

"Carson."

"Fuck this," I growled, and then I moved forward and took what I wanted.

Because that's the kind of man I was, apparently.

She didn't protest as I cupped her face and crushed my mouth to hers.

At this edge of the hallway, we were the only two here, and nobody could see, and I didn't care. I pushed her against the wall, and she didn't resist. Instead, she grabbed my suit jacket and pulled me closer. She tasted of sugar and sweetness, and I knew she hadn't been drinking tonight. She was clearheaded, unlike me.

Two sips of whiskey and I wasn't gone over. No, it was all her that brought me to the edge.

I cursed to myself as I deepened the kiss, needing her taste, needing her. She wore a flowing lilac dress, and I slid my hand up her thigh, caressing the soft silk of her skin. When my thumb brushed against the side of her panties, she stiffened and pushed on my chest.

I let out a deep breath, my chest heaving as I rested my forehead against hers.

"No."

"Okay."

I wouldn't force, and hell, I shouldn't have even kissed her. But I couldn't stop myself from needing her. If she'd said no, if she'd pushed me away, I'd have stopped. I wasn't that man. But I still wasn't a good man. I wanted her, but that was my problem.

It always had been.

"I...I came to dance. I needed to dance."

I brushed her hair from her face and slid my thumb over her swollen lips.

"You wanted this though."

I needed to make sure. It might have sounded as if it were an order, an accusation, but it was a desperate need.

She licked her lips, her tongue darting out against my thumb, and my dick pulsed.

"I wanted a lot of things."

Her eyes filled with something I couldn't read, and then she ducked under my arm and limped down the hallway.

I cursed under my breath and hoped to hell I hadn't hurt her more.

"Are you fucking kidding me?" a deep voice snarled, and I turned to see Dorian standing there, empty glass in hand, and a scowl on his face.

"She's a grown woman, Dorian."

I hadn't meant for anyone to see. Fuck. I hadn't wanted the Cages to find out. But now, there was no going back.

"You know what she's been through. And you attack her and put your hands on her in this hallway?"

"Like I said, she's a grown woman. And when she wanted it to stop, I did. I would never force her. Don't fucking put me in the same column as that man."

"That's my sister."

"Get over it," I snapped. "She's a woman. A fucking gorgeous woman. And I didn't do anything she didn't want."

I sounded like an asshole, but then again, I was.

"Fuck you." Dorian shook his head. "Get out of here."

"I'm already damned, so why not? But talk to Sophia. Don't be the asshole brother who thinks he knows what's best. I did that once, and I almost lost Cora."

Dorian took a step forward. "I'm not going to ask you twice. Stay away from my sister."

"I'll do what she wants. You and I are friends, Dorian. Don't cross that line."

"You already crossed it."

"Dorian," Harper whispered. "Stop. Sophia wouldn't want you to act this way."

"Sophia needs someone to take care of her."

"Maybe she can take care of herself," Sophia said from behind them, and I cursed. "Dorian, don't."

"Sophia—"

"I'm gone. Don't fight over me. I'm not worth it."

And then, I pushed past both Harper and Dorian and moved towards Sophia. She tilted her head up at me but didn't say a thing.

"I won't say I'm sorry."

"You told me to never apologize," she whispered.

My lips quirked up into a smile, before I turned on my heel, and walked away.

Knowing I had once again probably ruined another good thing I'd had in my life.

Chapter Six

SOPHIA

When my father died, it felt like the world had ended. Only it hadn't ended the way that perhaps one would've wanted. He had never been a truly caring and helpful man in my life. He had focused on himself when it came to his work and personal life and had barely been around. But when he had been there, he had, most of the time, focused on his children. Perhaps not in the way that some people would want, but he had been a good man. Sometimes.

At least that's what I had thought at one point. Because in the end, he hadn't been anything of the sort. It was as if he had decided to write how much he hated his children in personal letters over time.

His lawyer, the lackey that I could not stand and had thought he'd have more power than he truly held in the end, didn't supply each of the twelve Cage children with letters at the same time. No, he had decided to do it in small spurts, waiting for the perfect moment.

It seemed only obvious that a man who would help hide so many indiscretions would be as calculated as my father's lawyer.

And so now I looked at the envelope sitting on my desk and wondered if I should just burn it. He had delivered it to me personally over a year ago, and I hadn't bothered to open it. What was the point. The man hated me. Maybe not the lawyer, but for sure my father. And I wasn't sure I could stand him either.

From what Isabella and Blakely had explained to me, the letters sent to Aston and Isabella herself had been cruel and demanding. A clawed hand reaching even beyond death.

Only here I was, staring at this letter, wondering if I should just open it and get it over with. Because burning it would haunt me. Letting it sit here on my desk for so long gave it far more importance than it earned.

With a sigh, I took the letter opener that Isabella had given me one year and sliced open the seal. Part of me would've much rather have torn it open with my teeth, and then burned it, but I was trying for subtlety.

The man had typed the damned thing. Hadn't even bothered to hand write letters to his children, knowing that he was going to hate them in the end.

Sophia—

You were always our beauty. The one that brought praise and highlighted our family in all its glory.

And then you gave up.

All you do is give up.

You were supposed to be the touchstone for our family. To show your brother that there was such thing as art of grace, and not of filth and debauchery. Instead, you walked away at the height of your career, shaming this family.

Perhaps it was because you were not good enough. I would understand that. You were never as slender as some of the other dancers. Never as flexible. There was always something off with you, and perhaps you finally realized it.

And then you walked away.

I will never forgive you for shaming this family. It's no wonder that you were alone for so long. Because nobody will want you. You were just like your mother —second rate, second best.

Do what is good for this family, and find a way not to disgrace us. Not to ruin our honor. Do not shame this family. And be better than your mother.

Signed, Loren Cage.

He had actually signed it with a pen, and the angry scrawl looked as if blood had dripped onto the page. Of course, that was only me, putting symbolism on something that wasn't there.

This man was purely evil, and I still couldn't believe that he was my father.

I rolled my eyes, annoyed.

Of all the things he could have done to try to dig into me, calling me graceless or not good enough in dance wasn't it. Because before everything had changed, I had been one of the top dancers in the country, if not the world.

Isabella, Kyler, Phoebe, and Emily had taught me that I was allowed to be prideful when it came to my talent. I was allowed to show everyone that I was good at what I did.

I was one of the best. I could have gone to other cities. I had been invited to New York and DC. Even to Paris for a summer. But I had stayed with my family because they had needed me. I thought my mother had needed me, but in the end, she had dealt with her own issues. It was only after having the twins, and having to learn to be a single mother, that I realized my mother would always live with her mistakes, but she was trying.

I was not my mother, nor was I my father.

And as I looked down at the hatred in his words, I realized that yes, I was better off alone.

He had never even met Cale. Hadn't seen the mistake for what it was.

Part of me wondered if he would've seen the cruelty beneath. And if he had, would he have done anything? No. I didn't think so.

And that sickened me like nothing else.

Again, I was better off alone.

Of course, as soon as I thought that, a certain kiss filled my mind.

Had I ever been kissed like that? With such possession, such need? I swallowed hard, wondering what the hell was wrong with me.

I shouldn't have let him kiss me, and yet how could I have said no? Because part of me *had* wanted that, had thought about it, and then it was a reality.

But as soon as I had put my hands on his chest and pushed, as soon as I had said no, he had stepped away.

Just the act of a man listening to me, it nearly broke me.

I swallowed hard, annoyed with myself. The girls were at a play date, something that had taken all of my will to allow happen. I hated letting them out of my sight, even with the nanny or my mother. But they had wanted to be with their friends, and I had given them a couple of hours. A small sliver of me had wanted to stay at the other house, but I knew that being a helicopter parent wouldn't help anybody.

So the girls were two blocks away, and I would pick

them up soon. And now I was at home, working on household chores, and completely out of my depth.

My phone buzzed, and I groaned.

Of course, the first time that I kissed a man that wasn't my ex-husband, the first time that I had nearly come just leaning against a wall with a man's hand on my thigh, my brother had witnessed far too much.

It didn't help that I had so many brothers that it was hard to stay away from them, but now Dorian knew.

And he had told everybody.

I could have been annoyed, and was, but the other part was grateful that somebody cared. Somebody had noticed. I had hidden so much of my relationship with Cale as I had been blind to what he'd been doing until it was too late. Now my family kept their eyes on me to the point that it was nearly stifling.

I turned over my phone and looked at my sister group chat.

As with any large family, we had numerous group chats. One with all siblings, some with the siblings we grew up with, and other variations. They had organically happened, and honestly, I was grateful. We were doing the exact opposite thing of what our father had wanted. We had become a family.

And now that family was catching up to me. This time though, it was the women of the Cages. My sisters, and those women who had married into the family.

ISABELLA:

What is this I hear that you were accosted in the new club?

HARPER:

They were kissing in a hallway, and Dorian witnessed the aftermath. That brother of yours is so nosy.

EMILY:

You're the one who married him, Harper. I don't know what you were thinking.

PHOEBE:

I agree with Emily on this one. But we do need to hear about all this kissing. I've seen Carson before. He's hot.

BLAKELY:

Very hot. And hell, I had just talked to him at the office right before he went to the club, and he was all broody and growly. Tell us more, Sophia.

GREER:

Wait, is there a photo of this man? I feel so out of the loop these days.

SCARLETT:

inserts photo of Carson.

I rolled my eyes.

ME:

Where did you get that photo of him? And stop it. All of you. It was just a kiss.

BLAKELY:

!!!!

SCARLETT:

Mm-mmm.

EMILY:

A kiss? Was it good?

PHOEBE:

Of course it was good. That's why Dorian went all big brother.

HARPER:

It looked good from where I was standing. She was all flushed and swoony.

ME:

Please stop. It was just a kiss.

ISABELLA:

How did it happen? I didn't even know you two knew each other that well.

ME:

It just happened. And it'll never happen again.

ISABELLA:

I'll kill him.

I sighed, as that thought reminded me of exactly what Carson had promised. Danger radiated off that man, and even though I knew he most likely hadn't ever killed somebody in truth, he had threatened Cale enough to make it happen. And the rage, well, part of me liked that.

ME:

We'll talk about it at girls' night. It's nothing to worry about. It was just a nice kiss.

Nice had nothing to do with it, but I didn't mention that.

ISABELLA:

Oh, we will be talking.

BLAKELY:

Leave off. Let her live. She deserves it.

My heart ached, and I ran my hand over my chest.

ME:

I love you all, and now I'm getting back to paperwork. Go bother one of the boys.

HARPER:

I'm going to go bother Dorian. Because this is all his fault.

My lips twitched as they all agreed, piling on Dorian,

and I set my phone down. I loved my family, all of them. But with so many of us, not only did it get confusing, it got to be a little too much sometimes.

When my phone rang, I didn't bother looking at it. Of course it would be Isabella. My big sister needed to be protective, no matter that I had it on my own.

"I'm fine. Stop worrying about me."

"Oh, really? That's not what I hear."

That sickly-sweet voice filled my ear, and my entire spine went rigid. My hands shook, bile coating my tongue.

"You're not supposed to call me," I told my ex-husband, hoping that the fear wasn't evident in my voice. From the way that Cale chuckled, I had a feeling I hadn't been able to hide it.

"I'm not supposed to be near you because of some judge. So interesting. But I'm not calling to hear about you. Or why you think you're fine. I get to see them, Sophia. You know that. The law is on my side."

"Is it? Who did you pay off to make that happen?"

"I'm not the one with the money here, Sophia. You saw to that. I will get what I'm owed. I was part of that family for long enough, and I know what I deserve."

He didn't. He deserved so much, and yet, Fate had had other plans. His voice made my skin crawl, and all I could think of was how I was grateful that my little girls weren't here. The home they were at had a similar system to mine, Ford had made sure of it, and that was the only reason they were even allowed to be with their friend. I was overprotective, and I didn't care. Cale was up to something, and he wanted to see his girls.

"Talk to my lawyer." And with that, I hung up, trying not to let my stomach roil.

When the doorbell rang, before I could even let out a breath, the small gasp that escaped me, embarrassed me. It wouldn't be Cale. He wouldn't be that stupid. But I pulled up my phone again, sent Cale to voicemail, and looked at the screen readout to see who had come to my door.

On my doorstep, was a very familiar man. With broad shoulders, green eyes, and someone who was the exact opposite of Cale.

What was Carson doing here and how did he know where I lived?

I moved to the door, knowing ignoring him would be for naught, and opened it. "How did you find me?" My hands still shook, and he met my gaze, his arms full.

"I know things. And I wanted to see you. But what's wrong? What happened?"

"Stalking me?" I asked, tears threatening.

"No, I wanted to bring you something. And I know where all of the Cages live. I'm putting my family's trust in your company, so I did research. I wouldn't have used that knowledge, but there's just something about you. I couldn't stay away. But now I think I need to find someone and break them if they're putting that look on your face."

My chest tightened, and I had to wonder how exactly this man could do this to me. It was all too much at once, and I took a staggering step back. He was there in an instant, putting two large paper bags on my entry table. When he closed the door behind him, and cupped my face, I let him. What was wrong with me?

"What happened?"

"What did you bring?" I asked, feeling like an idiot.

"I asked Harper what some of your favorite snacks and drinks were. You don't eat enough."

I looked up at him then, confused. "What?"

"I wanted to feed you. Yes, it's idiotic, but it's something I wanted to do. You don't eat enough, you don't take care of yourself. You're too busy taking care of everyone else, including those girls of yours. I didn't mean to scare you, and I would've called ahead, but well, I'm an idiot. But why don't you tell me what happened? What put that look on your face?"

"I—" I shook my head. He had brought me my favorite things? What was with this man? Why did he have to be so caring in one instant, and so confounding in the next?

He was so unlike Cale it wasn't even funny, and yet, my brain couldn't focus.

"Nothing."

"You are a terrible liar." He slid his thumb along my cheekbone, and I swallowed hard.

"It's my ex. Cale." Even saying his name made me want to throw up. I hated that just the sheer thought of that man could affect me like this.

From the way that Carson's jaw tightened, he wasn't happy with that either. "What the fuck? I'll kill him."

Why that calmed me ever so slightly, I'll never know. "You need to stop threatening to do that. Because one day I may take you up on it."

"For you, I would."

He said it as if he meant it, and it made no sense to me. Who was this man? And why did he do these things to me? I took a step back, and his hands fell. It was those little moments, the fact that as soon as I needed him to not touch me, he would stop. And yet, part of me needed him to touch me just as much.

The contradictory nature of whatever I was feeling when it came to him frustrated me to no end. So when I explained the current situation with Cale, I couldn't understand why I was letting myself be vulnerable. Yet there wasn't another way.

"Why does he get to see them? He hurt you in front of them." He paled. "Did he ever hurt them?"

I shook my head and wiped my tears. I was so done crying over this. "He never touched them. He uses them as a bargaining tool. And yet no matter what lawyers the Cages have, the cruelty of men will prevail in the eyes of our laws. That's how it is. He has rights because he's a father, even if he is a monster."

"I can beat that monster. I can kill him for you."

"I somehow believe you. And that should worry me, but it doesn't. Because I don't think you've killed a man before."

"There's always a first."

I paused, swallowing hard. "Who are you, Carson?"

He tilted his head, then reached forward, brushing my hair from my face. "I'm no one."

"That's a lie," I said, a smile playing on my face.

"I'm just a man. I own a business. I'm a brother. And I want you. Even though I know it's not good for either one of us."

"I know it's not good for either one of us at all. I don't want anyone, Carson. I played at forever, and I broke."

"I can never promise forever," he whispered.

The truth of the blow ached, and yet it was a relief. Because I couldn't promise forever either.

"Who are you, Sophia Cage?"

"I wish I knew the answer to that," I said with a laugh that held no humor.

"Should I tell you who I see?"

"Who?" I asked.

"I see a mother, a woman, a dancer, and someone who strives for goodness. Someone who should not be standing in front of me."

"And yet you're the one who came here," I said honestly. He studied me for a moment, and then I took a step away and looked at the bags. "Is any of that perishable?"

"Most likely."

"I suppose I should show you the kitchen then."

"I suppose you should."

I had no idea what the hell I was doing, and I knew it was a mistake, but I led him deeper into my home, wondering when I would wake up from this impossible dream.

"I like your house."

"Aston helped me find it," I said after a moment, feeling awkward that a man was in my home. A man who wasn't related to me.

"He's good at real estate, it's one reason that I'm working with him."

My lips twitched. "And I suppose the fact that my brother can make money out of nothing doesn't hurt."

"No. It doesn't."

"Harper really told you my favorite foods?"

"Some of them. And then I saw what you ate at your brother's house, and what you picked up at the cafe. If I'm wrong, then I can eat it. Not a big deal. But, well..." He sighed, running his hands over his hair. I had never seen him look so out of sorts. It made me like him all the more.

"Carson?"

"I don't know what I'm doing here. I wanted to be here, so I came up with an excuse. I should go, but I'm not going to unless you tell me to leave."

I looked at him, the utter openness in that sentence breaking down a small wall.

"I don't want you to go either."

"Good." We stood there, staring at one another for a few more moments, before he began to pull out cheese, my favorite crackers, a chocolate bar, fruit, and turkey jerky that was my craving recently.

"How on earth did you know that? Harper doesn't."

"It was in your purse. You know, when you swooned in my arms."

I hit him gently with the jerky. "I did not swoon."

"Whatever you say, Cage."

"Are you sure you should be calling me Cage when there's so many of us?"

"Probably not. Not with what I want to do with you."

"Carson. I don't—"

He shook his head. "Too far. That's okay. But I do like your home."

"Oh?"

"I do. I didn't see enough of your older home to get the lay of it, and I don't care about that place. But this one? This one's for you and the girls." He gestured towards Violet and Hazel's drawings on the fridge and smiled. "I was expecting them to be here." He pulled out a few snacks for the girls, and my heart did that jumping thing that was brand new to me.

"They're on a play date."

"And you're stressing out about it?"

"Yes. Because they're growing up, and well—"

"Your brothers and I will not let that man hurt them."

"I know. But he's sneaky."

"I'm sneakier." He pushed my hair behind my ear and smiled. "I won't ask what else he took from you, because that's not my place, but part of me wants to know."

Cale had taken so much, nameless things that I couldn't speak of, but maybe I could say a few things. Ones that bothered me. Ones that I tried not to think about.

"He tried to take my studio."

He tilted his head. "He did what?"

"He tried to take everything from me that he could. Including the building that I owned."

"Did he?"

"He took half of it." Shame crawled over me. "I ended up giving it to him so he would stop fighting for custody. But he continues to come back, so I did it for nothing."

"You fought for your girls, it's not nothing. And I can buy the place from him. Force him to sell. Buy it for you."

I chuckled at that, wondering what it must be like to even be able to say things along those lines. "Just like that?"

"Just like that." He trailed his thumb along my jaw, over my lips, his other hand caressing my side.

I swallowed hard, need pooling deep within me. But I wasn't good at this. I hadn't been, not since... Well, not since. And how was I supposed to tell him that even though he could touch me, I wouldn't be able to feel it. Not where it mattered. Because focusing on a man with whom I could orgasm felt as if I were leaping off the tallest bridge, and it would never be enough. But I couldn't put that out there. Not when touching myself took hours. Just to get out of my own head. So no, I didn't say those words. Not yet.

"I want you."

My heart squeezed. "And you always get what you want?" I asked, knowing the answer.

"Yes. I do."

"You can't have me," I answered, speaking the truth. Because I could barely own my own heart at this point, my own soul. I had nothing left to give him.

His eyes darkened as he leaned down and brushed his

lips along mine. My toes curled, and I let out a sigh against his skin.

"I don't want your heart, Sophia. I don't know what to do with that. But I want you."

The raw honesty of his answer shattered me. But not the parts of me that had been broken before, no, a new sense of me that I didn't want to think about too harshly. And maybe his honesty was exactly what I needed. Because I had no heart to give. Everything I held within me kept me alive and kept me here for my girls.

I couldn't give him everything, but maybe I could give him what he wanted.

What I wanted to want.

"Okay," I said, surprising me.

And from the way his eyes widened ever so slightly, I had surprised him too.

And then his mouth was on mine, deepening the kiss. He squeezed my hip, and I wrapped my arms around him, arching for him. I could barely breathe, could barely focus, it was all on him.

And when he pulled away, his hand cupping me along my side, his forehead resting on mine, he smiled. That smile that did things to me, that made me wet, that made me want.

That smile was beyond dangerous.

"Tomorrow?" he asked.

I frowned. "Tomorrow?"

"You have to pick up your girls, and I have to meet your brother, preferably without a hard-on." He laughed, and I looked down between us, my eyes widening. The way that his cock pressed against his pants should worry me. Because just the idea of his size, well, I would be thinking about that for a long time.

"Eyes up here, Sophia," he ordered.

I looked up at him then, my cheeks blushing.

He ran his thumb along my lips. "I want you to look at me. Always. But we don't have time for what we need right now. So tomorrow? Can I have you?"

"I have the girls."

"When do they go to bed?" he asked.

"Oh. Well. Early." What was I saying? What was I doing?

"I'll see you tomorrow. I want to feed you. And then I want to taste you."

I blushed, my face heating.

"Should I say okay to that?"

"Say yes. Say you want me."

"You know I want you, Carson."

"Good." He kissed me again, slowly at first, then deeper.

"Tomorrow. Lock up behind me, Sophia. I need you safe."

I followed him in a dream, his hand on mine, and then with one final kiss he was gone, leaving me standing there, gently locking the door behind him, wondering what the hell I was doing.

I had just consented to sex. Tomorrow. In my house. And yet, I didn't think it was a mistake. At least not in this moment. Later, later I could worry.

It was something I was becoming far too accustomed to, after all. That...and pretending.

Chapter Seven

CARSON

THERE WERE MANY REASONS FOR ME TO WALK away, and yet I was ignoring every single one of them.

The best possible outcome for whatever would happen next would be a broken heart, a rash decision, and a punch to the face. Namely, I would have to deal with the Cages in all of their glory, as they always stood together. It was nice to see. Hell, it was needed considering everything that family had gone through. But I should not be walking up this path with food in hand, and a questioning glance.

No good could come from this, and yet I wasn't walking away. I couldn't walk away.

Before I could even knock on the door, it opened widely, and Sophia stepped out onto the front porch. She looked so damn striking. Sometimes it was hard to even breathe when I looked at her. And honestly, that meant I was just losing my mind.

The summer heat beat down on the back of my neck, sweat glistening, and yet I couldn't feel a damn thing. I could only look at her and wonder why I wasn't walking away.

Although truly it only took a single glance to realize why I stood here.

"You came," she said softly, her eyes wide.

You're going to be coming later, I thought to myself, and wondered when that juvenile thought had slithered through. I wasn't that type of man to make comments like that, or even think them, and yet here Sophia was, making me yearn for things that wouldn't be. Ever.

She had her hair down, and it flowed into soft waves as if she had it in a braid earlier. She wore a sundress that went to her mid-thighs, and her feet were bare. Her toes were painted a coral pink—a color I only knew about because my sister had mentioned it once—and her fingernails matched.

Such a small piece of clothing clung to the slight curves that shaped Sophia, and it was all I could do not to toss the food away and push her against the door so I could have my way with her.

That would be the first of many irresponsible and irredeemable steps I could make. And because I respected the woman in front of me, I wouldn't do that.

I sure as hell wanted to though.

"I did. I brought food. Although now I'm realizing that you might have meant for me to come over for you to cook for me. We weren't very detailed in our plans."

A small smile played on her lips, and she moved forward, her bare feet soft on the pavement.

"I'm glad you brought something, though I did cook as well. You said you would be here today, and well, it felt like an out of body experience. If that makes any sense."

I moved both bags to one hand, and took a step forward, lifting my arm towards her. She didn't flinch, and I was grateful for that. She was always so careful in the movements she made when it came to other people surrounding her, and I knew it was on purpose. All because of what that man had done. But I would take it in stride and force myself to remember why we were here to begin with.

Because I wanted her.

And I couldn't stop.

I brushed her hair from her face and tucked a strand behind her ear. Her head tilted towards my touch, and I cupped her cheek, wondering if she even noticed she had done that.

Her eyes widened, and both of us merely stood there, the distance between us vast and yet nothing simultaneously.

"We were vague with the plans. So I brought a few

things to snack on. You can have them later. I'd love to try your cooking. And yes, I am inviting myself to dinner."

She smiled then, and shook her head before taking a step back. I immediately felt the loss of her touch but ignored the feeling.

"It's just a veggie lasagna. The girls like it."

"I brought something for them too." Again, I had no idea what the fuck I was doing. Why was I here at all? With her kids in the house. It made no sense, and I was an idiot, but I couldn't take those steps back.

There was no other purpose in it.

"The girls are inside," she reiterated, and I nodded.

"I understand."

Did I? I didn't mess with single moms, nor did I even allow myself to truly want them. And yet here I was, wanting the unattainable.

"They know you now. You've held them." Her eyes filled, and then she blinked the moisture away before I could utter a word. "You can be a Cage family friend. You work with my family after all, and they've met you, so it makes sense."

I brushed my finger along her collarbone, loving the way her skin pebbled. "I won't hurt your children, Sophia." That was a promise I intended to keep no matter what. I did not hurt children. I did not hurt women. I took what I wanted, but I didn't leave sheer destruction in my wake. I was not my father. Nor was I the men that I had grown up with.

I might not be a good person, but I strove to be a better person than they had ever tried to become.

"Someone promised me that before—" She put her hand over her mouth, as if she had just realized what she had said.

I set the bags down and glared. "Did he touch them? I will kill him." She put her hands over my chest, went to her tiptoes so she could kiss my jaw. I leaned down and brushed my lips against hers. The softness settled something deep within me, and I had to struggle in order to just breathe at that moment.

"No. He never hurt them. But I thought maybe he would. He...he wasn't always cruel to me. He didn't hurt me like that. Yes, he ended up being a terrible person that went too far, and deserves far more than what he got, but he never touched my children. If he had ever laid a hand on them, I would've walked away. If he'd done anything close to what he'd done to me in that moment? I would've walked away. I was already planning on it. I promised. I wasn't staying forever." She continued to try to explain herself, and it broke me to hear her try. Because in that moment, she wasn't blaming Cale for the cruelty he relished in. No, she blamed herself for what pain he inflicted because apparently, she hadn't seen the darkness within. Well, screw that. That wasn't on her.

"Sophia. Breathe. Do not blame yourself. Please. You can yell at me, push at me, but you don't get to blame yourself for what that man did. He's just lucky he's alive."

"Please don't threaten to kill him in front of the girls. He's still their father."

"Not if he's dead," I growled.

"Carson. I'm doing all that's within me to ensure that he never sees them again, and yet, they still have questions about him. And I don't have answers. So please, don't make this any harder than it is."

I stood there for a moment, took a deep breath, and nodded. Then I pressed my lips to hers, the need growing within me. "Fine. We'll eat. I want to try this veggie lasagna of yours."

"And yet you still brought food?"

"I want to feed you."

"Why is that?"

I didn't know why, and that bothered me, so I spoke the truth even though it wasn't fully fleshed out. "You take care of others, but not yourself. So let me."

Something passed over her face, but she didn't elaborate. Instead, she reached for the bags. I took them before she could and then slid my hand over hers.

"Take me inside, Sophia," I whispered, knowing that even the words such as they were, might be too much. But instead, she looked me dead in the eye, nodded, and led me into her home, putting on the bravest face I'd ever seen.

This woman...

There were no words for this woman.

I should walk away.

And that's why I wouldn't.

"Mr. Carson. Do you like spetti?"

I looked down at Violet and grinned. "Spaghetti?" I asked, trying to decipher her words.

"Yes, spaghetti," Sophia teased from the other side of the table. Somehow, I had found myself sitting at the dinner table with Sophia and her girls, as if this was an everyday occurrence. Again, I didn't know why I was there, nor did I think Sophia knew. But here we were, figuring things out. Possibly.

All I knew was that I needed to be here. I needed to find out what this feeling was. I needed to get my hands on her.

Yet another part of me knew I needed to keep her safe.

It wasn't my job—it never had been, but now I was making it my job. I knew that would bite me in the ass later, but in this moment, I didn't care.

I cleared my throat and tried to remember how to speak to children—something I wasn't great at. I didn't know much about how children interacted with others, but I did recall that Hazel and Violet liked when I spoke to them like they were people rather than the figments of fear and illusion that most children felt like to me. "I do like spaghetti. All forms of pasta. Even vegetable pasta," I teased, and Sophia rolled her eyes playfully.

Vegetable lasagna had ended up being a meatless lasagna for sure, instead of regular noodles, they were using zucchini noodles. It wasn't my favorite thing in the world, but the meal itself was pretty damn good.

"I love pasta," Hazel said sweetly, grinning at me.

"Pasta hurts my tummy," Violet said simply, but she dug into her small plate.

I gave Sophia a strange look, and she blushed. "We are trying zucchini noodles because we don't know if Violet is gluten intolerant or not. So we're taking things one at a time."

"My stomach's fine," Hazel said.

"But you don't like milk," Violet countered.

And then the two discussed every single food and how it affected their stomachs.

My lips twitched as I looked up at Sophia, who just sighed. "These are good things to know."

"You say that, and yet you don't have the spreadsheet that I do."

"Spreadsheet?" This woman. Why was I supposed to resist her again? Oh yes, I knew why. Because going down this path would only hurt her. Relationships beyond a few nights were a lie. Watching my parents and every other couple around me fall to pieces over time proved that. I wouldn't do that to Sophia and these girls. Yet I couldn't leave this table.

"One that deals with every side effect of every meal these days. Being a mom is fun."

"We love you, Mommy," both girls said at the same time, and as Sophia's eyes filled, it felt like a kick to the chest.

Sophia was a mom. A damn good one. I might not know why I was sitting here, but I wasn't leaving. I wanted to be here.

I would have to deal with the consequences later though, and I would. But for now...

"Do you have a mommy and a daddy? We have a mommy. And we love her. But my friend has a daddy who lives at home, and we don't. But that's fine." Violet said all of those words practically in one breath, and as Sophia stiffened in front of me, I knew that it was important for me to answer this correctly. So I held up my hand, so Sophia wouldn't be the one to have to break this. I already knew she was having second thoughts for why I was here, and I wasn't going to make this any harder than she needed. Plus I didn't know if she had answers, and I was going to wing it.

"I do. Though I don't live with them. I have a sister

though. One that I love." The clarification there was lost on the girls, but not Sophia. Her eyes warmed, and I continued. "Not everybody has a mommy and daddy. Some of them have two mommies, two daddies, or just one."

"Or three. Like our friend."

I smiled then, remembering that yes, we had similar friends in poly relationships. "Or three. But they are loved, just like I know your mommy loves you. And all of your aunts and uncles."

"Because we're Cages." Violet said primly, and Hazel clapped her hands.

"Yes, we are," Sophia said softly. "And now it's time to get you cleaned up because there is pasta sauce everywhere."

"Do you need any help?" I asked, surprising myself.

From the look on Sophia's face, I had done the same to her. "No, you just relax. We won't be long."

"Will you read to us?" Violet asked as Sophia picked her up and set her on her hip.

"Of course," I said without thinking, knowing I was crossing a line. The girls didn't need a father. Sophia was very plain in that. But I couldn't help but want to make sure these girls knew they were cared for. Sophia was doing that all on her own, and doing a damn good job of it, but I couldn't walk away. And that was on me.

"Carson—" Sophia began.

"No. I'll read. I want to work on the dishes, and you work on cleaning up these little monsters."

"Rar," Violet growled, and then Hazel added her own monster noises.

Sophia rolled her eyes, her lips twitching. "Thank you for that."

"I hear the sarcasm," I whispered, but I ignored it. Instead, I cleared the table and washed the dishes, knowing that this domestic side of me wasn't usual, but that was fine. I would have to learn exactly what the fuck I wanted later.

Afterwards, I sat next to the girls' twin beds, and told a story of a bowl and his best friend, and the girls giggled, before falling asleep. It was still early, but then again, my bedtime was a little later than three-and-a-half-year-olds.

When we made our way to the hallway, Sophia stared at me, wide-eyed. "They usually fall asleep only after at least two books. Did you slip them something in their dinner?" Sophia asked, and I wasn't sure she was teasing.

"I'm glad to know my voice is so boring that they could fall asleep like that," I said with a soft snap of my fingers.

"That's not what I meant."

"What did you mean?" I asked, but then I didn't give her a chance to answer. I leaned down and took her lips with mine. And although the girls' door was closed, I was still quiet. I didn't want to wake them, and I didn't want them to have questions.

She searched for answers I did not have.

Our tongues brushed against one another as my hand went to her hip, sliding up her dress.

She moaned against me, and I took a step back, needing to breathe.

"Carson. I can't promise anything."

"I know." Although I ignored the odd sting deep within me at that. I was used to being the one who set boundaries, rules. But perhaps with both of us doing the same, nobody would get hurt in the end.

"Just this once," I reiterated.

"The first and the last time," she said. "Even though I have no idea why I'm doing this."

I slid my hand down her hip, then pushed her dress up slightly to bare her upper thigh. "We both know why you're doing this."

She nodded then, and I kissed her once more. When her head tilted back, I deepened the kiss and then moved my other hand to her hip and lifted her off her feet. She let out a sharp gasp into my mouth and wrapped her arms around my neck. I carried her by her thighs as she sank into me and thankfully found her bedroom.

She had painted the walls a deep blue, and the room was covered in royal and vivid colors. Nothing light and airy, nothing grayish or lacking in soul.

This was the Sophia that she had found over time.

The Sophia that man had tried to take away.

And this was the Sophia I would have in her bed.

I set her on the edge of her bed and then went to my knees.

"Carson," she gasped.

I leaned forward, my head between her legs, and pushed her thighs apart. And then before she could say a word, I moved her panties to the side and licked up her slit. I slid off her panties in a quick motion, needing better access to the glory that was all of Sophia.

She arched back, her pussy against my face as I licked and sucked and played with her clit. She moaned against me, and her sweetness settled onto my tongue.

And as she shook, nearly at orgasm, I continued to have my fill, knowing I would crave this taste until the end of my days. When she tugged on my hair, letting out a soft sigh, I looked up and licked her juices off my lips.

"What's wrong?" I asked, feeling the sudden tension in her.

"I don't think I can come that way."

Frowning, I looked down at her soaking pussy, and then back up at her.

"You were close. I can get you off. I promise you. Just because some man might've been selfish before, doesn't mean all men hate eating pussy. I love eating your pussy, Sophia."

The stark words made her blush, but her teeth worried her lip. "Well, I'm so far into my head these days, that it takes me forever to come. And well, I haven't come with a man in a long time. Even with, well—"

"Don't say his name."

"I won't. I promise."

Different scenarios warred within my brain, and then I shifted forward and kissed her inner thigh, then bent lower to kiss the scar above her knee. Her legs were covered in them, some because of her old job, but most because of that man. The fact that she even wore a dress at all told me that she was trying to be strong for herself, and for her daughters. Every part of me admired her for it.

And the deep down part of me knew it only made me care for her more. But I ignored that part.

Any form of additional feelings had no place here.

I stood up then, and stripped off my shirt, and my belt. Her eyes widened as she took me in, and I smiled before kissing her deeply. I knew she could taste her tart sweetness on my tongue, and it only made my dick grow harder.

But knowing this needed to be about her, I settled onto her bed, leaning against her headboard, and pulled her into my lap.

"Carson. What are you doing?"

"You're going to come, and I'm going to enjoy every moment of it."

With the way the dresser was situated, we could see each other in the mirror, and she blushed from head to toe.

"I don't know if I can."

"We'll take our time. We're in no rush." I kissed her neck, taking my time. Because at this point, this would be our only time. Our last time. And I would savor every moment of it.

I knew my cock pressed against her lower back, but neither one of us said anything. Instead, I settled her in between my legs and spread her before me.

"Oh." She blushed from head to toe, her pussy wet and swollen in the reflection.

"Just touch yourself, show me what you do."

"I—I've never done anything like this before."

"Then let me be your first." Another kiss to her neck, her shoulder. I slid the top of her dress down gently, exposing one breast, and cupped her softly. I rolled her nipple in between my thumb and forefinger lazily as I watched her hand slowly slide between her thighs. And when she gently began to cup herself, rubbing her fingers along her clit, I sucked in a breath, but didn't increase my speed. I would make sure she was the one in control. Because her first orgasm in this moment would be at her hands, with my aid.

Her head fell back to my shoulder, as her gasps increased, so I took my free hand and slid it over hers.

I increased the pressure, knowing it was her hand touching herself, and her gasps came quicker and quicker.

And as soon as she realized she could let go, and yet be in control at the same time, she fell. Wetness seeped from her cunt, soaking the bedspread as she came, her toes curling, her back arching.

As she came down from her orgasm, I moved her gently so she was on her back, and I was above her, my weight on my forearms by her head.

"Carson. I haven't—" Her eyes widened, so glassy, so full of heat. But I took her mouth knowing I couldn't let her say a damn thing. Because if she spoke, I would want more.

So instead, I stripped her dress off of her and quickly undid my pants. My cock sprang out, and I swallowed hard as soon as she gripped me.

With a shake of my head, I told myself that coming with one touch would be ridiculous, and so I stripped off my clothes and grabbed the condom that I had put in my pocket earlier.

Because tonight was just about sex. That's what I told myself. That was why I was here.

There was no need for any emotion.

And as that lie wrapped around us both, I sheathed myself in the condom and took her mouth.

I wanted to go hard and fast, to take her, but instead I kissed up and down her body, paying extra attention to her nipples, and then her clit. And when she came on my tongue, I nearly groaned in relief and satisfaction. Knowing that if I said anything I could break this moment, I settled in between her legs and met her gaze.

"Still okay?" I asked.

She nodded, her eyes wide.

"Say it. Say you'll take me."

"Please. Please be inside me. Please."

And with that, I gripped the base of my cock and gently eased my way inside her. She was so damn tight it was hard to breathe, but I didn't care. I would sit in this moment, in this agony, until she was ready for me. As her cunt slowly began to take me deep inside, I rocked back and forth, easing the way.

Because I would never hurt her.

No matter what pain radiated through my body, I would never hurt Sophia Cage.

And when I found myself seated at last, I began to move, meeting her gaze.

There was something in those eyes that spoke to me, that scared the fuck out of me. So I took her mouth, knowing it would be better if we both ignored it.

We rolled so she was on top for a moment, but as her body bowed in on itself, shaking, I moved again so I was on top, taking her with every ounce of dedication and control that I had.

And then when she came, surprising both of us, I

followed, burying my face against her neck, nearly saying words that would make no sense to me later. She clung to me, as I did the same to her, finally coming, filling the condom as she shook in my arms.

This was a problem. I knew it.

But soon I would walk away, all would be well, and nothing would change.

I kissed her lips and leaned back. "Let me clean you up, and then get you some water."

I couldn't breathe and I needed to find the space to think. Because everything that I had stood upon previously had been rocked to its core, and I didn't know what to do. As I slid out of her, we both groaned. I could barely stand, but once again, I told myself this was the only time for a reason.

I took care of the condom, then slid on my pants without buttoning them. I took a warm towel and cleaned Sophia as I tucked her in bed, and I knew it would take her a moment or two to come out of whatever haze she lay in.

Needing a moment to breathe myself, I walked into the kitchen.

"What the fuck are you doing here?"

I whirled, the glass falling from my hands, as I looked up to see Flynn and James standing in Sophia's kitchen, murder on their faces.

Well, hell.

Chapter Eight

CARSON

"What the fuck?" Flynn snarled, and then he was on me, his forearm pressed against my neck, my back against the wall near the refrigerator. The only reason it had even gotten to this point, was that I let him. Flynn deserved the first punch, maybe the second. After all, if I had walked into my sister's house and seen my so-called friend with Cora, I'd have an issue.

Then again, Cora always made better decisions than I did.

"I let you have that one, but that's it," I said softly, grateful that I could even breathe with the pressure at my neck. I had taught Flynn well, after all.

"Ease up, Flynn," James warned as he moved forward and put his hand on his brother's shoulder. He still glared at me, however. I was not out of the doghouse. Not that I deserved it. I had just slept with their sister, and now stood in nothing but my pants, still smelling of sex, while in her kitchen.

"I can't believe you fucking touched her. *My sister*."

James pulled his brother back, a scowl on his face. "Flynn. Stop. We're going to wake the girls. That's why we walked in without ringing the doorbell to begin with."

Flynn moved closer again, the snarl on his face deepening.

"Flynn? James? What are you guys doing here? Oh my God. Get off Carson. What the hell do you think you're doing?" Sophia came in then and pushed herself between Flynn and me. She lifted her chin, not a single ounce of fear in her body, and I cursed. With one movement, I twisted Flynn's wrist not to give pain, but so he would move back, and gently pushed Sophia to the side.

"Don't put yourself in between us," I ordered.

"Don't tell my sister what to do," Flynn snapped.

"Sophia? What's going on?" James asked.

I looked between the three of them and held back a curse. What the hell had I been thinking? No, I hadn't been thinking. That was the problem.

Here I stood in Sophia's homey kitchen, with her large island and deep green lower cabinets with lighter glass cabinets above, and felt as if I had never been more out of place.

I knew I shouldn't have touched Sophia. Hell, I had told myself repeatedly that I should walk away.

But over a year ago, I had seen her and had wanted to hold her. I'd wanted so much more. All because I saw the fire in her, and that connection had clicked in an instant. It shouldn't matter though, because when it came to Sophia Cage, I was not the right person for her. And yet here I was, taking what I wanted because I was just as much of a fucking asshole as everyone had always accused me of being.

The moment that I wanted something I took it. I had either worked hard for it, or called it my own by right.

It was just how I had built my business, my gym, and my friend circle. I had done everything in my power to create what was mine, and hadn't let the consequences matter.

Clearly they did.

Because here Sophia stood in her home, her hair looking as if I had run my hands through it for the hours that I had, her lips swollen, her legs bare, and she was here, standing up for me. As if I had any claim to that heart of hers. As if I had earned her protection. But I hadn't. I had been the one to pursue. I was the one here now, and I would be the one to deal with the consequences. Sophia waited. No matter what I did, Sophia would have to be safe.

I might not be able to promise her forever, or even beyond this moment, but I could promise her that.

"So? Is anybody going to answer me?"

"We were just checking on you," James said simply, as if there were anything simple about what was happening.

"By breaking into my home?"

"And you just let him in?" Flynn asked, the derision in his tone hurting more than it should. They were my friends, but then again, I'd gone behind their back and slept with their sister. I deserved a punch and hadn't gotten it yet.

"We weren't breaking into your home," James said softly. "We didn't want to wake the girls. And when you didn't answer your phone or your door, we got worried." James met my gaze and glared. "Clearly we were unaware of the changes in circumstances."

"As in our friend taking advantage of our sister."

"You're lucky that I'm trying to be quiet because I don't want to wake the girls, but don't you ever say anything like that again," Sophia said softly, her voice fierce. "What happens between Carson and me has nothing to do with you."

"So something *is* happening?" Flynn asked.

"As if you couldn't see it for yourself?" I drawled.

Sophia elbowed me in the stomach, though it didn't do much. I looked down at her, and she glared up at me. "You're not helping."

"What is there to help? I sullied their perfect sister." I leaned forward and brushed my thumb along her jaw. "But I'm not sorry about it."

"Stop touching her," Flynn bit out.

"What the hell is happening here?" James asked.

"It's none of your business," Sophia said. "We are two adults, and again, none of your business."

"It is our business. You don't know what Sophia—" Flynn stopped himself, and Sophia stepped in front of me. I put my hand on her shoulder to steady her, because I knew she shook, but from the way that both Flynn and James glared at that action, I knew it was a mistake. But not for her. And whatever happened, Sophia was the important one here. I might have just broken my friendship, potential business assets, and so much more, but I would not break Sophia.

"Don't. I might have made a terrible decision once, but I will not make that same mistake again."

Both faces paled, and James swallowed hard before holding up his hands. "That is not what we meant." He looked over at Flynn and raised a brow. "Correct?"

"Right." Flynn nodded tightly, and then glared at me. "We're just worried about you."

"Then don't be. I'm sorry I didn't answer a text, or the door. Although it is late enough that maybe I was sleeping. Or, I don't know, being an adult and having an evening to myself. But don't worry, it's never happening again."

The certainty of her tone slapped at me, but it was nothing I didn't already know. It was what we had already decided. So I nodded and stared at both of them. "I'm sorry that you walked in on me in her kitchen getting water. Now, if someone will point me to the broom, I'll clean up my mess."

Sophia whirled at me, and I reached for her, so she didn't step to the side and onto the broken glass with her bare feet. "Watch out. I don't want you to hurt yourself."

"So now you care," Flynn muttered.

Sophia went to turn and say something to her brother, but I kept her steady. "Broom?"

"You don't have to clean this up."

I knew she wasn't speaking of just the glass, but I had a feeling there wasn't much to fix after this.

"Sophia. Go put on clothes, and I'll clean this up, and then I'll leave. I'm sorry for hurting your brothers."

She studied my face, her eyes covering every inch, before she nodded tightly, her throat moving as she swallowed hard. "Fine. Thank you for reading to the girls."

And with that, she moved towards her bedroom, ignoring her brothers completely. I didn't glance at them as I went to the pantry, and was grateful that I happened to find the broom as nobody had pointed the damn thing out to me. James was already on the ground, picking up the large pieces and using a paper towel. We each worked to clean up my mess, at least this part of it.

"Why don't you walk outside with me once you find your damn shirt," Flynn said softly.

"Flynn—" James began.

"No, that's fine. I'll meet you outside."

"If you kill each other, it will only make things worse." James shook his head and helped me take care of the rest of the broken glass.

"I'm not going to kill him. I like your brother, contrary to what it may be looking like at this moment."

"You didn't like me enough to stay away from my sister."

"I wasn't aware I was warned off from her. Next time maybe you should be a little more territorial when it comes to your family. Then again, I never did like rules."

"You are not this much of a psychopathic asshole," James said with a dramatic sigh. "Go put on your shirt, get your things, and talk calmly to Flynn. Neither one of you are going to hurt one another. That would just harm Sophia and the rest of this family. However, we both know that you being in this house right now isn't going to help anything. Especially since Sophia seems to have already said her goodbyes."

With a glance at both of them, I moved back to the bedroom, knowing that tonight hadn't ended how I wanted, but perhaps it was for the best. Sophia stood there now, in soft linen pants and a tank top, her arms folded underneath her breasts. She'd put her hair up in a bun. "I'm sorry about them."

"Don't be. It's good you have people in your corner."

"You say that, and yet, I'm not used to people walking into my house to be so growly and protective."

I reached forward and cupped her face. "It's okay that you do."

"I..." She blushed. "I had a lovely time tonight. If we ignore the whole brawl that was about to happen in my kitchen."

I leaned forward and took her lips with mine. Just a gentle kiss, a caress, a goodbye. "I had a good time tonight too, Sophia. I'll never forget."

She studied my face but I couldn't read her eyes. Maybe that was for the best. "Considering you are so entwined with my family, I don't think I'm going to be able to forget either."

I let my thumb glide over her lower lip, loving the way her mouth parted.

"Thank you. For tonight. For sharing yourself and part of your evening with me. Those little girls are amazing."

Sophia's entire face brightened. "They really are, aren't they? I just... I'm not good at this."

"Neither am I. I'll fix this with your brothers. They're not going to hurt you."

"They never would. I just don't want them to hurt you." She hooked her fingers into my belt loops, and I leaned down, pressing my forehead against hers.

"It was a pretty damn good evening even if it was just for one night."

"I guess you're right about that. I'll see you around, Carson Woods."

I kissed her again, because I couldn't help it.

"You too, Sophia Cage." And then I shifted back and grabbed my clothes. I quickly dressed as I walked out through the kitchen, and then to the porch. James had clearly stayed in the house to grill Sophia, or maybe just to comfort her since I was leaving like the recluse that I was.

Flynn stood by my car, arms folded over his chest much like Sophia's had been.

"Are you fucking kidding me? You slept with her?"

"We both wanted each other, and we both said it would be just for one night. There were no broken or hurt feelings until you walked in and embarrassed your sister." The snap in my voice increased, and I realized *that's* why I was angry. Or at least part of why.

Yes, I would regret walking away, but it was the smart choice.

But they had embarrassed her, and I couldn't let that slide.

"You're a fucking asshole. You've told me more than once that you don't want to settle down. That you don't see yourself as a one-woman man. Or even someone who wants a relationship. And then you go and sleep with my sister."

"Sophia is a grown woman and we both made a choice."

"And you were never going to tell us?"

"Why would I tell you about what your sister and I do? It's none of your business."

"She's family. Of course it's my business."

"You say that, and yet you're never going to tell your family about—"

Flynn's fist slammed into my jaw. I regretted the words as soon as they were out, and I staggered back, knowing I deserved the hit.

"I'm sorry." I held up both hands. "I won't mention it. I'm sorry," I reiterated.

"Don't you ever..." Flynn's hands shook as he took a deep breath and rolled his shoulders back. "I didn't see what Cale was doing until it was too late." He held up his hand before I could snap out my anger. "And I know you would never do what he did. But she's still in a vulnerable place."

"And she's a woman. Who asks and gets what she wants."

"I like you, Carson. I really do. But I don't want my sister to get hurt."

"And I don't want to be the one that hurts her."

And with that, I pushed past him and got into my car. As I drove away, I watched Flynn stand there, his hands in his pockets, looking far more defeated than even I felt.

I knew I should have never gotten close to Sophia, and I would regret part of it till the end of my days. But I would never regret touching her. Being with her.

Walking away however? This was what would break me more than ever.

My phone rang as I turned towards the highway, and I answered on Bluetooth. "Cora? Are you okay?"

"Oh, I'm fine. Just hadn't heard your voice in a couple of days. Juliet is working, and I was craving ice cream. I thought maybe my big brother would want to come over and have a sundae with me?"

"What happened?" I asked, knowing she wouldn't just call out of the blue and invite me over like this.

"Mom called. I answered because I'm an idiot. She didn't say anything new, but I really want ice cream."

"I'll be there soon. I promise."

"I know you will. I love you, big bro."

And just like that, she believed in me. Because she could trust me.

But she couldn't trust our family. No matter what she did to reach out, to try to prove to them that she was worthy of their love, they hit back, and they proved that they were nothing in comparison.

And that was why I would never settle down. I would

never give in as Cora had with Juliet. Those two were luckier than most.

Love and family would break you. I had my sister, and I would protect her to the end of the earth. Just like Flynn and James were doing with Sophia.

They were doing the right thing by protecting her. And if I made a move towards Sophia again, or gave in to the temptation burning within, I knew it would only break us. Because one of us would disappoint the other, and then it would be all for naught.

No, this was better. A single taste, a single touch. And now I was walking away. But why did it feel like I was making another mistake? One that would possibly break both of us in the end?

Chapter Nine

SOPHIA

"Be good for your grandmother," I said as I knelt down in front of Hazel and Violet and kissed their little cheeks. I loved spending time with my girls. In between work, and the constant drama that was my ex, sometimes I didn't feel like I had enough of it. But they were the light of my life, and I hoped they knew that.

"Of course, Mommy," Hazel said softly as she kissed my cheek right back.

"Love you," Violet added and kissed my other cheek.

"Are you ready to spend time with Grammy?" my mother asked as she ran her hands over my little girls' heads and smiled.

My mother had been a good mother growing up. She had cared about us and ensured that we were able to lean into our strengths. We'd played sports, danced, and Kyler had always been able to focus on his music. She had loved us and helped us strive to become who we needed to be.

A side of me had always wondered if she had focused so hard, had pushed with so much devotion, because she knew she held a secret.

She had tried to take the place of both mother and father when our dad couldn't be bothered, but then again, she had known about the secret family the entire time. Had worked out a way to still be with the man that she loved—despite his faults—and keep the secret from her kids.

As a mother myself, I partly understood why she had done it.

Growing up, if we had known we were only second best in his eyes, or worse, I don't know if we would've thrived like we had. She had put blockades in front of us to protect us, and perhaps it hadn't been enough, but she had done her best, and honestly had to atone for her sins.

It wasn't my job to judge her or the choice that she had made as a wife. And as a mother, well, as I looked back on everything that she had done for us, I realized that she had tried her best. Maybe it wasn't enough for some of my siblings, but knowing that I would raze the earth to protect my girls, I understood some of her choices.

"You guys are going to have a blast today," I said as I looked up at my mother and hoped she saw the truth in my gaze. I didn't hate her. I didn't resent her. Maybe part of me would always wonder why she had made those choices, but I was not my mother.

"We will. We're going to be playing with slime."

I groaned. "Really?"

"It's a grandmother's prerogative. Plus I set aside a whole part of the house, so it looks like Dexter's basement.

The girls looked confused, and I tried not to laugh because my mother was doing her best. And honestly, she was a fantastic grandmother. She deserved all of the love and adoration for that. She even cared for the grandkids that weren't hers by blood.

Melanie Cage had essentially been kicked out of the family. She hadn't been a good mother. Had been cruel, and vindictive, and had hated my own mother. So no, I would never forgive that woman for the pain and terror she caused. But I was not part of that circle.

My mother held Aston's son as if she were his grandmother in truth, and from what I could see, that baby would grow up knowing that he was loved by so many people, including his grandmother Constance. It was the same with Ford's child, and any other child who would come from the Cages.

My mother now had twelve sets of Cage families to watch over, and all of their next generation. So while mistakes had been made, there had been a purpose none of us could ever hope to understand.

"Do you have any good plans for the day?"

"Paperwork. My team is running the studio today, since I worked late into the night, but household chores and paperwork are calling my name."

My mother reached forward and touched my face. "Take care of yourself too, my darling."

"I will. I promise."

"Is Mr. Carson coming?" Violet asked and it took me a moment to get through the buzzing in my ears to answer.

My mother gave me an odd look, the curiosity in her gaze blinding.

"I believe he's working. *With your uncles.*" I looked at my mother and hoped that she didn't ask any questions at this moment. I still answered a few unasked ones anyway. "He's friends with James and Flynn and has met the girls a few times because of the merger."

"Ah." I didn't know if my mother truly believed that, but she wouldn't ask. Because once the truth had been laid out about the formation of our family, she would never pry. And while some of me wanted to bare my soul to her, the rest knew that doing so would open up all the pieces I wasn't ready to speak on.

Namely, the fact that I'd had the best sex of my life with a man I might never see again.

It was totally normal.

"Okay, have fun, girls. And try not to make too much of a mess for Grandma," I teased.

The girls chattered in their own secret language, speaking a mile a minute, and I only caught every fourth word or so. My mother leaned forward and squeezed my hand, the touch startling.

"Enjoy your time alone. The quiet is always nice."

As a mother of five, I knew my mother understood that more than most.

"I will. The vacuum is calling me."

"It always does," she said with a small laugh. She studied my face once more, and I knew she had other questions, but she didn't ask and I didn't answer. Instead I watched as she took the girls for their afternoon with their grandma, and I went back to my small office.

This home wasn't my dream home, wasn't our forever home. But it was the one I could afford after the divorce. Cale had taken so much from us, but I never wanted to sleep under that old roof again, not after the attack. My girls had never stepped foot inside that house after we had taken them away. No, they would never even look upon it again. If I could bulldoze it, I would. Cale had sold it and moved to a bigger place once he was finished with the courts. I didn't want him to have the girls, didn't want him to see them, but I knew once I was done with this phone call with my lawyer, I was going to end up being rageful.

But Cale would never walk into this home of mine. He would never see what I had made with my own two hands. One day we would move to a bigger place, where the girls could have their own rooms, and my office wasn't a mere closet off the kitchen. I loved this home, and I knew that if I asked, any one of my siblings would help me buy a bigger one for the girls, but I needed to do this on my own.

With a sigh, I looked at the clock and understood if I didn't call my lawyer soon, I would be late. So I sat down at my desk, pulled out my notebook, and hoped that this would have a better outcome than last time.

When I hung up the phone, I rubbed my temple, and realized that no, it hadn't gone well at all.

In fact, the concept of things being truly evil settled in.

Cale would be taking the babies for his night soon. We would go over a time through our lawyers, but it would be coming.

He didn't even have supervised visitation.

That man had nearly killed me with my babies in the next room, and yet he was allowed to see the girls without somebody there to make sure that they were cared for, that they were safe.

How the courts had failed us this deeply, I would never know, but I would never trust them again. I wanted to bundle the girls up and run away, to keep them safe forever, but I knew that there would be no hiding.

Laws didn't exist to keep us safe.

They just existed for men to thrive.

My phone rang, and I looked at it as if it were a snake ready to strike. As Cale's name appeared on the readout, perhaps that was truth.

He wasn't supposed to be calling, no, he should have been contacting me through our lawyers. But Cale never did listen.

I needed to send him to voicemail, but I was also about to give him our babies—no, *my* babies—for a weekend. And if I angered him now, I didn't know what he would do to retaliate.

Fear and anger warring within me, I answered.

"Yes."

"I see the lawyers have spoken with you. We'll be arranging a time soon for me to see my girls."

I gritted my teeth, knowing he was going for my reaction. He had wanted sons, and had never called them his with that proprietary tone. No, he would only do so to try to get me to fight back.

He wanted to get a reaction, and I wouldn't give it to him.

"The lawyers will let us know on the calendar. I will have a list of things that the girls need, what they're allowed to eat, and things for their allergies."

"I know what my girls want. Don't patronize me. You might think that you're acting the good mother, but I know for a fact that they're rarely under your roof, yet a certain man seemed to be."

Ice crawled up my veins as I knew he had been watching us. It didn't matter what security I had on my house, what my family did to protect us, it would never be enough.

Because evil prevailed.

"Our lawyers will handle it then." And with that, I hung up the phone, knowing I would just anger him. Yet maybe not. Because he'd gotten the rise out of me that he wanted.

Heart racing, I pulled away from my desk, grabbed my phone, and began to pace.

My lawyer was doing what he could, but Cale had more connected friends than I had ever guessed. He had married me for my money and all my connections, but he hadn't been able to get anything out of that, so he had tried to ruin everything.

He tried to ruin me.

I knew he was taking my babies.

With a deep sigh, I stared at my phone and realized I needed to talk to someone.

Isabella and Blakely would be working, as there was a large meeting coming up with the Cages. I could call any one of my siblings, even my mother, but as my phone went to my contact list, I called the one person I shouldn't

—and hadn't even realized I was doing so until it was too late to back out.

"Princess?"

At the sound of his deep voice, my heart slowed ever so slightly. No longer feeling as if I was going to pass out, I leaned against the counter and wondered if I had lost my mind. Why the hell was I calling this man at this moment?

"Don't call me princess," I said halfheartedly. Why did hearing his voice calm things in me?

I should hang up. I shouldn't have called at all.

"Why are you calling, Sophia? Is there something wrong?"

I shouldn't tell him a thing.

"Cale— Is he there? Are the girls safe? What did he do?"

I could hear him rustling in the background, as if he was moving, and my hand tightened around the phone. "He just called. And I heard his voice, and it was after we talked with the lawyers." I explained everything that had happened, the words falling from my lips without thought. I could have called anyone else, and yet why did I call him?

"I should have just left it alone. I'm sorry, I shouldn't have called. I shouldn't lean on you."

"No, you should have called me. And you did. And don't apologize, Sophia."

"You don't deserve that burden." He paused for so long I was afraid he'd hung up.

"Maybe it's not a burden, Sophia." Another pause. "I'll pick you up in ten minutes. Bring a suit."

I stiffened, looking down at the phone for a moment, trying to contemplate what the hell he had just said.

"What?"

"Are the girls with you?"

"No, they're with my mom."

"Pity, they would've had fun. But this is for you."

"Carson..."

"Just breathe, Sophia." *A deep breath.* "No promises. Right?"

This time that phrase didn't wrap me in comfort, it wrapped me in apprehension. Yet I answered anyway.

"No promises." And that was how I found myself on a boat on Cage Lake of all places, wearing a sundress over my bathing suit, a large hat covering my head and shoulders, staring at Carson as he maneuvered the decently sized speedboat across the lake.

When he showed up at the house, I thought I had been dreaming, and yet he had taken one look at me, brushed my hair from my face, and piled me in his SUV.

During the drive up we talked about the merger, and the girls' upcoming recital. Nothing important and yet everything. I didn't understand who this man was, or why he was here. But he seemed to be a fixer, one who needed to make sure everyone around him was taken care of. Maybe that was why he had done the same with me. Just like he did for his sister.

"When did you find out that your family owned this town?" Carson asked as he stopped the boat, and we rested on the water. He sat next to me, his feet outstretched, and I couldn't help but look at the man. He had on long cargo shorts, a white muscle top, and a linen shirt over it. He'd put a ball cap on, but put it backwards, his hair longish underneath the brim. He also wore expensive sunglasses that just made him look sexy as ever. I had told myself, just like we had told each other, that we would not want anything more than that one night. And yet I couldn't stop staring at him. What was this? And did I want the answers?

"I found out when the rest of my family did. I never even knew there was a small town called Cage Lake up in the mountains. But here it is, the perfect tiny town with its own lake and everything plastered with my last name on it. It's a little disconcerting."

"I should build a town for the Woods family. Just to rival yours."

"I'm sure the family would love seeing that happen. Isabella, however, would do all in her power to keep Cage Lake in the top spot. She's slightly competitive."

"So says the principal ballet dancer."

"Well, she is even more so than me. Just saying."

"Good to know."

"So your family, you have your sister Cora, right?"

He stared at me for a moment, as if I had crossed a line, and maybe I had. But he seemed to know so much about me, and I barely knew anything about him.

"Yes, Cora is ten years younger, getting married soon. In fact, she keeps pestering me to bring a date."

I smiled softly.

"Oh really?"

"Well, I suppose bringing a date to the wedding is expected for most people. But I want to bring someone who knows that there will never be a promise. Someone that understands. I don't want what my sister has. She and Juliet are perfect for each other, and that's great, but I've seen the other side of things. Just like you have."

My heart shuddered, and I knew he was telling the truth, so why did I feel so disappointed?

"My parents are still alive. But they're terrible people who don't understand that my sister loves another woman. Nor did they understand that I don't want to be part of their business. My father and your father were friends for a reason."

I leaned into him and squeezed his hand. When he tangled his fingers with mine, his thumb rubbing my palm, I didn't even think he'd realized he had done it.

"You're a good big brother."

"I try to be. You should come with me."

I frowned, trying to meet his gaze.

"To where?"

"To the wedding. You would like Cora. And I like seeing you in dresses."

I didn't say anything, as I watched the sun glisten over the water, and realized that neither one of us knew what we were doing. But I did not want forever either, I reminded myself. I had thought I had once, and it had nearly broken me. So maybe this was the best case scenario.

"I can go. For your sister. She needs all the people that she can get in her corner for sure."

"Good." His eyes darkened, and then he leaned down and nipped at my lip.

"Carson."

"We're both adults. We can say no, but if you want me for this? To be your friend? Then I'm here."

I swallowed hard, need warring with reality, and yet, this was exactly what I had wanted. Carson, but on our own terms. No forevers.

I nodded, and then he smiled before kissing me softly and standing up.

"I made a chicken Caesar salad on a baguette, and I have that sparkling water you like. The flavored stuff. You should eat."

"How...how did you know that's one of my favorite sandwiches?"

"I told you, Sophia. I pay attention."

And then I found myself eating my favorite sandwich, with my favorite drink, wondering how he could continue to do this without asking for a single thing in return. And what did I give him?

Worry? My body? I could give him that freely. But it wasn't enough. Because he never said a damn thing about what he needed. Nor did I know what I would give if he truly spoke his feelings.

After we finished eating, and I slathered on more sunscreen, I finally relaxed. A sense of peace washed over me, and while I knew I had a thousand things to do when I got home, and work piling up, it didn't matter in this moment.

When he began to rub my feet, I pulled them away.

"I have dancer's feet, they're so ugly."

He scowled at me and pulled my legs onto his lap.

"I box, and I fight MMA occasionally. My nose is broken, and I have calluses on my feet and hands. Your feet look like they do because of your strength and your discipline. Don't be embarrassed."

Blushing, I let him rub my feet and god, I couldn't help but moan into him as he pressed his thumb into my arches. He smirked at me, and I knew exactly what he was going for.

And then his hands slid up my legs, massaging my

calves, my thighs. When he gentled his touch over my scars, my back straightened.

"You don't have to do that."

"I remember you."

I frowned. "What do you mean by that?"

"I saw you dance. More than once. You were so fucking beautiful. I couldn't keep my eyes off of you."

I had no words for that. He had seen me dance? Before the accident? Who was Carson Woods and why was he holding me?

"I saw you then, and I knew you. I still see the strength within you. Even if you don't dance anymore, I still see you, Sophia."

And then his hands were moving again, this time parting my thighs. I leaned back on the soft cushion, as he positioned himself between my thighs, and kissed and sucked his way to the apex.

"So warm, so wet already."

"Carson. You don't have to."

He kissed over my bathing suit bottoms, then tucked them to the side. "I told you I love eating pussy. I love eating *your* pussy. So don't tell me not to. Unless you truly don't want me to have my tongue on your cunt."

"You with this dirty talk." I slid my hand down my stomach to his hair, tangling my fingers. "I think I like it."

"Good."

And then his mouth was on me, and I gasped out his

name. He spread me with his tongue and moved so his fingers did the same. When he blew cool air over my heat, I arched for him, my toes curling. And then he sucked my clit into his mouth, sending me over the edge. Just like that, I was coming over his face, my wetness sliding down his chin, and he continued to eat his fill. And when he hummed against me, my thighs clamped around his head, the orgasm still shaking me.

He leaned back onto his knees and wiped his chin. I should be embarrassed, but he was so damn sexy in that moment, I couldn't breathe.

"Sweet and tart. My favorite dessert."

I knew he'd never want me to feel embarrassed, so in answer, I scrambled to my knees and pushed him so he was on his back. He let out a rough laugh, and I undid his pants before he could say anything. When I pulled him out of his boxer briefs, his eyes darkened once more.

"Sophia. You're playing with fire."

"I think I'm playing with your cock."

Even the words sounded foreign on my tongue, but as he smiled greedily, I pumped him once, twice, and then licked the slit at the tip of his dick. His eyes crossed, and I knew I had done the right thing. When I lapped at the barbell right at the slit, his whole body shuddered.

"Sophia. Damn."

"Can I swallow you like normal with this?" I asked, honestly curious.

He moved forward slightly, his hand outstretched to tug on my hair. The slight sting sent shivers through my body, and he smirked as if he knew exactly what he was doing.

"Just be careful of your teeth, and the back of your throat. I promise not to hold you down and fuck your face like I want to. I don't want to hurt you, Sophia."

I ignored the implied double meaning behind that and slowly began to work my way down his length. He tugged on my hair, but kept it loose as I sucked and licked at his cock. I used my other hand to cup his balls, and he shuddered in my hold. I felt so powerful with him under my control, so I hollowed my cheeks, and let my throat relax so he could go farther down. When my nose touched the base of his cock where that trimmed patch of hair lay, he cursed under his breath.

"Jesus Christ," he said aloud. "That's it. Look how pretty you are with my cock down that throat. That's it, look at those lips. All swollen. Do you like my cock, baby? Do you want more of it? Would you like my cock in that pretty cunt of yours? You're so tight. Every single time that I watch my cock sliding in and out of you, it's all I can do not to pound into you harder, and claim it as mine."

He continued to murmur those things as I worked faster, needing him. When I felt his balls tighten, he pulled me away and crushed his mouth to mine.

"I want to come on those tits or in that pussy of yours. Let me," he murmured against my mouth.

"My pussy, please. Fuck me."

"Dirty words for such a princess."

I could barely think with the heat running through my veins. "Don't call me princess."

"Maybe I'll just fuck you like one then."

And then I was on my back, my bathing suit completely off next to my dress, and Carson was there, naked as well, where anybody could drive by on their boat, but I didn't care.

He sheathed himself in the condom I didn't even realize he had, and then he was at my entrance.

"Tell me if I hurt you."

"You can't, Carson."

Again, a double meaning, one that we both ignored.

And when he pressed deep inside, I gasped, the intrusion nearly too much. He was so thick, so long, that it took a moment for me to accommodate him, but then he was sliding into me, balls deep, and I couldn't ask for more. My nails dug into his shoulders as he pounded into me, and I reached for him, thrust for thrust. And when he pulled out and flipped me on my hands and knees, I gasped.

"That's it, look at that beautiful ass of yours. I want to fuck that ass. Will you let me? Will you let me, Princess?" He slid his thumb over my hole, and I stiffened.

"Don't worry. Not today. But one day, I'm going to fuck that ass, and you're going to take every inch of me."

"I don't think so," I teased. But when he used my own wetness to lube up my hole and slide his finger inside, I gasped, pushing back at the intrusion.

"Look at you, taking my cock and my finger at the same time. You're always so beautiful, Sophia, even more so now. I'm a bad man and I don't fucking care."

Blushing from head to toe, I arched against him as he grabbed my hips with both hands and pounded into me. He leaned over me, kissing up my spine, playing with my breasts in just the perfect way. I wanted to reach back, to play with the barbells in his nipples, to just play with him, but he was the one in control now, and that was just fine with me.

"Play with yourself, make yourself come as I fuck you." I did as he asked, leaning on one forearm as I used my other hand to play with my clit. And when I finally came, clamping around his cock, he sucked in a sharp breath through his teeth and pounded harder. I found my cheek on the cushion, my ass in the air, and he was moving fast, hard. But before I could say anything, still coming down off my orgasm, I found myself riding him, my body shaking, meeting his gaze.

"Let me see your eyes. I need to see your eyes when I come. Let me feel you, Princess. That's it. Move."

Tears threatened at the words, and I knew it was just

sex to him. That's all this was. We may care for each other, in a way of friends, but that was it. No promises.

When I met his gaze, I couldn't read the emotion there, and I nearly closed my eyes.

Somehow I found the strength within me to do what I should have done in the first place. I met his gaze, rolled my hips, and watched him come. Warmth spread within me as he filled the condom, and part of me ached for him to fill *me*, but I knew that was just the orgasm whispering.

As he had one hand on my breast, the other hand on my hip, claiming me in all aspects, this was just this moment, it was all it could be.

I couldn't read his face, couldn't tell what he was thinking. So I leaned down and buried my head against his throat, needing a moment just to breathe. He was still deep inside me, stretching me, holding me, and in this moment, it was everything that I needed.

Chapter Ten

CARSON

While I wasn't a romantic man, nor did I truly believe that people could find their forevers in a blink, I would never begrudge my sister her happiness. If she wanted love and forever and whatever else came from being with Juliet, I would do anything to make sure that happened.

Even if it meant burning down the world to get there. And while not everybody would agree with me, they would just have to deal with the consequences.

Today was the big day.

My baby sister would be marrying the woman that she loved, and there would be no going back from that. I liked Juliet. I respected her, and I wanted her to have the best future she could possibly have.

And that meant blocking anybody who would dare come for my baby sister.

It also meant that I'd had to learn what certain flowers were called, and help figure out seating arrangements, as well as far too many of the minute details that came with getting married.

Cora and Juliet hadn't wanted a huge wedding that would go on for hours and put them in debt—not that I would truly allow them to pay for anything in this wedding, but they didn't know that.

My lips quirked into a smile as I thought about what they would say when they realized that I had paid for everything, and they were just going to have to deal with it.

I had no plans on getting married, having children, or walking those imaginary daughters and sons down the aisle. I wasn't quite sure I could be that person at all. No, that wasn't what I needed or craved.

There had been the bridal shower, something I had been forced to do and had been the only man in attendance. I had sat in the corner and glared, and my sister had looked happier than I'd ever seen her. She truly loved goading me, but I probably did the same to her. It's why we worked so well as siblings.

There had been the rehearsal dinner, and the rehearsal itself. I honestly hadn't realized how many logistics went into creating a wedding, and thought there should be far more details when it came to creating a marriage. Cora and Juliet seemed to be on the same page when it came to that, and I was grateful. Not many people had come to the rehearsal as the wedding party was small. Each wife had their best friend—other than each other, of course—standing for them. I was the one who would walk my sister down the aisle, while Juliet's parents would walk her down. I had seen the anguish in my baby sister's eyes for a mere moment before she had blinked it away and acted as if she wasn't in pain watching Juliet's parents love their daughter so unconditionally.

But I had also seen the way that the older couple had brought Cora into their arms, and ensured that my sister knew that she was now family. There would be no questioning their love for both of their daughters now. She had found her person, the one person that would be hers forever, and she was marrying into a family that adored her. That respected her. And that wanted only the best for her.

So of course I was damn proud of her. Why wouldn't I be?

My date hadn't gone to the rehearsal, nor had she come to any other part before this. Getting her away from her family, her job, her work, and much more seemed insurmountable, but Sophia would be here today. I had offered to pick her up, but she had shaken her head, kissed me softly on the mouth, and told me that I would just have to wait for her. After all, I needed to be there early to guarantee that Cora had everything she needed, and that someone was in her corner, while Sophia had needed to make sure her daughters were taken care of, as they wouldn't be coming to the wedding. Cora had offered, but I knew riding herd on two twin little girls would be a lot. And there was no way that Sophia would allow someone else to watch her girls while she was enjoying herself at the wedding. Because I would make sure that Sophia would have fun tonight. She deserved it.

Just as much as she deserved a moment away for just herself.

The wedding began in a couple of hours, as Cora and Juliet had wanted to spend the day together. No, they wouldn't see each other in their dresses until the wedding, but they wanted to make their own superstitions and luck by enjoying a moment to themselves before they were with their family and friends.

Family. What an odd thing to think, as I was Cora's only family here. She had many friends attending, the family of her own making, but I was the only one of blood. We had no cousins, no other parts of our family. And now we had to figure out what our lives would be with Juliet joining us. Or rather, would it be us joining them?

"Such a contemplative look on your face."

I turned at the sound of Sophia's voice, as if I had plucked her from my memories into fruition, and nearly fell over.

She stood there in a champagne dress, her hair flowing around her shoulders, her makeup done to perfection, but not overly so, and took my breath away.

I had always known Sophia Cage was one of the most beautiful women I had ever seen in my life, but I hadn't realized until this moment that there would never be another like her. All others would pale in comparison to the woman before me.

For she was the one who haunted my dreams, my waking memories. The dress literally hugged every curve she had, and it took all within me not to move forward, put my hands on those hips of hers, and press her against the wall.

From the look in her eyes though, I had a feeling she knew exactly where my mind had gone.

"You're here." I cleared my throat as my voice had broken ever so slightly, and then I was moving closer to her without thought. I cupped her face, and she smiled up at me.

"I'm sorry I couldn't be here earlier. But I promised the girls I would spend the morning with them, and now they're off with their Uncle Aston and Aunt Blakely and cousin Stone. I'm truly afraid of the mayhem they're about to be create."

I ran my thumb over her cheek, relishing in the softness of her skin. "They're going to teach Stone all of their tricks."

"That's what I'm afraid of. Because I have a feeling all of the Cage cousins are going to run wild and learn far too many secrets."

"As I have a feeling the Cage siblings have done the same, you can't really blame them."

"No, I can't. Speaking of siblings, are you ready for today?"

I swallowed hard and let my hand drop. I needed to stop touching her. She wasn't mine and never would be. It would be smart to remember that.

"I don't know how Cora got old enough to find herself getting married, but I suppose Juliet is good enough for her."

"Excuse me, Juliet is the best for me. Is this Sophia?"

Before I could say anything, my little sister was shoving me out the way and wrapping her arms around Sophia.

"You look gorgeous. I'm so glad you're here. That annoying big brother of mine hides all of his friends and never lets me meet anyone." She pulled back and gripped Sophia's shoulders.

"Seriously, gorgeous. I love this champagne color on you. And you match the wedding perfectly."

Sophia's face was a lovely shade of pink, and while part

of me wanted to pull Cora away and protect her, I knew that my sister needed people with her. Especially because as we got closer to the wedding itself, the lack of family on our end would begin to create a cacophony within her.

"Congratulations, Cora. It is lovely to meet you."

"Carson was saying you have two little girls. Just know that they were welcome to come here, but it's also good to have adult time."

I turned slightly so I could watch Cora wink at Sophia, and the woman I could not stop thinking about just beamed right back.

"I have photos if you want to see."

"As any good mother does. Of course I want to see. One day my brother over there is going to be an uncle, and I can't wait to see him be all flustered with kids."

"He's oddly perceptive when it comes to the girls. In fact, they love him."

Cora gave me a look, raising her brow. "Interesting. I didn't realize that Carson was so good with kids."

"I think it's quite shocking to all of us," Sophia teased.

"I knew I should have come alone to this wedding," I grumbled. "Look at you two, ganging up on me."

"Hush, hush," Cora said, waving me off. "I'm kidnapping Sophia, and I'm bringing her to my get ready room. You can have her later."

"Oh, Cora. You don't have to do that. You're with your friends."

"I am, and you're my friend now too. I'm sorry, but I've already adopted you." There was an odd sense of panic in her tone, one that I wasn't sure anyone else could hear, but from the way that Sophia's head tilted, studying my sister, I realized that Sophia had also heard it.

My baby sister was stressing out about the wedding, most likely about a million things, and so of course Sophia would lean into caring. Because that's who she was.

And it was another reason why I needed to stay away.

"I'll see you at the wedding, I suppose," I grumbled.

"Your seat will be right by his in the front. Don't argue," Cora said, waving her finger at Sophia. "You're going to need to keep Mr. Blubbering over there calm."

"I have never once blubbered," I drawled.

"I wouldn't mind seeing that," Sophia teased.

"I knew I'd like you." Cora grabbed Sophia's hand. "We'll see you soon, big brother. I'm going to get my dress on."

"Carson," Sophia said with a slight panic in her tone as she stared at me.

"Have fun," I said softly. "You look beautiful, Sophia. In case I didn't get to say that out loud."

Sophia's eyes widened, even as Cora wiggled her brows, and then the two were gone, Cora dragging Sophia to the other side of the hall, leaving me alone and wondering what the hell I'd gotten myself into.

I could have invited any one of my friends to join, so I

wasn't alone, and I knew any of the Cages or other businesspeople would have shown, but that wasn't what today was for. Cora needed me, and I didn't want to bring anyone who would stress her out.

I truly hadn't even thought to bring Sophia until the words were out, and now she was here, and my sister had kidnapped her.

I had a feeling this wasn't going to end well.

By the time the wedding itself came to fruition, my chest tightened, and I looked down at my baby sister and her beautiful cream gown, and just shook my head.

"When did you grow up?" I asked, my voice rough.

"Long ago, big brother. Thank you for this." Her eyes filled, and I cursed under my breath.

"Don't cry."

"I won't. Well, I will, but not for anything other than happiness. Because I have my family here. The family that matters."

"Damn straight."

"Sophia is beautiful, you know."

"I hate the fact that we have the same taste in women," I teased.

"Always have. She is gorgeous though. And seems nice. You should bring her to more family events."

"We're just friends. It's not like that."

"It should be. It *could* be."

"We're at your wedding. So we're discussing your relationship. Not my lack thereof."

"I love you, brother of mine. And I truly believe the two of you would be amazing together. Just saying."

I shook my head, then leaned forward and kissed the top of her forehead, careful of her makeup and hair. "Focus on the love of your life."

"And not yours?"

It was like a kick to the gut, and I scowled at my beautiful baby sister.

"Cora."

"I know. I know. I'll tease you later." She went up to her tiptoes, kissed my cheek, and then the music began.

It was an out of body experience, walking my sister down the aisle. Her friends all stood, staring at her, as I led Cora to Juliet. Juliet had walked first, without us near so we wouldn't be able to get the first look. But as I realized that the two had not only chosen similar styles, the colors themselves, an off-white and cream that complemented each other so well, I knew that they were soulmates beyond anything.

Cora began to cry as soon as she saw Juliet, and Juliet just smiled wide and held out her arms.

My sister practically ran to her future wife, and I held back a chuckle even as others laughed, before I handed over the person I adored more than anyone else in the world to someone I knew would care for her in all the ways that mattered. The two clung to each other, laughing as they complimented each other's dresses, and as everybody else joined in on the laughter, I moved to sit in the first row, taking Sophia's hand without thinking. She leaned into me and whispered, "I have never seen such a beautiful couple."

I swallowed hard and nodded, careful not to look at her.

"You're right."

And with that, I watched as Cora and Juliet professed their love and dedication to each other, their values and futures entwined, and a small part of me believed it could work.

Because forevers might not be ordained or destined, but I had a feeling these two would make it work.

And throughout it all, I held Sophia's hand and refused to look at her. Because if I did, I was afraid of what I would see. And worse, what it would do to me.

By the time the reception began, I needed a fucking drink and a place where people didn't look so damn happy.

"Congratulations," a man I didn't recognize said as he shook my hand. "Those two have a bright future."

I nodded tightly. "They do."

The man gave me an odd look, before he said something similar to Sophia, and moved on to another couple.

Sophia tugged on my jacket and scowled up at me.

"Stop looking like you want to beat up everybody who compliments your sister."

"I don't know why I'm so angry," I muttered, and Sophia just patted my chest and stared at me. And then it clicked, and I was a damn idiot. "They should be here."

"No, they shouldn't. Her family is here. You're here. Her friends are here. Heck, I'm even here. That girl adopted me in two seconds flat, and I would do anything for her. Just like I would for my daughters. She's not alone."

And with that, the urge for a drink lifted, and it was all I could do not to pull her into my arms and hold her until my dying breath.

But that would never be happening.

Instead, I slid my knuckle over the side of her dress over her hip and licked my lips.

"Have I told you how beautiful you are?"

"A few times." She blushed, looking so fucking delectable. "And you better stop looking at me like that, or you're going to have a hard time walking soon." She gestured towards my crotch, and I snorted.

"I think I can deal with a hard-on."

"I think you mean you want me to deal with that hard-on," she teased.

I closed my eyes and groaned. "I didn't know you were a sadist."

"I try my best," she teased.

I shook my head, ready to say something, but Cora patted my shoulder. "I'm sorry to interrupt, well, because, well... you know. That was way too much information." She blushed the same deep red as Sophia, and I sighed.

"You weren't supposed to hear any of that."

"You didn't exactly whisper it," she said pointedly. "But it's time for the first dance, and so you're stuck with me. Sorry."

I looked down at my sister and knew that tears threatened, but we weren't going to think about our parents.

They loved me, or at least they professed they did. But they had said point-blank that they didn't love or like their daughter, so they could burn in hell for all I cared.

So I squeezed Sophia's hand, gave her a nod, and then moved towards the center of the dance floor as Juliet brought her father out.

"You ready for the family dance?" she asked, her voice low.

"I've already given you away, and now you want me to dance. So needy."

She shoved at me, and I pulled her into my arms as the music began. We swayed back and forth, before I used those dance lessons that our parents had forced us to take to waltz her around the edge. From the look on Sophia's face, I had surprised her, and I couldn't help but let the pride filling me explode.

She wasn't the only person who could dance out of

the two of us. Of course, I was nothing compared to her, nor in the way that I knew dancing made her feel, but that was neither here nor there.

Because she wasn't mine and that shouldn't matter.

When the song ended however, and Juliet's mom moved towards Juliet for another dance, I realized that I would be on the dance floor for a while. Juliet had other siblings who wanted to dance with her, and I was Cora's only family.

"It's okay. I can dance with my friends."

"What about with me?" Sophia said as she moved forward, her chin lifted slightly. "I mean, I have no idea how to lead, but I figure all of those years in ballet could be used for something. What do you say?"

"Sophia, I would be honored."

I moved back as the two of them began a complicated waltz around the dance floor, and I just shook my head, at a loss for words. Because without even trying, Sophia had showed Cora that she would never be alone. Even a woman that she had just met would be in her corner.

My heart ached and I rubbed it before I forced myself to turn away and head towards the bar. I ordered a whiskey, and downed it in one gulp, before going for a second.

It was time.

I had broken a promise to myself, and there was no going back.

We would have tonight, and maybe tomorrow, but that would be it.

It was time to break it off before anything got worse.

Before Sophia realized the man that I was.

Or before I did something monumentally stupid.

Like fall in love with a Cage.

Chapter Eleven

SOPHIA

A HAND SLID UP MY THIGH, AND I MOANED, THE crest of sleep beckoning while I was warm and sated. And yet as soon as that hand touched my bare thigh, my body ignited. Eyes closed, I shifted slightly, knowing that Carson would have already sensed my alertness. It didn't matter that I might look like I was asleep, he would know.

Soft stubble brushed against my shoulder, his lips grazing the outer shell of my ear. "Princess, it's time for you to wake." I let out a soft sigh, sinking into him, as his hands continued to roam over me.

We lay spooned against one another, the hard line of his cock pressed against my backside, and I knew he was aching just like I was. But he didn't shift, didn't move. Instead, he explored.

One hand lazily caressed my nipple, the other went to

the apex of my thighs, spreading me. I let my outer thigh fall lightly, as he used his middle finger to slide up and down my slit, gently probing.

"For someone who is pretending to sleep, you sure are wet. Look at you, soaked for me."

I groaned as he gently speared me with one finger, using the caress to gently tease me. It was hard to breathe with him touching me, but that wasn't new. *That was just Carson.*

"Mm-mm," I moaned.

"Look at you. Finally waking. Your cunt is tightening around my finger. Greedy. Hungry. Do you want this finger to be my cock instead?"

In answer, I shifted so my backside pressed against him even more, and he groaned. I could feel a slight wetness against my lower back, and I knew his cock was already leaking precum. I wanted to turn, to take him in my mouth, and to show him exactly how awake I was, but that meant I would have to move from this moment and not allow him to touch me anymore. I was greedy for him, aching just like he said.

It should scare me, and perhaps part of me was terrified. I wanted this man. But I knew if I didn't pull back, there would be no stopping.

I wanted to touch him, to hold him. I wanted him to be inside of me. I wanted him to know that he had already wrapped himself around my soul just like he had my body.

I was terrified of the truth.

His fingers clamped down on my nipple, the slight sting bringing me out of my spiraling thoughts, and I let out a deep breath.

"There she is." And then he was lifting my thigh, his cock sliding against my pussy.

"I want you bare, holding onto my cock with that beautiful pussy of yours as if you can't let go."

I moaned again, wanting that, but knowing that I couldn't. Shouldn't. I wanted him inside me so I could feel all of him, but I didn't beg, I didn't ask. So when I heard the crinkle of a condom, I didn't let the disappointment settle in. Being safe was smart. And sometimes being with Carson felt anything but safe in some respects, and the safest in all others.

He continued to rub against my cunt, this time with the condom wrapped around him, and I arched for him, needing more.

"That's it. That's my Sophie." *My Sophie.* As if I was his. It didn't feel like that was the case, but perhaps it could be. Perhaps if I let myself be his, I could let myself be who I was when I couldn't focus.

I had fallen for Carson Woods. I had done the one thing we had both promised each other we wouldn't do.

But I wouldn't think about that now. Instead, I reached between my thighs and maneuvered him so he was at my entrance. "Tell me yes. Tell me I can have you for this moment."

I nearly frowned at the qualification, but then his hand was on my clit, and I couldn't think.

"Please, Carson. Take me."

He murmured against my neck, and then he was filling me. Slowly. Inch by inch. There were no more words, no other thoughts. Just Carson. There didn't need to be anything else.

It took a breath for my body to acquiesce, my inner walls tight for a moment until I began to relax around him. He shifted slowly, small bursts until he was seated deep within me, his balls pressed against me, and I couldn't think of what else to say. What else to think. There was nothing. Just Carson, just these moments.

"That's it, that's my girl."

Mine. I let the smile spread over my face, knowing I was making a mistake.

Because in this moment I was his. Just like he was mine.

He kissed my neck, my ear, but didn't tilt my head back to take my lips. That was fine, because he took me. He moved slowly, gently, both of us rocking into one another as my orgasm began to crest.

My pussy fluttered, stars dancing behind my eyes, I leaned back, my head on his shoulder, as I came.

He murmured against me, his hips thrusting harder, faster, and the sounds filled his room, as he filled me.

And when he came, his hand a bruising force on my hip, I smiled against him, and I was lost.

This was all too much, and I knew it. I shouldn't be doing this, I shouldn't have fallen. But I had.

It didn't matter that I had lied to myself for so long. I had gone and fallen in love, and yet, as he held me, I could believe that maybe he felt the same. And perhaps he did.

What more could I ask for than this man who held me?

We laid there for a moment, our breaths coming in pants as he held me close, but didn't say a word. He didn't kiss me either, but it didn't matter. I could still feel him hard within me, both of us shaking as we came down from our orgasms.

It had been reckless to stay the night, and I knew it, but after the wedding, we had been so tired, and I had already planned to be with him.

Aston had given me a curious look when I had asked him and Blakely to watch the girls overnight. They had wanted a sleepover with their baby cousin anyway, and I had acquiesced. My big brother—a man who I had not grown up with and hadn't known until I was nearly married and a mother myself—hadn't scolded me or teased me. He hadn't given me a worried look. Instead, he had promised to watch over my girls with everything he had. And considering I wasn't sure what would happen with Cale next, as we still hadn't formed a plan for his supposed weekend visitation, that meant everything.

Blakely had given me a knowing glance, and I had promised to tell her everything.

Though I had known it for a lie right away. After all, how could I tell her what I didn't know?

I wasn't supposed to fall for this man, and yet I was. It would be so easy to continue to fall and to never let myself feel the pain, but he had not promised forever. In fact, he had done the exact opposite, and once again I had been broken.

But in this moment I could pretend. I could pretend there was such a thing as forever.

I had danced with Cora at the wedding, and then Juliet. And then I had found myself in Carson's arms, never letting go.

Others had recognized me, surprising me, but as some of the brides' friends had loved to dance, they knew who I was, and I had even given a few digital business cards for upcoming classes for their children. All in all, it had been a successful wedding, and although there was always that ever present backdrop of darkness that came from parents who never understood, Carson had filled that moment and role with such sincerity, that it hadn't signified.

Cora was loved and she knew that with every ounce of her soul.

Her parents would never be part of this, not in the end.

And I had been blessed to witness it.

After the wedding, I had gone home with Carson, to his large house only a neighborhood away from Aston's, and we had gone to sleep after hours of clinging to one another. I had never had so many orgasms in my life, and I knew my inner thighs would be sore for days to come, but it didn't matter. I was happy. It should scare me, and perhaps it did, but did it matter? He made me happy, and that perhaps was all that was worth counting.

And I wanted to tell him. To explain to him that I could see more.

But then again, maybe that was just my body reacting and not my soul.

Because I had trusted before and I had failed. Failed to the point that scars covered my heart, my body, and could have touched my children.

Suddenly chilled, I sank into Carson, still feeling his length deep within me, and he wrapped his arms around me, holding me close. We were no longer covered with a blanket, both of us naked and stated, but we didn't say anything. Instead, he buried his face in my neck and let out a deep breath.

Perhaps it would be okay for me to tell him. He was a rational, good man even though he didn't think so.

Maybe he would understand.

He kissed the back of my neck, and gently, oh so gently, slid from between my thighs. I immediately felt the loss, the ache, and I let out a deep sigh.

He didn't say anything as he shifted off the bed, and then did away with the condom. Water ran as he washed his hands, and I moved to lay on my back, my hands on my breasts, and smiled up at the ceiling.

I had never meant for this to happen, but here I was, in Carson's bed and happy.

Carson moved from the restroom then, wearing dark sweatpants and a flat expression on his face.

Chilled, I slid the sheet above me, covering my body. I didn't like to be naked when he wasn't, that's just who I was. Usually he came back to hold me afterwards, but we did have to go to work later. He had meetings all afternoon, I knew, and honestly I didn't even know what time it was.

I had been so lost in him, I hadn't even called Aston. I had earlier, right before seven in the morning when Carson and I had woken up in each other's arms, but hours had passed, and I needed to again.

I was just about to shift to reach for my phone, when Carson moved to the side, and reached over the bed to brush my hair from my face.

"This was nice," he said, his voice devoid of emotion. My hand hovered over my phone as ice slid up my spine at his tone.

I looked up at him and frowned. "Yes," I said, and I cleared my throat. "It was."

"I need to head to the office. You can stay if you want, but I'll make sure you have a car to pick you up. I'll be out of the state for a while, I have a few meetings and mergers to worry about. But maybe I'll call you when I get back?"

This didn't sound like the Carson I knew. No, I didn't recognize this man. That was a lie. He sounded like the man that I had first met. The one who had promised me nothing and told no lies.

And just like that, the glass shattered around me.

And I realized what this was.

A brush off. A casual goodbye that was anything but casual.

I sat up then, not letting the sheet fall. I needed that armor.

"Oh. Sure. I need to see the girls."

"I'm sure you do. Thank you for coming to the wedding. You helped alleviate that burden for Cora, and I'll be forever grateful for that. You let me know if you need anything, and tell the girls hello." He took a step back, as if to say nothing at all, and I stared at him, wondering exactly who this man was.

There had been no promises, and yet this seemed something different. Something I had missed.

I had been the one to change the rules, even if he hadn't known. And I couldn't breathe.

I had let a man hurt me before, because I hadn't seen the truth, and I wouldn't do it again. It might be a completely different moment in this breath, yet the agony twisted. I shifted off the bed and walked towards my clothes, letting the sheet fall. I didn't need the shield, he had seen everything. Touched everything down to my soul.

And I hadn't been enough.

I didn't turn around as I dressed and gathered my things. I still wore the dress itself, not even a spare change of clothes or a toothbrush. Because that's not who we were.

"Let me call you a car," Carson said, and I finally turned to him, realizing he hadn't moved at all. He had stood there, watching me dress as I tried not to shake, and I knew this was goodbye.

It should have been goodbye with that first kiss, but it hadn't been. I had played with temptation and been burned.

I should have known.

"No need. I can do that. I want to go home and shower before I pick up the girls anyway. Give Cora my best. Juliet as well."

Carson nodded and didn't say a word. He didn't move forward to kiss me goodbye, to tell me he would see me again.

He did nothing but stare at me blankly, as if he had no

idea what to say.

Well, good. Because I didn't either.

I gathered myself, left the bedroom, and quickly called a car, before pulling up my group text.

ME:

I need you. I'm safe. But I need you.

Just those simple words, and then each one of my sisters, by blood and marriage, answered back.

ISABELLA:

I'm on my way. I'll kill him.

BLAKELY:

I'm coming too. I have the girls with me. You won't be alone.

SCARLETT:

I'm in town. I'm stealing one of Dorian's cars.

HARPER:

I'll pick you up, Scarlett. I'll be there soon, Sophia.

PHOEBE:

I'm close to the house. Do you need me to pick you up?

EMILY:

I'm already out the door. See you soon. We love you, Soph.

They would be at my home soon. And I wouldn't be alone.

See? I wasn't below nothing. I had family. I had friends.

I had people who cared about me. I slid into the car, once again realizing Carson hadn't asked me to come back, hadn't said a damn word to me after he'd made his peace.

I wasn't alone, except in all the ways that truly mattered.

But this time, I didn't break.

Chapter Twelve

CARSON

Lack of sleep meant that I was a real bear to deal with, then again, it wasn't anything new, right? After all, I was the asshole that people whispered about before I walked into the room, and then suddenly they were busy at their own jobs.

If I were any nicer, things wouldn't get done. I knew how that worked. At least that's what I continued to tell myself. But I hadn't slept at all since watching Sophia walk out of my house, as if I hadn't been the one to push her out. I deserved whatever hell came my way. She had been so fucking strong.

Yet I had seen the absolute devastation in her eyes, when she'd given me that one look and realized that I was blowing her off. That I was pushing her away and doing my best not to reach out and never let go.

Because if I did, it would be a mistake. One of us would end up breaking the other. We would end up hurting the other person when things got too real, and I didn't want to be the one to do that. She was so much better than me.

She had already dealt with one of the worst possible things imaginable, and had survived. And I had just been a distraction, a stepping stone into who she needed to be. And I hadn't minded it. Fuck, I had relished in it. And that had been the problem. I had wanted too much. I connected too much. She had been everything, therefore I had to ensure it was nothing.

I knew that being as cold and callous as I'd been had been cruel, but I needed to ensure there was no space for miscommunication, or second guesses. We had both told each other there would be no promises, and yet the fact that we had promised it called us both liars.

She deserved someone better than me. Somebody who actually believed in something beyond a few nights. I shouldn't have touched her at all, but I hadn't been able to stop myself, and the way that she had melted in my arms had proved that we had been meant for at least those quiet moments.

So walking away when I had was smart.

Only she had done the walking, hadn't she? I may have been the one pushing, but she had held her chin high, like the damn goddess she was, and left. And I hadn't even driven her home. Not because I was an asshole, far from it. But because if I had gotten in the same car with her, I never would've let her go.

And that scared me like no other.

I was not the man who wanted forever. I was not the man who needed it. I walked away and didn't look back. Because that was what me or my partners wanted. There had never been a time where somebody came back to me, wondering what the hell I had been thinking because they had thought our relationship was something far different. There had never been any confusion until now. The confusion was on my part. Not hers.

Because Sophia had walked away. Maybe to protect herself, maybe because she was done with me. Either way, I had hurt her, and there was no coming back from that.

And yet I hadn't been able to sleep. Hadn't been able to think without her coming to mind.

And it was going to break me.

What the hell was I supposed to do now?

"Sir?"

I turned towards Rose, trying to pull myself out of whatever thoughts I had been spiraling down, and shook off the concept of thinking about Sophia more than I should.

"What is it, Rose?"

"I was just making sure you were okay. You were staring off into the distance for longer than usual."

Rose had been with my company since the start of it. Much like Andy, my driver, they had wanted to work for someone who would treat them with respect.

Rose had also worked with me long enough to be given grace for any snark or worry.

Because I wasn't the monster that I pretended to be. Not always.

"How long have I been staring?" I asked, honestly curious.

She raised a brow. "Long enough I was getting worried. Are you coming down with something?"

That would've been an easier answer than what I was truly feeling, but Rose didn't need to know that.

"I'm fine. Are we set for the next meeting?"

I hadn't lied to Sophia completely. We had flown out to Seattle the day I had forced her out of my home, and part of me knew there would be no coming back from that. I might have ruined everything because I couldn't stay away from a woman who shouldn't be mine.

I was now dealing with another merger, an acquisition, and a company I wasn't fond of. I preferred working with the Cages, and even the Montgomery family in Colorado, but there were other families in other states that required help, and who I knew we could be profitable with.

I knew my head wasn't in the game, and that's when mistakes happened.

"We have everything all set, and the rest could be done remotely. I can have the plane ready soon."

I didn't always travel private. In fact, I hated it. It wasn't good for the environment, and it was all pretentious. But because I needed to get more than a few people in different places in a hurry, and we did our best to offset any issues, it usually made sense financially, economically, and environmentally. It just wasn't my favorite thing to do.

"Give me a few hours. I want to make sure it settles with them, and being in person will help."

"Will do. I'll give you an update when I have it. Oh, and sir?"

There was a hesitancy in her tone that worried me, so I finally turned to look at her and frowned. "What is it, Rose?"

"You have two Cage brothers here. I wasn't sure whether to tell you or not since they aren't on the agenda, and frankly, I don't know why they're here. But they don't look happy. I can do more reconnaissance to see if the next phase of the business deal we have with them is in jeopardy."

I pinched the bridge of my nose, wondering why it had taken this long for them to show up. I was surprised it was only two Cages and not all fifty of them. I wouldn't have been surprised if it had been all of them. After all, I had hurt their sister, her pride, and her feelings. I hadn't hurt her heart. Because there was no way that she had fallen for me. She was smarter than that.

Then of course, I was reminded exactly why she had protected herself. "Send them in," I said, the sudden urgency in my tone surprising her.

Because if Cale had done something and I had been looking the other way, I would never forgive myself.

"Are you sure?"

"Rose. I am. I promise."

"I'll have security waiting."

I snorted. "I could take both of them, we know that."

"I didn't tell you which Cages are out there."

"You didn't have to."

Not only would I know who they were no matter what, I also knew I could take them. Not that I would harm any of the Cage women. I wasn't that much of a monster. Although I wasn't sure Sophia would agree with me in that moment.

With a sigh, I leaned against my desk, hands in my pockets, as I waited for two Cages to show up and explain to me exactly how much of a terrible person I was. It wouldn't be anything new, honestly.

"Well, looks like I'm going to have to kick your ass after all," Flynn said far too calmly, his voice smooth as silk as he strode into my office, complete in a perfect suit and tie. James followed him, a deadly snarl on his face.

"So. It's the two of you. I thought it would be. But

honestly, I would've expected Isabella here with a pitchfork too."

"She's with Sophia, but if she had her way, she'd be here as well," Flynn said.

I studied both of them, my jaw set. "Meaning no one else knows that you showed up. Does Aston?"

"He's not our keeper," James put in calmly. "But I would love to know what you were thinking when you broke our sister's heart."

I stiffened, my own heart squeezing ever so slightly. Because no, that wouldn't have been the case. I hadn't done so.

I would've known.

"What happens between Sophia and me is none of your business," I said boldly. I ducked the first punch, Flynn glaring, but wasn't fast enough to escape James's hold. He hovered over me as he tugged at my shoulder and glared.

"You have no idea what you're talking about. We weren't able to protect her when that asshole hurt her. Physically, emotionally, financially, everything. But you? You were a friend."

Were. "Past tense then?" I asked.

"You asshole," Flynn said as he moved forward. I pulled away from James, and the other man let me go. I fixed my suit, pretending I cared about the lapels.

"Sophia and I are friends." Or perhaps that was past

tense as well. "We had a few moments, and then our time ended. We both made promises. I didn't want to hurt her."

"Maybe you did, maybe you didn't, but you shouldn't have touched our sister to begin with," Flynn snapped.

I nodded tightly. "You're right. I shouldn't have."

Both men looked at me in surprise, and I shook my head.

"Sophia's way better than me. She deserves more than me. We had our time, and I walked away before things got more complicated. I'm sorry if I hurt her." I shook my head. "No, that's a cop-out. I'm sorry *that* I hurt her. But being with her would have hurt her even more. Believe me."

"You shouldn't have touched her," Flynn repeated.

"What happened between Sophia and me was between two consenting adults, and I won't answer to you for that. She deserves better than that. But please, don't ever compare me to the spineless asshole that is her ex-husband. Because I'm not like that man."

Flynn opened his mouth to say something, but it was James who spoke instead.

"You're right. You're not Cale. I'm not disappointed in Cale because I hate him so much it doesn't matter. But you? Why did you have to walk away like that?"

I rubbed my hand over my heart, not even realizing I was doing so until it was too late. "I'm no good for her."

"So you hurt her?" Flynn asked.

"I walked away. It made sense to walk away."

"Maybe. Or maybe you should have found the courage to stay. To figure things out. She deserves everything and more," James reiterated. "And you don't deserve hell either, Carson. Maybe you need to think about that."

And without saying another word, James dragged Flynn out of my office, and I stood there, wondering what the fuck had just happened.

I didn't deserve more. I didn't deserve better. Sophia deserved the world.

But I wasn't it.

And yet...

I missed her.

"Fuck."

That was the crux of it. I missed Sophia Cage. And I wanted her.

And I didn't know what the hell I was supposed to do about that.

Because part of me needed her. Hell, *every* part of me needed her. Everything had felt so much lighter with her near, but that wasn't how I operated. I'd done what I'd always done, and walked away before things got heavy, and now? And now I had hurt the one person who had actually seen me.

I was the asshole that didn't deserve anything but pain. I knew that, she had to as well.

"But what the hell was I supposed to do about it now?" I asked, shaking my head.

With a sigh, I texted Rose to get the flight ready. Because I needed to go back to Denver.

I needed to talk with Sophia. Because I had made a mistake. Just like that, I had made a fucking mistake. And I needed to fix it.

Only I had no idea what the fuck I was supposed to do about it.

By the time we made it to the airfield, my hands shook, and my knee kept bouncing as we sat on the tarmac.

"Do you want to tell me what's wrong?" Rose asked from her seat beside me.

"Nothing," I lied.

"So it has nothing to do with Sophia Cage?"

I frowned at her, wondering where the hell she got her information.

"I've worked with you for how long now, boss? We know things."

Andy snorted from behind me. "She's a good person. We like her. And maybe if you gave in just a little, you'd like her even more."

"Since when do you two care about my personal life?" I asked.

"Since always," Rose teased. "You introduced me to my wife, and I will forever be grateful for that. You might be the big bad bachelor in most rooms, but you're also a good person. Sometimes you forget that. And I like the Cages. We've done so much background work on the family, I feel like I know them. Sophia? I've watched her dance for ages. Hell, you're the one who introduced me to her and the ballet. She's freaking amazing, hot, and probably too good for you. That's why you should try harder."

"I have no idea why I keep either one of you employed," I grumbled.

We were up in the air then, on our way back to Denver, and I needed to figure out what the hell I wanted. Because if I wasn't careful, I was going to break her.

Maybe I had already done so.

Sophia didn't want anything serious or permanent, she had plainly said so, but part of me was afraid she had lied just like I had.

I missed her. With every ounce of my soul, I missed her and it had only been two days.

Two days since I had touched her, two days since I had broken both of us.

I missed her, her smile, the way she made me laugh. I missed the way the little girls made me laugh. And that wasn't who I was normally. I wasn't a man who knew what to do with a family like that. And yet here I was, wanting something more.

And that's how I knew I was in trouble. The plane

dipped for a second, and I frowned, looking up at the pilots.

"Everything okay, Josh?"

"We're hitting a bit of turbulence, everybody make sure that you're settled in."

There was an odd note to his voice, and that worried me more than anything. Because I had worked with this team for years now, and they did not get worried.

I met Rose's gaze, her eyes wide, the fear there startling more than anything. Rose was stronger than I was in so many ways and now I had to be the one who held it together.

"Everything will be fine, let's get home. Then you can tell me exactly how I'm supposed to fix this with Sophia."

"Well, good. You came to the right person for advice," Rose said, although there wasn't a hint of humor in her tone.

Then the plane dipped again, this one sharper. Rose let out a scream, and I reached out, gripping her hand. Andy was behind me, doing the same for our other team members.

And when the plane dipped once more, there were more screams, and all I could do was think of Sophia.

Chapter Thirteen

SOPHIA

SOMETIMES A GIRL JUST NEEDED HER FAMILY. And with the number of family members I had, I'd take any assortment of them at this point.

"Since when were we making this a girls' day?" Kyler asked as he pulled another beer out of the fridge and gestured towards me with it. "You want one?"

"I'm good with my Diet Coke," I said softly. "You know my addiction."

He raised a brow, his eyes brightening. "Ah, yes. The white woman's addiction to Diet Coke. It must be studied."

"Excuse me, if you add a Caesar salad and French fries, it is the perfect lunch."

"You know, I had that before. Add some steak on top, perfection."

Kyler opened his beer, then moved into the room to slink gracefully onto the armchair.

He had one leg resting over the arm, and he slouched as if he had practiced it. Considering I had grown up with the man who was now a world-famous rockstar, I knew for a fact he had practiced. He'd even practiced that little smirk that he did in the mirror when he was a child. That was what happened when you were the only boy out of five siblings and was the middle child on top of it.

"There is nothing wrong with a girls' night, or a Diet Coke," Emily said as she strode into the living room with us, a glass of sparkling wine in hand.

"I see you're not the one drinking a soda," Kyler commented.

Emily shrugged and took a seat on the couch, with Isabella following her.

Phoebe had a family dinner with Ford's family, as the Montgomerys met just as often as the Cages did, so we weren't quite a full family of five, but close enough.

"Do you think you would be so good at dealing with women and sisters if you hadn't grown up with us girls?" Isabella asked, and I held back a smile. It surprised me that I could even do so, considering I hadn't smiled at all in the past two days.

It broke me ever so slightly to know that we were meeting as a family to yes, be close to one another, but they were here because I was in pain, and they loved me.

The fact that we were at Kyler's place was kismet. As he was rarely in town these days, it was nice that we were able to get together at all.

"If you mean that I'm used to having to deal with all of you up in my business? Of course being the sole brother of the five of us growing up helped with that." Kyler winked and took another sip of his beer, as I sipped my soda.

Of course, Isabella immediately answered Kyler, pushing at him in the lovable way that the eldest daughter did, and I met Emily's gaze.

She rolled her eyes, yet gave me a concerned look at the same time.

Because we were here for numerous reasons. The fact that Kyler was back in town, the concept that our families actually liked being with one another, and because they were all worried about me.

When I had texted the girl group chat that I needed them, they had all shown up in full force.

The girls had run to me, talking a mile a minute, and I had held back my tears and pain until they had gone down for their naps. And then I had fallen into Isabella's arms and confessed it all.

My being with Carson, the promise that we would never want each other for more than we had.

The idea that I had failed so wholeheartedly that I had fallen in love with a man who could never love me back.

He had said so. It wasn't like he had ever lied to me. And that was the hardest part. Because no, he didn't love me. He never would, and I needed to be okay with that.

It was on me that I wanted more, and these feelings were my problem. Not his.

I wasn't allowed to hate him for my own failures. Of course, explaining that to Isabella was impossible. Because she had merely glared at me and promised to cut Carson's balls off.

That was a big sister for you.

And while I knew Kyler visited, I had a feeling that one, if not all of my sisters and sisters-in-law had contacted Kyler to tell him that I needed him.

Of all of my siblings, sometimes I felt like Kyler and I were the closest. It wasn't always the case. He had a special connection with each one of us, just like I did with my sisters—and now the brothers I had never known about before the will reading.

None of them were here today, but it wasn't because we didn't want them here. It just so happened that this family meeting had been this group.

All of our brothers had been invited, but each had had plans, or had promised to try to show up later.

Because we were a family, and we loved each other.

Something my father would've hated. That made me smile, and perhaps I was a terrible person in thinking that, but I didn't care. Just like Cale, my father had tried to break me. And maybe he succeeded in some ways, but like Kyler, I had found my own future and ways to breathe. Kyler and I were artists—something that had always pained me to even say. I didn't like the concept of being an artist at first because I had my father's voice in my head. But my mother had been the one to push us, to prove to us that we could do anything—even if we hadn't known why she had been so sad sometimes.

And now here I was, a teacher rather than an artist, and my brother had sold-out shows all over the world with people clamoring to be part of his life.

I was pretty sure our father would've hated every bit of this. Perhaps that's why I liked it so much. Call me petty.

My phone buzzed and I looked down at the read-outs, realizing that the childcare video app had alerted me, and my girls were up from their nap.

"Oh, I'll be right back," I said, and each one of my siblings gave me a worried look. "The girls are up."

"Here, let me help." Kyler set down his beer, ran his hands over his jeans, and followed me down the hall to the nursery.

A nursery that he had put in the moment I had told him I was pregnant, because he wanted to be the best uncle there was. Of course, he had to fight for that title with the rest of our brothers, but he was doing a decent job of it. Each one of my siblings had space in their homes —however large their homes may be—in order to have space for the next generation. I walked into the small nursery and looked at the tiny beds that were set up on one side, and the cribs on the other.

"You know, one day you may run out of space with the way the Cages procreate," I teased.

Kyler rolled his eyes. "You say that, but I feel like there's a slight break. I don't plan on having kids anytime soon, and I think the rest of the newlyweds are taking their time. That gives me more space to spoil your baby girls, as well as Stone and Micah."

I leaned into my brother, hugged him tight, and he gripped me so hard I was afraid he might bruise me for an instant, but then he kissed the top of my head, and I shook it off. Kyler had his own demons, he always had. There was a reason there was so much emotion and guttural rage and pain in some of his music. We all had our own paths and burdens, and mine happened to be my choice in men.

Cale hadn't called me or contacted our lawyers since that last time, and I was forever grateful. Maybe he had given up wanting a weekend with the girls, and that would be just fine with me. I didn't want to deal with him, or his needs. I was done dealing with the man at all.

"Hey there, my little rock stars," Kyler said with a wide grin, and sidled up to my girls. They jumped up and down on the bed, and even as I frowned at them, they didn't care.

"Uncle Kyler!" Violet squealed, and Hazel jumped without fear, and her uncle caught her.

Kyler picked up Violet as well, hung them both on his hips, and began to spin in circles.

Both girls giggled with glee, Kyler laughed, and I pulled out my phone to take a photo.

Then of course, I had to record the whole thing, grinning at this side of my brother that he hid from the rest of the world.

When he gave me a look, I rolled my eyes. "I was planning on selling this to one of those terrible news organizations. What do you think?"

"You'd make big bucks. I'm pretty."

"So pretty." Hazel reached up and patted his bearded cheek, and my little brother blushed, before he scowled and ran out of the room, leaving me behind.

I smiled softly, my heart aching as I watched him walk towards the living room with my girls on his hips.

Each one of my brothers—whether I had grown up with them or not—were unique and special in the way that they were uncles. My children did not have a grandfather, nor did they have a father. I refused to call Cale their father any longer. If the world were perfect, he would never have access to them again. And because I wasn't reacting the way that he wanted, he hadn't come for them. They were his leverage against me and whatever I could give him, and I would be stronger than whatever he tossed at me. But the men in my life—the ones who had married into the family or were Cages by blood—were showing my little girls what it meant to be a protective and strong male figure.

And they would grow up with their cousins, and hopefully never feel the lack.

I ran my hand over my chest, once again feeling a connection to my mother even though she wasn't here today. Maybe we would invite her for dinner later and reiterate that she was welcome. She hadn't wanted to intrude on sibling time, and she didn't know about me and Carson. But perhaps it was time for me to open up to her. To tell her she wasn't alone in her not-so-great scope of choosing men. Not that Carson was in any way like Loren Cage or Cale. No, he was a man who knew what he wanted and was honest about it. Yes, the way he had practically tossed me out of the house was cruel, but it had been the wake-up call that I needed.

And I would find a way to survive knowing that I loved him. Just like I had found a way to do so when I didn't love Cale.

I walked back into the living room, as my babies played with my siblings, and leaned against the doorway, wondering what I was supposed to do next.

"Is Mr. Carson coming?" Violet asked out of the blue, and it was like a kick to the chest. Isabella gave me a look, and I ignored her.

I hadn't introduced Carson as anyone other than a friend, and he would still be in our lives as part of a connection to the family business. So we would find a way to make this new phase of our lives work.

"No, but I hear we're having pasta."

"And pasta for me?"

I smiled at my daughter's question and went to sit on the floor and play.

When the doorbell rang, Kyler frowned, looked at his phone, then went to answer.

"Who is it?" Isabella asked.

Like all of our homes, Kyler's had security. It was also in a gated community, considering his celebrity status.

"It's Flynn."

"Oh. I'm glad he's here," Emily said with a smile. "He's been so grumpy lately. We'll feed him the carbs and make him happy."

"Grumpy grumpy," Violet teased, and my lips twitched. Oh yes, Uncle Flynn would love that.

But as Flynn walked into the room, his face ashen, an equally worried Kyler right behind him, my entire body froze.

"What's wrong?" I asked, visions of Cale coming at my family screaming in my head.

With that look on Flynn's face, I couldn't help but worry.

Flynn glanced at the girls, and then Emily was there,

picking them up and carrying them to the back room, mumbling something about secrets and treats, and I knew I would pay attention to that later. For now, I stood up on wobbly legs and moved towards Flynn.

"What is it?"

"It's Carson. We just landed after getting back from Seattle." He held up his hand, waving me off. "Please, you can yell at me later for getting in Carson's face about what happened. I'm your big brother, and sometimes I'm an asshole. But this isn't it. We took different planes because Carson has an entire team. And they had a private plane. Sophia—"

Flynn had gone to confront Carson? Yes, he was right, we would deal with that later, but for now I put my hand on his wrist and held on tight.

"What is it?"

"I just got word from a buddy of mine, there was a plane crash. They can't get ahold of the plane itself, and there isn't any other news. But there're rumblings, Sophia, and they're saying there are no survivors. I'm so fucking sorry."

As a tear slid down Flynn's cheek, my knees gave out, and then Isabella was behind me, Kyler beside me, and I broke.

I had done the one thing I hadn't done before, and I shattered.

Chapter Fourteen

CARSON

Forty-eight hours.

Forty-eight hours in which I would have to wonder exactly where everything had gone wrong. Forty-eight hours in which I had nearly lost everything.

And now I stood here on her porch, lost, never found, wondering what the hell I was doing. The car had dropped me off, only lingering for a moment before it took the hint and left. I knew my team wanted me to go home. To shower again and pretend all was well, but I couldn't. Not until I saw *her*.

There were a thousand things I needed to be doing, other places all over the country that I needed to contact and be seen, but that didn't matter.

There were only two places in the world I needed to

be, and one I couldn't contact yet. Here I was, trying to figure out what the fuck I was going to do.

But before I could even ring the doorbell, or walk away, the door opened, and then Sophia was in my arms. I clung to her, inhaling that sweet vanilla scent of her hair, and sank my face into her neck.

She let out a cry as my arms tightened around her waist. "How. How?" I set her down, careful not to hurt her. I had already done that enough.

"I'm sorry it took me so long to get here."

That felt like an understatement, but I held back, trying to formulate the words I needed.

She ran her hands over my beard and glared up at me. "They said your plane went down. They said—" She shook her head. "They said so many things, and yet you're here. How are you here?"

I cleared my throat and felt awkward as hell. The last time I had seen her, I had walked away. No, that wasn't right. I had pushed her away. I had made everything awkward as fuck and ensured that she would never want to see me again, and yet from the tears streaming down her face, the whole incident had worried her. I did not deserve those tears.

I reached up and used my thumbs to wipe her cheeks. "Don't cry. Please, Sophia. Princess. Don't cry."

"Come inside. I mean, if you have time. Cora. You need to go to Cora."

And just like that, every instance of when I had been an idiot slammed into me. Because I loved this woman.

She was here, breaking, in pain because I was a monster, and she could only think of my little sister.

It was no wonder that I loved Sophia Cage.

"I already talked to her. I promise. She's on her honeymoon."

"I know. We've been texting." She pressed her lips together, as if she hadn't meant to say that, but of course I had already known. I kept my hands on her face, trying to collect this moment. Because once she came back to reality and realized I was still the asshole I always had been, she would walk away again. Because I had been the one who pushed.

And I wasn't good at groveling. Nor did I think any groveling or apologies I made right now would be enough. Not for the way that I had hurt an already broken soul.

"Can we talk? Do you mind? I'll tell you the whole story. Are the girls here? Are they okay?"

Her face softened, and I swallowed hard. "They're in the playroom. They don't know. I didn't tell them. And of course. If you can, if you have time. Carson. What happened?"

I slid my hands down her shoulders to her hands and squeezed. "I'll tell you everything. I promise. I'm sorry for keeping you waiting. Sophia, I'm just so damn sorry."

She frowned at me once again, before pulling me into

the house, and I took those steps, knowing that they had to mean something. I would ensure they were worth it.

I wasn't going to be the evil person that I was ever again.

I couldn't.

"Can I get you something to drink or anything?"

I pulled her into my arms, selfish as always, and held her close. She stiffened for a moment, before sinking into my hold and letting out a deep breath.

"I'm okay. I'm fine. I promise."

"I need to tell the girls you're here because they're going to hear your voice."

"I won't tell them anything." I kissed her temple, and she pulled back, studying my face. I couldn't read those gorgeous eyes of hers, but I watched as she walked away, down the hall to the girls' playroom.

Part of me wanted to follow, but from the way that she had rolled her shoulders back, I knew she was trying to center herself, to find strength.

And hell, I needed to do the same damn thing.

I looked around her home, the one that she had made herself without that man, and with the family that she had cared for. Her little girls were growing up underneath this roof, within these walls, and were loved. They thrived.

I didn't know how to tell Sophia that I wanted more. I didn't even know what I wanted. Just more. I wanted her. I wanted those promises that I had failed to allow myself to keep. Because I had never meant them, and that was the problem.

How was I supposed to make sure she knew it was something I had been thinking about before the plane went down?

"Mr. Carson! You're here!" Violet squealed as she ran towards me. I knelt down, ignoring the twinge in my back, and held open my arms. She ran to me, and I gathered her up, Hazel right behind her. They talked a mile a minute, and kissed my cheeks, before going down to their feet and bouncing around me.

I only understood around a third of what they said, but I merely smiled, loving how the girls were so animated. They looked like their mother in that instant, and I was so grateful that Sophia had even let me in the house, because I wanted *this*. I wanted to be part of this.

And I had no idea what the fuck I was supposed to do about that.

"Okay, girls, I need to talk with Mr. Carson, but thank you for welcoming him," Sophia said, her voice oh so careful. I hated that I had done that to her, but I would make up for it. Somehow. And not with gifts or anything that came from who I was outside of this house.

No, I would need to find other ways.

I was not good at this.

No wonder the Cage brothers were ready to break me. Because I deserved it.

"I can talk to you soon," I promised both of them.

"I'm happy you're here," Hazel whispered before she grabbed her sister's hand and skipped down the hallway.

I tilted my head, studying them. "While they have never seen *The Shining*, my brothers thought it would be funny to teach them different weird things. Meaning they like to do that terrifying twin thing without even knowing they're being terrifying."

I pressed my lips together, trying not to laugh and failing. "Was it Dorian?"

"And oddly James," she said with a laugh. "Theo may have helped as well."

There was an awkward silence as I stood up, looking at this woman that I adored, loved…

"I thought you were dead," she croaked out, and I took a step forward as the first tear fell. But she held up her hands, waving me off. "Just tell me what happened so I can breathe. I am—I don't know what to think, Carson."

I ran my hands through my hair and nodded. "I don't know either. The plane did go down, but not fully," I corrected.

That didn't make any sense.

"There was a malfunction, and the engine just stopped midair. We went down hard. I was with my team, the people that I have handpicked for my business. They may not be family, but some of them are the closest people

I have to it. And all I could think of the whole time was that they were going to lose... The people that they loved were going to lose them, and it would have been my fault."

"How on earth would it have been your fault?"

"Because it was my plane. My pilots. My engines. Everything was mine. It doesn't matter that we had countless checks on it, and we didn't skimp on safety, it happened. Thankfully, I have the best fucking pilots in the business, and they were able to ensure that we didn't crash into the forest beneath us, but we landed hard, in a place with no service, no communication, and we couldn't get out to anybody. Then some asshole decided to tell the world that our plane went down. Crashed. No survivors. I don't know who started that rumor, but I'm going to find out. Because it broke my little sister to think I was gone." I swallowed hard, knowing that Cora would forgive me, but I didn't know if I deserved it.

My baby sister had spent part of her honeymoon thinking I had died.

And our parents hadn't reached out once.

I might have been the one presumed dead in those instances, but now those people were dead to me. Just like they should have been years ago.

"Carson. That must have been so terrifying." She moved forward then, and I held out my arms. When she sank into me, my heartbeat slowed slightly, and I realized how tense I had been.

"We spent one night in the forest until emergency services could find us. We were all okay, a little sore from the rough landing, but nobody was worse for wear. I contacted Cora as soon as I could, as well as most of the company, but apparently I had already been declared dead on the internet."

"It was terrifying," Sophia said softly. "And I know that rumors can just be rumors, but when you didn't reach out—"

"I just landed like an hour ago at DIA. And the first thing I did was come here. I was going to call, and well..." I sighed. "I didn't even know if you would've cared. Or noticed. That was selfish of me, I know. But I didn't want to worry you with a phone call to tell you that I'm alive, if you didn't even know I was hurt, or if you even wanted to hear from me."

"Are you serious right now? Even if I hated you, I would want to know you were alive."

"I know that. I'm just a chicken shit. And then as soon as I talked to Cora, I knew that you heard about the accident. And I had to find the words. But all of this to say, no matter how meandering this conversation goes, it's because I wanted to see you in person. I wanted to hold you and tell you that I was safe."

"Carson—"

"Please? Just this once."

And as she gave me an odd look, and nodded in

understanding, I cupped her face and took her mouth with mine. She sank into me, and I brushed my tongue along her lips. When she parted them for me, I deepened the kiss, needing her taste.

"I was so scared I would never see you again," I whispered against her mouth, and she pulled back and frowned.

"I thought you didn't want to see me again," she said after a moment, her voice devoid of emotion. "It's why you pushed me away. We had no promises."

I cursed under my breath and ran my hand over my chest. "Because I'm an idiot. Because I'm fucking scared. I shouldn't have done that. Even if we were going to end things in that moment, I should have driven you here. But I was afraid once I got you in my car, I was never going to let you go. All I wanted to do was just be with you, and it's ridiculous because I've never felt like this about anyone."

She shook her head, confusion etched on her face. "And this epiphany came when you thought you were dying?"

"No. I mean, yes, I thought of you because I didn't know if those were my last moments. But before I even got on the plane, before your brothers showed up to yell at me, I knew I'd made a mistake and I was going to have to find a way to atone. To fix it. And I still don't know how to do that."

"Carson, I haven't slept, and I know you haven't

either, so you're going to have to be plain. What on earth are you talking about?"

"I love you, Sophia. I was so fucking scared that I was going to lose you, and then I nearly lost myself. I know you didn't ask for this. You didn't ask for me or any of the drama that comes from me being in your life, but I love you. I've never loved anyone before, I've never felt like this before. And all of this was intensified even before I thought I was going to die. And I don't know how to prove that to you. But no matter what, I will do all in my power to show you that I'm worthy. Because I'm not right now. But I will be."

Tears were falling down her cheeks again, and she took a step forward, her hand on my chest.

"You love me?"

"I shouldn't be so surprised that you sound flabbergasted at the thought, but I do. I hope to god that you can take a chance on me. I know you didn't want forever either. And you didn't want a relationship. Hell, you're still dealing with that asshole. And you have your babies, and your family, the studio. You have everything. But if you let me, if you let me just be part of it, I will do all in my power to show you that I love you, and that I can be your helpmate."

I took a step back, ready for her to reject me. After all, I would deserve it, but when she reached for me, I took her hand, unable to watch her reach for anything. To ache for anything.

"You love me," she repeated.

"Of course I do. I think I loved you the first time you swooned in my arms."

"I did not swoon," she corrected, though a smile covered her face.

"Maybe a little. But I think I loved you then. Your strength, your tenacity. Your humor. I know I can be a better man for you, and with you."

"You need to be a better man for yourself, but I don't think you're as evil and corrupt as you think you are. Or at all," she corrected.

"Maybe. Maybe you see the light in me, and I wouldn't mind fading out the darkness just a bit."

She still hadn't told me how she felt, and I was okay with that. I would wait, and I would earn it. But the fact that she hadn't kicked me out had to count as a plus.

"I can go. I know I have a few things to do with the company later, and well, you said you hadn't slept. I should leave you be."

Then Sophia was in my arms. "I know you said you were scared. But Carson? I'm always scared." She pulled back, staring at my face. "I'm scared that I'm not being a good enough mother. That I won't be enough. I'm scared that I'll lose what I have, and he'll take more. I'm scared that I'm not present enough for my family. Because you know the Cages have their drama, and sometimes I feel like I can't focus on theirs when I'm breaking within mine. But Carson? I was so scared that I would never see you again, and then I was afraid that I would never tell you how I felt."

I ran my thumb over her bottom lip, my chest tightening. "How do you feel?"

"I love you. I love you so much, and it scares me. Because you keep showing me parts of yourself when you don't mean to. You bared yourself to me, and it just proves how scared I am."

"You have nothing to be afraid of, Sophia. I promise I will do all in my power to show you that."

"So what does this mean?" she asked.

I let out a rough laugh. "I have no fucking clue. I've never been here before. But I love you, and I want to prove that to you. And frankly, I just want to hold you."

"Don't think you're going to be walking out of this house tonight," she warned. "Because I thought you were dead, and I'm going to need a moment to break down about that."

I held her close, my grip tightening to the point of near pain. "All I thought of was you in the end," I whispered.

And when she cried against my chest, I kissed the top of her head. "Don't almost die again, okay? I'm still getting used to this whole love thing. Because I realized I didn't love him before. But you? I would shatter the earth itself with what I feel for you."

My knees nearly gave out, and perhaps I would be the one to swoon, so I held her close and sighed. "Those little girls mean the world to me too, you know."

"And there I go," Sophia said, before she sobbed harder, and I just held her, each of us swaying in the other's arms.

I'd nearly died, and the world thought I had for those mere moments. But no matter what, I would prove to whatever gods were looking down and to the woman in my arms, that I was worthy of this second chance.

Even though I knew that this was only the beginning. Because I was missing something. I knew it.

That meant I would have to prove to Sophia I was worth it. And to whoever else may be fighting against what we could be.

Chapter Fifteen

SOPHIA

A HAND SLID UP MY THIGH, AND I ROLLED INTO his arms.

I was getting far too used to waking up in this man's hold, and yet part of me had pushed those thoughts away. Even before we had almost lost everything, I hadn't realized that I'd wanted this with such an intensity that it would nearly break me.

"You're awake," a deep voice murmured against my ear before Carson began to nibble up my neck.

I moaned into him, twisting so I faced him fully, one leg wrapped around his hip. When his cock slid between my legs, I arched.

"Good morning," I said softly. "I feel like I should brush my teeth."

His hand squeezed my hip and he shook his head

slightly. "My cock is sliding against that warm, soft, wet cunt of yours. If you roll away to go brush your teeth, I will not be responsible for my actions."

My lips twitched, but I understood.

"Well, if you're sure," I teased. And then his lips were on mine, and nothing else mattered.

Soft morning light slid through the blinds, and I knew our alarms would go off soon. We would have to face reality and everything that came with it, but for now, we were in this moment, just the two of us. I reached between us and gripped the base of him, and he groaned.

"You're going to kill me."

"I just might if you're not inside me."

"And here I was thinking I would wake you up, licking between your legs, and yet, you changed the game."

I blushed, wondering how long it would take me to get used to the way he spoke about things, but in the end, it was all I could do not to shake near him. I positioned him at my entrance and when the tip of his cock slowly, oh so slowly, entered me, I sucked in a breath, loving the way that he stretched me.

Because Carson knew exactly what to do with that thick cock of his, and even thinking the words made me blush. I had never been like this with any other man, but as Carson held me, as he made love to me, no other man mattered. And they never would.

"You know, maybe I just have to surprise you later and

show up to be with you. Because there's so many things I want to do with this delicious body and soul of yours that there's no stopping me."

I reached around and squeezed his ass, smiling. "You are ridiculous, but go on. Do tell."

And then he did, doing exactly what he wanted to do with me, as we leisurely made love, arching for one another, his thickness stretching me in all the best ways. And when his fingers played with my clit, I came around his cock, both of us shaking. And when he followed me, slowly pushing me to my back so he could piston deeper, harder, warmth spread within me as he came.

His lips on mine, my hands roaming over his back, it wasn't until he stiffened that I realized that we had forgotten something very important.

"Fuck. I'm sorry. I forgot the condom."

I kissed him on his jaw, my fingers playing along his cheekbones, the worry etched in his eyes stark.

"I'm clean." I shivered, realizing that I hadn't explained everything before. We knew so much about each other, and yet there was so much more to explore. And I couldn't wait to figure that out.

"I had to check everything after. Well, after him."

The scowl on Carson's face could have committed murder itself. Then he kissed my jaw and stared down at me. "Please don't mention him while I'm buried balls deep inside you. In fact, never mention him again."

"I will do my best to make sure that I never speak of that man again. But I'm clean. And on birth control. I love my babies, but well, having more children was never in the cards."

He kissed me again, slowly sliding in and out of me even as he hardened again. "I'm clean as well, and I can show you my latest physical. I've never gone bare with anyone before. And my god, I don't want to go back to a condom."

"Then we don't have to." Warmth spread again, and I kissed his cheek as we began to make love once more, surprising me.

Afterwards, we showered, this time with me on my knees and his cock deep down my throat, and then I found myself sitting on the inlaid bench as he had his fill of me, his tongue doing amazing things.

We got ready together, as the girls began to wake.

"I need to get them ready for daycare and my mom. I have four lessons today."

"We should align our schedules, because I know you work more hours than you should—" He paused. "No, I'm not complaining. You do what you need to, because you love it. I'm not telling you what to do."

My heart warmed again and I realized he understood me. I didn't know how I had fallen in love with this man, but I knew there was no going back. I didn't want to go back.

"Yes, I do love calendars. They're needed in my business."

"Mine too." He kissed the tip of my nose and dressed in the same casual outfit he had shown up in. Apparently, once he had finished with the doctors and showered after he had been rescued, he'd been given casual clothes that weren't his and came straight here.

"You know, you can leave a few things here if you want." He raised a brow.

"You and the girls can leave stuff at my place as well. I realize that I don't have good enough beds for them, but that can change. In fact, I can call my team and make that happen."

"Carson."

"Or we can stay here, I don't care. But I want to be with you, Sophia. I love you. We'll go as fast or slow as you want. All that matters is that I love you, and I love those little girls."

Tears threatened, and I went to my tiptoes, grateful when he lowered his head so I could kiss him. As a dancer, I was taller than my sisters, but Carson still loomed over me, and he had to bend to *allow* a kiss. Somehow that was hotter than I thought possible.

"Let's table that until we get a full night's sleep and figure things out. Because I'm not running away, Carson. But I'm also sort of in a daze."

"Agreed." He ran his thumb along my cheek. "As for more babies? Well, we can talk about that later too."

My stomach tightened even as butterflies threatened. This man knew how to disarm me, but in the best ways.

We made our way out of my bedroom, the one that I would share with Carson whenever he was here, and went to get the girls. They were so happy to see Carson, that they didn't ask a single question as to why he would be here so early in the morning. After all, they were too young to truly understand. We would have to figure out a way to explain what was going on, but first Carson and I would have to put labels on it just for them, at least. And my family. Well, that was going to be a tough conversation with Flynn and the others.

With Violet in my arms, and Hazel in his, we made our way to the kitchen, and I went to start breakfast. But then Carson was there, his dexterity in the kitchen surprising me.

"I've lived alone a long time, Sophia, I know how to cook for myself. Plus, I need to figure out what these little munchkins like to eat."

I shook my head, loving the way that the girls already clung to him. It had worried me beyond all measure of what I was going to say to them when I had thought Carson and I were over. Let alone what I would have been forced to do if he had been killed. I shuddered, trying not to think about that.

The doorbell rang, pulling me from my thoughts, and I realized that my mother had shown up early.

"I told the family group chat that you were alive," I whispered against him as he gave me an odd look.

"I can face your mother, Princess," he teased.

This time I didn't correct him on the term. When I opened the door, my mother was there, concern in her gaze, and yet not a single lick of tension.

"Sophia. I know I'm early, but I didn't know if you would need me."

"Carson's in the kitchen cooking breakfast for us. You're welcome to join."

I braced myself for judgment, but instead my mother just smiled wide, moved forward, and held me close. It took me a moment, but then I was holding her back, nearly letting the tears fall.

"He makes you smile. I love him already." A pause. "Just like you do."

I froze, my hands shaking. "How did you know I loved him?"

"A mother knows. Sometimes it takes a kick in the ass, but we figure it out."

With that startling revelation, I threw my head back and laughed, then hooked my arm with hers before we headed into the kitchen.

"Mr. Woods," my mother said.

"Hello there, Ms. Constance. You're welcome to call me Carson."

I love that he called my mother that rather than using either of her last names. While I used Cage to be close to my siblings, not my father, my mother had her own issues with her name. I had a feeling she would stick with Dixon for herself, but keep the connection to the Cages, a name she had never taken legally, for her own children. There wasn't anything a mother wouldn't do, and it had taken me a long time to realize that.

"It's good to see you here. And look at you, little girls, already covered in syrup."

I shook my head as my mother and I began to clean up the girls, and Carson just shrugged. "I'm learning here."

"I'm still learning something new every day," my mother said, and just like that, things settled.

I hadn't expected this, and yet I loved it.

"You better be good for my baby girl," my mother whispered as she walked past Carson, and as I opened my mouth to say something, Carson shook his head and squeezed my mother's shoulder.

"I will do my best to be worthy. I promise."

Was it any wonder that I loved this man?

By the time we finished breakfast and cleaned up, Carson already had a car service waiting for him. "Well, I need to go deal with coming back from the dead, I guess."

I shivered, hating the humor in his tone, because I knew he was coping the best way he could.

"I'll see you soon?"

"Count on it. I mean, your mother likes me but I'm going to have to go through the gauntlet with everyone else."

I laughed and silently agreed.

My mother left soon after. I would be dropping the girls off at daycare, and Mother would be picking them up. She liked to have breakfast with us, and I had truly appreciated her being here.

After I got the girls settled in their playroom, I went to my room to finish getting ready, knowing I had a long day ahead. I was already behind with everything that had happened with Carson, but it was all worth it.

Because he was here.

There were so many unanswered questions, and I knew we had to plan our future. I didn't know what would happen next, or how quickly things would roll into the next phase, but all that mattered was that I trusted him.

It should surprise me, but it didn't.

Because that's just who Carson was.

Humming under my breath, I went to my closet to get to my dance clothes when a shadow passed out of the corner of my eye. I whirled, wondering if it was one of the girls, and before I could scream, a hand clamped over my mouth.

"I don't think so, Sophia. Don't forget, you're mine." And then Cale slid a needle into my arm and hit the plunger. Darkness and dizziness warred within me before I could take my next breath, and the first thing that I could think of were my babies.

My girls.

And then there was nothing.

Chapter Sixteen

CARSON

THE LOGISTICS OF CLAIMING THAT ONE'S DEATH was prematurely announced to the world, was probably far more difficult than it should be.

I was not dead. My team had not died—thankfully. And the world could begin rumbling normally. And yet, not so much.

There had been discussions with the board, with people at my company who had not been on the flight but wanted explanations. There of course had been phone calls with my sister, and ignoring phone calls from my family. If my parents needed to talk to me, they could go through our lawyers.

Other companies that I worked with had wanted to reach out, to say their condolences, and frankly, I had a feeling they wanted to ensure that they weren't using the same planes we were. After everything that had happened, I was just grateful that we had survived, and now I sat here across the table with lunch in front of us, and the Cages looking no worse for wear.

"I'm glad you're alive," Aston said, leaning back in his chair.

Blakely snorted. "Really? That's what you're going with?"

"Dear wife, you do realize that it wasn't a bad thing to say. After all, our friend is alive and has seemingly groveled well enough for Sophia." He gave me a pointed look. "Of course, we will have to ensure that's the actual truth later, won't we?"

I didn't say anything, a soft smile playing on my face as I thought about Sophia. No, I hadn't groveled well enough yet. But I would continue to do so because she deserved it. Fuck, she deserved everything. And despite what I knew I probably deserved in this moment, I wasn't going to take her for granted. Nor was I going to wallow in my own pity. Because I had been gifted a second, third, even fourth chance. And I wasn't going to give that up.

"I'm seriously glad you're okay." Blakely reached out and squeezed my hand, and I let out a breath.

"I'm glad I'm okay too. And my whole team. It was scary as fuck, and I'm just glad the two of you weren't on the same flight." I gestured towards Flynn and James, who each nodded in turn.

"Damn straight." James shivered. "Not that I would begrudge you for being angry at us for coming at you."

"Oh, he deserved it," Aston said, glaring at me. I might have seen the care and relief in his gaze, but I had still hurt their baby sister, and I needed to atone for that sin—and not merely towards the woman that I loved.

"We'll have to have a lovely family dinner to truly see how things are working out," Aston said, and Blakely rolled her eyes.

"We're going to have a family dinner because apparently that's what we do now. It's our form of entertainment. But what we're not going to do is put Carson in the hot seat."

"Excuse me, we *will* be doing that," Flynn said, an odd note in his voice that I couldn't read. "It's our right as big brothers. You, the sister-in-law, will have your own gauntlet for him to go through. However, we are not done yet."

"And what will happen one day when you mess up with the person you love, and you're forced to face her family?" James asked.

Flynn stiffened, before I watched him force his shoulders to relax. "Then I guess I should get some practice being an asshole to Carson. That way he understands the true magnitude of the situation."

I watched the family volley back and forth, as if I

wasn't in the room. I didn't mind that. Again, I deserved it. And more.

But here I was, eating a damn fine lunch, most of the paperwork for the day done, and soon I would be heading towards Sophia. She hadn't texted back earlier, but I knew she had more than a few dance lessons for the day. Once classes were over, she would get to her phone, and I'd hear from her.

I had no idea who this man was, the one who desperately needed to hear from a woman, but here I was.

"I am glad you're here though," Blakely said. "And not just because I need every single detail. We're glad you're safe. You're part of the Cage group now. I won't say Cage family because that puts pressure on Sophia and the girls and I'm not that crazy, but you're a good person, Carson. And Cora needs you. So does Sophia."

My chest ached at those words, and I ran my fist over my heart. "You're right. They do. So I'm not going to mess up. Not anymore."

"And we will all be doing new checks on our planes," Aston said dryly.

"Damn straight," I agreed.

By the time we finished lunch and went over the final paperwork for another partnership between the Woods and the Cages, everything felt fucking fantastic. I had a literal new lease on life, and I was going to be heading to Sophia soon. Not home, no, not yet.

But I already had a line on a decorator to help outfit one of the spare rooms into the girls' room. Because while Sophia might not be ready to move in, hell, I wasn't even sure where I was on that, other than the fact that I wanted her in my life at all times, and I wanted the girls to know that they had space with me.

It might be moving too quickly, but then again, I'd almost lost her. And I'd almost lost myself. So perhaps I wasn't moving fast enough in the end.

As I made my way to my SUV, footsteps sounded behind me. I turned to see Flynn jogging towards me, an odd expression on his face.

"Hey there. Did I miss something?"

"No, I was wondering if you could drop me off at Sophia's? I figured you're heading there."

My lips twitched. "I am. Are you going to start another interview?"

"No. I promise. I had to take my car to the shop today, as it was making a sound, and I'm not a mechanic. And while I could use one of the company cars, I figured you could drive me to her place, and then I'll order a ride back to mine."

"Why do you need to see Sophia?" I asked, confused.

"Because I've been kind of an asshole to both of you. And while I haven't quite apologized to you, I am going to fully apologize to her."

"I should be angry that you would even dare be a jerk

to her, but I know you were just being the big brother. As someone who's an asshole and a big brother myself, I understand it. Come on, I'll drive you."

"I promise I won't stay long. Though it is nice to see my nieces."

"They're pretty amazing."

"I'm glad you understand that. Because their father sure hasn't."

As we pulled out onto the main street, my hands tightened on the steering wheel. "I know you have good lawyers, but I'm going to add mine to help out. I want that man nowhere near Sophia and the girls."

"Any help is appreciated. I hate the laws in this country most days now."

"Cale deserved far more than he got, and I'm not going to let him at that family anymore."

"Especially since I have a feeling you're going to be part of our family now," Flynn said dryly.

"I love her," I said simply. "And I'm not going to change that. So yes, you're stuck with me."

"I like you better than Cale. You don't have a veneer over yourself. You are who you are."

"Damn straight I am," I said with a growl. "Being any different would just hurt us in the end."

"You're right about that. After everything that happened with her ex, well, I may be an asshole, but I have my reasons. And I'm glad that she has you."

I didn't know why Flynn thought of himself like that, nor what was going on in his head. I hoped one of his brothers did. Flynn was a good person, and while we fought at the gym, it was for a reason.

All I knew in this moment though was that I needed to get to Sophia. I missed her like hell.

When we pulled into her driveway however, I frowned. "I thought her last class was over? Her car isn't here."

"Weird. Maybe she's running late?" Flynn asked. But without another word, we were both out of our seats and heading towards the front door, which was open.

"What the fuck?" Flynn asked.

"Call the cops," I said, alarm prickling, the hairs on the back of my neck standing up. Because her alarm was off, the door was open, and the girls were screaming.

Flynn already had his phone in his hand as he moved behind me, and I took in my surroundings. Nothing looked out of place, and yet, she wasn't here. Her purse was still on the counter, and I could hear Hazel and Violet banging on their door.

I ran down the hallway, and my blood went cold.

"Help me move this," I shouted though Flynn was already by my side. Somebody had positioned the breakfast bar in front of the girls' door so it couldn't open, and that meant something was wrong. Beyond wrong.

We shoved it out of the way, and then I forced open the door, terrified of what I would see.

Both girls slammed into my legs, and I bent down and picked them up. They were shaking, crying, and it looked like they had been trapped in here for most of the day.

"I wet my pants," Violet sniffled as she clung to me.

"Where's Mommy?" Hazel asked, and I turned to Flynn, whose face had gone pale.

"They're on their way," Flynn whispered, and then mouthed the words *the cops*.

With a hard swallow, I handed the girls over to Flynn. "I need to check," I said, terrified of what I was going to see.

"Carson, don't—"

But I shook my head sharply and hoped to hell that Flynn understood.

Because I wasn't about to let the girls go into the back of the house with me, nor did I want Flynn to see what might be in Sophia's room.

Not his sister.

Not the woman that I loved.

Sophia.

As I moved into her bedroom, I walked past the bathroom. The sink faucet was running, and the makeup mirror that had been on the edge of the counter was shattered on the ground.

Someone had left the closet light on, and that's when I

realized that most of the clothes had been pulled down, with shoes and bags tossed around as if someone had tried to fight, or someone had been fucking angry.

But that's not what had chilled me.

Because next to a fallen shoe, the same shoe that she had been wearing when we left, was a needle.

A used one.

And my world ended.

Chapter Seventeen

SOPHIA

I had been in and out of consciousness over the past however long hours, if it had even been hours and not minutes or days. I had only known I was even awake because my body ached. I was tied up, my arms in front of me, my bare feet bound. But Cale had put a blindfold over my eyes, and a gag in my mouth. I couldn't scream, couldn't see anything. I knew I was in a trunk because I couldn't lift my body, and every time we hit a bump or a hard curve, I'd bang into the lid or the sides, and I knew I would be bruised and bloody.

If only I could remove my blindfold, maybe I could figure out how to use the latch to get out. Any car these days had an escape latch in case you were accidentally—not even purposely—put in a trunk.

And yet I couldn't do any of it.

Were Hazel and Violet okay? They had to be. I couldn't hear them, so they weren't calling out for me, not in this car. But he wouldn't have hurt them. He didn't even like them. They were nothing to him but a way to get at me. And since he had me, there was no way he would hurt them. Right?

Bile filled my throat, and I swallowed it down. The last thing I needed to do was choke on my own vomit and brushed along my shoulder, and I flinched, pulling back from him.

"Fucking bitch. You think you can just get away die and not even be able to fight for myself."

I was strong, a dancer, and yet where Cale had already broken my bones in the past, I could feel every bump and turn to the point that my entire body ached, thrumming on a stressful drum.

What was he going to do with me?

It wasn't as if killing me or hurting me would get him what he wanted. Maybe he would ask for a ransom note? But my brothers and sisters would never let him get away with it. They would find him and end him. They wouldn't even let the judicial system have its way because it had already failed us more than once before. And as for Carson? I held back a soft cry.

No, Carson wouldn't allow it to happen either.

He had already threatened to kill him more than once, and I knew he wouldn't stop until he found me.

But I couldn't wait for them.

They didn't even know I was gone. I'd have to do this myself.

But how?

Where the hell was I?

We had to be going up a hill of some sort, because my ears continued to pop with the elevation changes, and as we took a sharp turn, I slammed into the side of the trunk and blood seeped down my face.

I would be okay. I had to be okay.

My girls needed me.

Carson needed me.

And fuck, I needed myself.

I had so many plans, and I wasn't going to let my terrible decision in one man and a choice of what I thought was forever ruin this.

And then we stopped.

A slam of a car door.

Boots crunching on gravel.

Fear coated my tongue, and my pulse raced to the point I was afraid I would pass out, but I needed to remain calm. I needed to get out of this.

"There you are," Cale said as he opened the trunk, and light began to seep around my blindfold.

His fingers brushed along my shoulder, and I flinched, pulling back from him.

"Fucking bitch. You think you can just get away from me like that? No, that's not how this works."

"You are going to just lay here for a bit longer, and think about what you did."

I tried to scream through the gag, but he punched me in the gut, and then slammed the trunk lid back down.

Pain rocked through me, and I nearly threw up. The gag fell from my mouth, and I knew if I screamed, he would just hurt me more.

I needed to figure out exactly where I was, who was around, and then I would make more noise.

But for now, I needed my bearings.

He opened up the trunk once more, stuffed the gag back in my mouth even as I screamed, and then he slapped me.

He hit me once, twice, and on the third time I blacked out.

By the time I woke again, there was darkness, nothing.

I would continue to scream, behind the gag, anything I could do, but nobody would hear me.

Nobody was coming for me.

I tried to reach my pocket, where the one thing that may save me lay, but I couldn't reach, not at this angle. My shoulders burned, and maybe if I tried to dislocate myself like in the movies, I'd be able to figure it out.

But I couldn't.

I was helpless, and for now, there was nothing.

When he opened the trunk once more, I didn't scream.

He pulled me out by my shoulders, and the moans sounded like screams to my ears.

"Shut up," Cale snarled. He tossed me onto the ground, and I was grateful that I was low enough that I didn't break a bone. But sharp pain and nauseating agony slammed into me from my shoulder, my head, all throughout my body.

And when he pulled up my feet and began to drag me, I twisted and fought, and I tried to kick. He slapped at me, but it wasn't enough at this angle.

And when my gag fell out finally, I screamed.

"You fucking bitch. You don't even know where you are. They're not going to find you here. Nobody comes up here. Not since the last incident."

I froze, as Cale pulled off my blindfold.

I stared into the eyes of the man that I thought I loved. The man that I thought had believed in me, but there was nothing. No hope, no emotion, just pure vacancy and hatred.

"You don't even know where we are, do you?"

I tried to look around, my entire body shaking, but when I met Cale's gaze again, he smirked.

"Your pretty little town. The one with your fucking name on it. The one that you didn't let me have a single slice of because you're a fucking selfish cunt. You and your family. Your dad and all of his cronies took everything for granted. They had all this money, and you didn't take a single penny of it. What a fucking whore. A wasteful disappointment." He backhanded me, and my head slammed into the picnic table behind us that I hadn't even realized was there.

A ringing sensation echoed in my ears, and then Cale spit next to me.

"I could have had everything, and yet you did nothing for me. You were a waste. Not even a good fuck. You couldn't even give me boys. Instead you gave me girls."

"The girls. Please tell me—" I blurted, trying to get my wrist free.

Cale had always been good at knots.

Another shiver.

"The little brats are fine. I didn't touch them. I'm not a monster."

He said the words as if he believed them.

But this man was going to kill me.

And I was never going to see them again.

"You're going to die on the land that bears your name. Because you were worthless to me alive. But when you're dead? I'm going to get everything."

He smirked, that wild smile on his face looking nothing like sanity.

"Cale. We're divorced. That's not how this works. You know that. Killing me is going to accomplish nothing."

All I could feel was relief that he hadn't touched my babies. But they were alone. All alone.

"Oh fuck off. My lawyers were always better than yours. We have our ways."

He was believing his own lies at this point, anything for him to have power, and yet it was for nothing.

He was going to kill me for nothing, and it was all I could do not to sob and scream.

And then he pulled out a knife so large it glinted underneath the dying sunlight.

"If you move, I'll gut you. You're going to die anyway, but let's make it quick."

I tried to back away, and he backhanded me again. This time blood flooded my mouth.

All I could do was stare at the man that had ruined everything, and I hadn't been able to see it until it was too late.

He cut the bindings at my feet, then my arms. It made no sense until he put the knife against my throat.

"I've already written your note, one that's going to explain what you want to do with our children and your income and your businesses. Because you made mistakes. And now I'm going to need you to walk to that cliff. Does it look familiar? I read in the news it's the one where your sister almost died. The small town of Cage Lake apparently has a newspaper where it explains when people are so stupid at the end of cliffs that they fall off. But you're not going to fall off. You're going to jump, Sophia."

I tried to look, but the knife dug into my skin. I didn't want to die, I couldn't. But I refused to cry in front of this man. He'd already taken so much from me, I would not give him any more tears.

I would not give him myself.

I would not die.

But it seemed he had an odd plan, one that wouldn't work, but as it did in his head, it didn't make much sense to fight it. At least outwardly. Or maybe I was too exhausted to think clearly.

"Cale. Please."

"I like you begging. You never begged enough before. You wanted the perfect man, the beta who would take what you can give, and yet, you didn't see me for who I was. You were always such a fucking idiot. Not a good wife, not a good fuck, a terrible mother. And you gave me nothing. So now you're going to walk to that cliff where your sister almost died, and you're going to jump. And if you don't do it, I'll push, and you'll be dead. But then I'll go to your little girls, the little brats you love so much, and I'll end their lives just like their mother's."

Ice crawled up my spine as I saw the truth in his gaze.

He would kill them. If I didn't kill myself, he would kill them.

And I wanted to cry. Hell, I wanted to die in that moment. But I didn't. I couldn't.

I needed to find another way out of this.

So when Cale pulled me up to my feet, I didn't fight, as the knife was still touching my neck, but my gaze shot in all directions, praying that someone would walk by.

We were on a trail after all, and it was in the middle of summer. Somebody had to come.

But nobody was coming.

Not my family, not Carson.

It would just be me.

"I would ask for your last words, but I don't even want to hear your fucking voice."

And then Cale let the knife drop, his hand went to my back, and he pushed.

I couldn't even open my mouth to scream. My foot dragged on the edge of the dirt, and I twisted, not even realizing I was falling until it was too late. My arms slammed onto the ground, blood seeping into the soil as I skidded down the side, an awkward marionette with its strings pulled.

But Cale had made a mistake.

Because as I had fallen, my arm had reached out, and I hadn't even realized I had grabbed onto his shirt in the process.

The high-pitched scream hadn't come from me. For I had no breath.

No, it had come from the man that I hadn't even realized had been a monster until it was too late.

Because Cale's mistakes were his final ones.

Because as I had fallen, my fingers digging into his shirt, he hadn't been prepared for the imbalance.

So I slammed into the ground, barely holding onto the edge of the cliff by my fingernails, and Cale screamed beside me, arms outstretched, knife falling beside us, and then there was nothing.

He was gone.

And I was still going to die.

I tried to hold on, but my arms were weak, and there was no grip.

"Sophia!"

It didn't sound like Cale's voice, but maybe it was an angel's. Did the grim reaper speak to you before he took your soul?

Tears fell down my cheeks as I struggled to keep hold, and then one arm slipped, and I knew this would be the end.

I would never see my babies again.

I would never see my family.

I would never see Carson.

"Sophia!"

And then strong arms were lifting me up, and I cried out in pain, agony.

And then somehow Carson was holding me, both of

us shaking, and I was on the ground, in Carson's lap, and somehow I was alive.

Somehow he was here.

"Holy shit," Flynn burst out, and then he was on the ground next to us, awkwardly holding the two of us.

I could hear sirens in the distance, but it made no sense.

"How are you here?" I rasped.

I tried to look over the side of the cliff, but Carson moved me so I couldn't glance over.

"Don't look. Don't look," he whispered as his gaze raked my body, anger in every inch of his posture and eyes.

"How?" I rasped, tears now fully shaking my body.

"Your phone," Flynn answered. "You had it in your pocket. But I guess you couldn't reach it?" Flynn asked as tears covered his face as well.

"I tried," I panted.

As the authorities ran towards us, Carson cupped my face and kissed my bruised and bloody lips.

"So strong. You did it. Although I should have," he growled.

I would deal with that statement later, and what it meant, but I leaned against him, Flynn holding us both, and I let myself break.

"The girls?"

"They're safe. The girls are safe. I love you. Don't fucking do that again."

"I love you, and I won't. I won't."

And I let myself fall, in the arms of the man that I loved, the man that I trusted, with my family at my side, knowing I would never be alone.

The nightmare was over, and perhaps a new one would begin, but it didn't matter.

Because I had made my choice, I had tried to fight.

And somehow, against all odds, we had won.

And maybe in the morning it would all make sense.

Chapter Eighteen

CARSON

ALTHOUGH HER EYES WERE CLOSED, AND HER breathing even, I knew she was awake. I could always tell. She looked so damn beautiful underneath the soft duvet, her eyelashes pillowed on her cheeks, her hair flowing over her shoulders. I knew she usually slept with a bonnet, but we had been up late the night before, enjoying ourselves a little too much. In fact, we'd stayed up far too late and had barely gotten any sleep. I was loath to wake her up this morning, but we had to. We had an important day ahead of us.

I knelt by the edge of the bed and leaned forward, staring at the woman I loved.

I couldn't quite believe that this was our life now. Sophia sleeping in our bed, with the girls making noise in their room, giggling at one another. They were still young enough that the twins wanted to stay in one room, and I knew one day it would probably break Sophia's heart to have them separate, and frankly, it would probably break mine as well.

I was never meant to be a father—not with the father that I had growing up—and yet here I was, becoming the man I never knew I could be.

Because of this woman.

I was now a girl dad, and I loved it. And anybody who ever came near those little girls of mine would have to deal with my wrath.

"I can hear you growling. Who are you thinking about maiming?" Sophia hadn't opened her eyes, though a small smile played on her face as she spoke. I leaned forward and traced my fingers along her jaw.

"I'm just wondering what I'm going to have to do one day when Hazel and Violet are old enough to date."

Sophia's eyes fluttered open as she laughed softly. "Oh yes. I can see you being that growly man. But you have to let them open their wings. If you cage them, they'll just rebel. You know your sister."

"My sister is in a loving relationship with an amazing woman. Maybe we'll be lucky and our daughters will be lesbians, that way I don't have to deal with boys."

Sophia's entire body shook as she laughed, and I leaned down and kissed her softly on the mouth.

"That sounds quite bigoted, mister."

"You know I'll love whoever they love. But they will have to run the gauntlet."

"And not just your gauntlet. Have you met the Cages?"

"You know, that's true. I bet Aston and I could start an entire interview process for the next generation." Actual plans began to take form in my mind, but then Sophia was leaning forward, her lips on mine.

"Stop. We will raise them to be smart, caring, and careful. We will not have an actual lie detector and interview process."

I grinned. "I didn't say anything about a lie detector, but I like the idea of one."

"You are ridiculous."

"But that's why you love me," I said honestly.

Her entire body softened, and she sat up. I couldn't help but notice the way the sheet pooled at her waist. Her pink tipped breasts were so damn beautiful, so I leaned forward and sucked one into my mouth.

She groaned, leaning forward.

"Carson," she whispered.

"You always taste so beautiful."

"And I just looked at the clock, so I know we'll be late if we're not careful. We need to get the girls ready. And that means you need to get your mouth off my breasts."

"I'm sure we can find some time."

And with a growl, I was on her, the sheet torn away,

and my sweats tugged beneath my ass. I was in her in a blink, her legs wrapped around me, and as she arched, I groaned into her neck.

"Carson," she whispered.

"That's it. Mine." And then we rolled so I was sitting, and she was on my lap with my hands on her waist, lifting her up and down smoothly, her pussy fluttering around my cock.

I took her breasts into my mouth again, ignoring her phone alarm going off. We would be late, but I didn't care. This was the love of my life, and I wasn't letting any moment go to waste.

When I slid my hand between us, flicking my thumb over her clit, she met my gaze, eyes wide, her mouth parted, and then she was coming. Her wet, hot cunt gripped my cock as I slid in and out of her. She continued to come, her hair flowing down her back as she arched for me, and I moved at a rapid pace, unable to hold back. My balls tightened, and then I was filling her, body shaking, cum leaking between us.

There was no condom, there was no need. Not anymore.

Body shuddering, I held her close, my face buried in her neck.

"That's one way to wake up," she teased.

I kissed her neck, her jaw, and then her lips. "I love you," I rasped, my voice breaking.

"I love you so much," she said softly, her eyes filling. "But I hate the fact that we're going to have to wash the sheets again."

I threw my head back and laughed, my still hard cock pulsating deep within her as I did.

She giggled, her head resting on my shoulder, and I knew this was how I wanted to wake up every morning until the end of our days.

By the time the phone buzzed again, I knew we would truly be late and I didn't care. We cleaned up the bed, and then each other, and I was very good and didn't pin her against the shower wall like I wanted to.

Instead, I used my fingers to make her come one more time, just because I could, and let her lick her sweetness off my fingers.

Since Sophia needed to blow dry her hair, I was the one who got the girls ready for the day, loving the way they explained about their dreams, and what they wanted to do for the day.

I was not their father, not in blood, but I would be. I would take care of these girls until the end of my days.

Because Sophia wanted me to be their father. And I was never going to let them go.

"Uppies?" Hazel asked, that wicked gleam in her gaze. She was so like her uncles it wasn't even funny, so I picked her up, knowing she could speak in full sentences at this point, she just liked the word.

I rubbed my beard against her soft cheek, and she giggled as Violet twirled around me, showing me her new ballet moves.

"Well, look at you three, you got ready so quickly," Sophia said as she moved into the kitchen, wearing a soft dress and a bright smile. Her cheeks were also glowing, and I knew once we made it to Aston's house, they would all know why we were late. Brunch would just have to wait, and I did not care.

"Are you ready to see all of the Cages?"

"We're Cages," Violet said before she curtsied.

Hazel and I clapped, as Sophia went to her knees and hugged her daughter close.

"You are Cages."

"But Carson isn't," she whispered.

My heart clutched, and I swallowed hard.

"No, but I love you Cages."

"Will you be one?" Hazel asked, playing with my beard.

I looked over at Sophia, at that blush, and knew she would have to be the one to answer this.

"He can be ours, and you know, our family loves to make people honorary Cages. Even if they have different last names."

In that moment, I knew I would change my last name if they wanted me to. I wasn't going to make the girls do it again when I made them mine. Because I would adopt them, Sophia had already agreed. We were just waiting to lean into this new moment of our lives.

Cora had taken Juliet's name, and I had been grateful for that. We hadn't wanted another connection to the family that had tried to take so much from us.

Maybe I could add Cage to my last name. It would surely confuse some of the older people I worked with and piss off my father.

I grinned at that, the smile probably wicked, and Sophia gave me a look.

"I'm a little afraid of what you're thinking right now."

"Oh, just thinking how I can be a little wicked."

"Carson," she whispered.

"I'll tell you later." I leaned forward, and kissed her jaw, before running my beard along Violet's cheek to make her giggle just like her sister.

"Scratchy!" Violet giggled.

"Okay, I guess I need to shave."

"No, I like it," Sophia said, and I swallowed hard, knowing that for her to say something like that was a big step.

She had spent so long hiding who she was, never expression her wants or desires. That she felt free to do so with me meant the world.

Because she never had to deal with ramifications when it came to me. I would always be there for her. And if she wanted to tell me her preferences, or asked me to change or not to change, I would.

Because she trusted me, and I would do all in my power to make sure she knew that she *could* trust me.

That these girls could trust me.

"Okay, let's get ready to head to Uncle Aston's," Sophia said after a moment, and I smiled, knowing that I would find a way to make a dating triathlon of some sorts in order to keep the kids safe.

From the look on Sophia's face, she knew exactly where my mind had gone.

It didn't take long for us to get everything ready. I lived closer than Sophia had, so that was a plus. After the kidnapping and attack, Sophia hadn't wanted to go back to that house. It was the second home of hers that had been broken because of Cale, but that man wouldn't hurt her anymore.

He was dead.

I would never regret not reaching out to save him. Part of me probably should, but I had been there to make sure Sophia had survived, and moving would have meant possibly risking her life and mine in order to protect the man who had threatened his children and nearly killed Sophia more than once. I would not feel guilt over that man's death. Sophia would though. And that was why we talked, why she and her family went to therapy, and why I went with her.

Whatever Sophia needed, I would be there. Because she was the strength within us, and her being able to shine that light meant the world.

We got to Aston's place, and he gave us a knowing look as to why we were late for brunch. But I ignored him. He wouldn't tease his sister, not for a little while yet, and I was grateful for that. One day he would see how far she had come and would tease her like he once did. But then again, they hadn't grown up together. Everything felt new when it came to this family, and I was the one joining in now. I was the one learning how to be part of this family.

But they had welcomed me with open arms. Even Cora and Juliet were invited to most meals that we were, though today they were out of town on a second belated honeymoon. Cora had been so damn scared about what had happened, but had opened her arms for Sophia, welcoming her as a sister. And Juliet had done the same.

Our parents didn't matter. If I never heard from them again other than through their lawyers, I would be fine. And I knew Cora and Juliet would be too. They had been adopted by the Cages just like I had. And just like Sophia had said at the wedding, Cora would never be alone.

We were all family for a reason, and we were figuring out exactly who we were together.

Not all the Cages were here, with Flynn being late from what I could tell, and Kyler out of town. Those who lived farther away from Aston weren't here today, but there were enough of us. The entire Cage family could take over our conference hall at this point, and I knew that once people started having more kids, it would just get louder.

I was excited that one day I would be in this home, with Sophia as my wife, and the girls as my legal kids. And that day would come soon. The ring was already wearing a hole in my pocket. But I would wait.

I would wait until Sophia was ready.

When she wouldn't wake up in a sweat because she could hear that man scream.

But we had time.

All of us.

The man who had shattered her once was gone. And wouldn't be coming back.

And the girls would one day ask where their father had gone, and we would find a way to tell them.

And I would find a way to be the man that they needed.

And that wasn't daunting at all.

"Are you okay?" Sophia asked, pulling away from Isabella and Blakely to come towards me.

"I am. Have I said I love you recently?" I asked, brushing her hair back from her face.

"Only twice or so this morning. I love you too, you know."

I leaned down and took her lips with mine.

"Get your mouth off my sister," Dorian snarled, even as he laughed, with Harper glaring at him.

I ignored them all and just looked at Sophia.

"When can we leave again?" I asked.

"You're ridiculous. We are here for family brunch, and you're going to help with the dishes."

"Big bad Carson, Mr. Former MMA fighter, and the CEO to end all CEOs, doing dishes? I can't wait," James said with a laugh. I leaned back and let them tease me, knowing that I would have to get used to this.

I hadn't grown up with a family that pushed one another like this, that wanted to be with one another.

Then again, everyone in this room hadn't grown up in a way that would lead to this either. We'd all begun with secrets that would hopefully end with us.

I had found my forever in a woman who tempted me, teased me, and found strength within me I hadn't known was there. She challenged me every day, and I could not wait to see where she would take me.

Because I knew, no matter the gauntlet the world put her through, and no matter what her family spoke of, I would be her pillar, her strength. Because she had enough spine for every person in this room. And now I would be the one she could lean on. Because I had accidentally fallen in love. And this fling, the single night that should never have happened, would be our future.

And I supposed being a Cage couldn't be all that bad in the end.

Epilogue

FLYNN

I RAN MY HANDS THROUGH MY HAIR, ANNOYED once again that here I was, stressed out about who could possibly be at my door.

It wasn't as if this were new. It was just different. Or perhaps, something that would never become routine. It couldn't. If it did, it would destroy so fucking much. And well, probably piss off more than a few people in my family. And I was Flynn Cage, I did not piss off my family. If anything, I was the mediator. Much like James, I was the one who made sure my family didn't implode. And we sure as hell had gotten close more than a few times.

I let out a sigh as my phone buzzed, and I looked at the screen.

L:

I'm here.

I slid my phone into my back pocket and went to the door, trying to act casual. It wasn't as if she could see me through the mahogany door, but with the way that I swore she could see through everything other than the facade I tried to keep on, maybe she could.

I opened the door and stared at the woman standing underneath my porch light, her hair tucked under a knit cap, glasses perched on her nose, and her eyes wide.

"You're late."

She rolled those gorgeous gray eyes of hers and pushed past me.

"There was traffic. And I'm not that late. If I were going to be, I would have texted you. Because I like to be on time, and I don't leave people waiting for hours by forgetting to mention that they weren't coming."

Guilt stabbed at me, and I closed the door behind us a little harder than I'd meant to.

"I didn't ghost you."

She turned and stared at me. "Yes. You did."

"Our plane literally malfunctioned, and we couldn't get into the air. I tried to call you, to text you, even tried to email you that I wasn't going to be here on time, maybe not even for the entire evening, but I couldn't get ahold of you. I've apologized multiple times, but I didn't purposely stand you up."

She pulled off her jacket, and laid it on the end of the couch, before toeing off her shoes.

I was already barefoot, in black joggers and a white tee, as I'd quickly showered after work and hadn't bothered dressing for dinner.

She set her purse by her coat, then turned to me.

I shook my head and moved forward without saying a word. When she tugged on the bottom of my shirt, I helped her slide it over my head, then undid the buttons of hers.

"How much time do we have left?"

"Less than an hour."

"I wasn't late."

"I could have already made you come by now if you had been on time."

"Jerk." She slid her hand down and cupped me over my sweats. I groaned, leaning into her touch.

"Wicked."

"I thought you liked it when I was wicked."

"Why don't you get on your knees and show me how apologetic you are for being late."

I was only teasing, not expecting her to actually do it, so when she slid to her knees and pulled down my joggers, I groaned.

My cock sprang out, and she caught it at the base, squeezing slightly.

"Luna. You don't have to do this."

"I want to. I never get to taste you." And then her mouth was on me, licking at the slit and causing me to nearly come right then and there. Her shirt was open, her lace covered breasts begging for my hands, so I leaned over slightly to cup her, even as she hollowed her cheeks and continued to suck me down.

"You're so damn good at that," I growled.

She pulled back, letting me go with a gasp. "Well, I know you like licking pussy, so I figured I would return the favor."

She winked as she said it, causing me to grin as I slid my thumb over her plump lips. She opened for me, and I pushed my thumb into her mouth, watching her suck it, just as she had been sucking my cock a few moments ago.

My twin brother's wife's twin sister did not do dirty talk. She didn't curse often, and she looked like a prim and proper chemistry professor.

And yet, here she was, on her knees, sucking my cock again.

She bobbed her head, and I tangled my fingers in her hair, tugging slightly because I knew that's how she liked it.

I shouldn't know exactly how she liked that edge of pain. Just as she shouldn't know how to cup my balls with one hand and move her other hand around to play with my taint. We were learning each other far too quickly, and that was a problem. Because what we were doing right now? Beyond wrong.

There were boundaries when it came to who you

could fuck, and the twin sister of your sister-in-law who happened to be married to your twin brother, was on the list of never fucking.

And here I was, pulling her back because I was ready to come, then pulling her into my arms.

"I need to fuck you," I whispered against her lips.

"Then do so."

I crushed my mouth to hers as I slid my hands under the soft linen of her pants, letting my thumb and fingers play against her wet slit. She gasped into my mouth, her hand gripping my cock as she jerked me off.

We were quick, and fast, stripping one another as we practically fell onto the couch, our hands roaming, our touches frantic.

I reached for the condom that I had left in my pocket and sheathed myself before we made a mistake. Then Luna was on her back, her breasts full, her pale nipples tight, and I swallowed hard.

"Are you sure about this?"

"Never. But please."

And with a nod, I grabbed the back of her thigh, pushed her leg up so her knee was at her shoulder, and positioned myself at her entrance.

Her pussy was plump, swollen for me, and I wanted to lean down and taste her, but we didn't have time. We never had time.

This was so fucking wrong.

Luna's gaze darkened as she reached forward and brushed her fingers along the scar on my leg. I swallowed hard and told myself to ignore that.

The scar didn't hurt anymore, and neither one of us needed to think about that moment. So I arched my hips, filling her in one stroke, thrusting hard and fast, going balls deep inside that sweet cunt of hers.

She gasped into my mouth, and I smiled against her. It wasn't sweet, it wasn't gentle. Because that wasn't what we were to each other.

This was a means to an end. A tease and a taste that had gone on far too long.

I didn't know what this craving meant.

This would be the final time. We were just two people who needed to scratch an itch, and soon we would find people that wouldn't be a problem. Where the fallout of whatever the fuck this was wouldn't break our families.

She arched into me, her breasts pressing against my chest, and I leaned down and took one nipple into my mouth.

"Flynn."

My name on her lips nearly sent me to the edge, but I shook my head and slid one hand between us, flicking my fingers over her clit. She came then, hard and fast as her body shivered in my hold, her cunt squeezing my cock.

I moved faster, my balls tightening, and then I was

coming, burying my face into her neck, afraid to look into her eyes and see what both of us tried to forget.

We were not for each other. And to think so would break one another.

And as I finally came down from my orgasm, my cock twitching as I filled the condom, both of us fought for breath.

She slid her hand up and played with the barbells in my nipples, smiling against my cheekbone.

"You always surprise me with this," she teased.

I let out a rough chuckle, knowing my weight was probably too much for her, and yet I wasn't moving.

"I do my best." I kissed her neck, knowing it was far too intimate for either one of us, and pulled back.

"I need to take care of the condom. And then we need to go."

She nodded, her face pale. "I took a ride-share here. My car's in the shop."

I nodded, having known this already. "I'll take you. It won't be suspicious."

I pulled out of her, and she whimpered. I looked down at her pussy, at how warm and soft and swollen she was, and slid my hand over her, cupping her sweetness.

"Did I hurt you?"

She smiled, though it didn't reach her eyes. "No. You're just really fucking big. So it takes me a moment to get used to you not being there anymore."

I wanted to take that as a compliment, but I was afraid I'd hurt her. So I took her lips with mine, a gentle kiss that should have meant nothing but still scared me.

"I'll be right back."

"I need to get dressed anyway."

We scrambled off one another, that awkwardness settling in.

We didn't talk about this, or what it could mean, or what it should mean.

Luna Blair was not for me.

Nor could there be anything that came from this.

I couldn't help but admire the roses and thorns tattooed between her breasts and cupping them, just like I had cupped them earlier with my hands. And when she turned, I found myself wanting to lean down and lick up her spine, over the vines that covered her skin.

She was one of the most striking people I'd ever met in my life, and I knew we needed to stop this.

Because nobody in our family knew that we did this. Or when it had started. Or when it needed to end.

This was a mistake, and we both knew it.

By the time we were dressed and sitting in my car, Luna looked as if she had just gotten off work and didn't have a care in the world.

She was fiery, and all magic, and a fucking amazing person.

She annoyed me to hell sometimes, but I figured she did that on purpose.

Or maybe I just needed her to.

"Thank you for the ride."

I smirked.

"Excuse me, but you didn't let me be on top this time, so I don't think you can actually let your mind go that way."

"I'm sorry that you didn't get what you wanted."

"I don't think getting what each other wants is what this is," Luna said, before she met my gaze, and turned away.

I cleared my throat and started the car, and we awkwardly made our way to my brother's house for a family dinner.

Luna didn't attend them often, but Scarlett was in town and wanted to see her sister.

So we would go and sit with the Cages, and I would pretend I didn't know how she tasted. I would pretend I didn't want her.

"How was work today?" she asked, the awkwardness settling in.

"We didn't buy another company today, so that was something."

"The Cages are taking over the world, and it's a little scary."

"So says the woman who probably knows how to make a very big bomb."

"There's no probably about it, but we don't talk about that sort of thing."

I looked over as she winked, and my lips quirked into a smile.

"It's good to know not to piss you off."

"You live and breathe to piss me off, Flynn Cage. But that's okay."

My hands tightened on the steering wheel, and I forced myself to relax. This was just us teasing. Just what we did.

"Hudson and Scarlett are going to be in town for a little while."

"I know. It'll be good to see my sister. I don't get to make it up to Cage Lake often."

"I don't that much anymore either, not with Hudson taking over my job. Isabella too."

I had been the one who took care of the businesses in Cage Lake since my father had done his best to destroy them. But now that Isabella and Hudson lived there full-time, I wasn't needed.

I tried not to think about what that meant.

"Anyway, Scarlett wants to see me a lot, and we're going to do a bunch of sister things. Mom's finally coming down too."

I looked over at her, surprised. "Really?"

Mrs. Blair was an agoraphobic, though she had been getting better ever since the shooting that had changed all of our lives. However, I wasn't sure if she ever came down to Denver.

"It's a big thing. And I'm glad. And well, I think Scarlett also wants to set me up with a friend."

My throat tightened, and I nodded. "Oh?"

"She knows somebody that Hudson knows as well. And I don't know. Maybe I should say yes."

There was a discomfort in her tone, or maybe I just wanted to hear it.

Nothing good could come from what Luna and I were doing. I knew this.

We weren't exclusive, and hell, we weren't even promising each other another night.

This would be good. I knew that. And apparently she did too.

Then why did it feel like I was being stabbed?

"If Scarlett likes him, I'm sure he's a good guy. Have fun on your date."

"Oh." Silence. "I guess I will."

"I'm heading out with Theo and Luke in a couple of days, since The Teal Door is having that singles' night. I don't know exactly why I'm going, but I figured I'd support my brother and his best friend. You know?"

"You're right. You should go do singles' night. I'm going to go on this date, and maybe I'll find that perfect person. Thank you for tonight, Flynn, but we both knew it was going to have to end sometime, right?"

I couldn't look at her, because I heard the hurt in her words. Or was it anger? I couldn't fucking tell anymore. "A clean break, you know?"

"Sure. Makes sense." Her eyes widened then, and I turned back to the road, unable to look at her face any longer.

Headlights flashed and the car on the other side of the road had veered towards us.

"Flynn!"

I turned the wheel hard, but it was too late. Metal crashed against metal, and the sound of screeching tires filled the air as burnt rubber and oil and whatever the hell else filled my nostrils.

The SUV flipped once, twice, maybe more, I couldn't tell. I reached out for Luna, trying to stop whatever the hell was happening, but it was a lost cause.

Luna screamed, and as my hand finally grasped hers, there was nothing.

My eyes cracked open as pain radiated through me, and I looked over to see Luna hanging from her seat, the seatbelt keeping her in place. The airbags had deployed and blood covered them.

I gasped in air, trying to catch my breath. "Luna. Luna!"

But there was nothing.

Her eyes were closing, and I couldn't see if her chest was moving.

Somebody else screamed, and sirens echoed in the distance, and I reached for her again, trying to make sure that she was okay.

Because she had to be okay.

But there was nothing.

Just darkness.

Next in the Cage Family Series:
Things get interesting with Flynn & Luna:
Wish it Were You

And if you'd like to read a bonus scene you can find it HERE!
I love this scene so much!

If you'd like to read the next Generation with the Montgomery Ink Legacy Series:
Bittersweet Promises

In the mood for more small town romance? Check out the Ashford Creek series with LEGACY. Or as I like to call it "The Small Town of Single Dads".

A Note from Carrie Ann Ryan

Thank you so much for reading **Pretend it's Forever.**

This wasn't an easy book to write and yet their romance flew onto the page. I knew exactly where Sophia & Carson needed to be and I am so grateful I was able to tell their story.

Thank you so much for being here and loving the Cage Family as much as I do. I truly appreciate you!

Next up is a twisty romance because Flynn has so many secrets. I cannot wait for him and Luna to tell their story in Wish it Were You!

In case you'd like to read Phoebe's romance, you can read about her and Kane in His Second Chance!

And Ford finds his match with Greer and Noah in Best Friend Temptation!

Book 1: The Forever Rule (Aston & Blakely)

Book 2: An Unexpected Everything (Isabella & Weston)

Book 3: If You Were Mine (Dorian & Harper)

Book 4: One Quick Obsession (Hudson & Scarlett)

Book 5: Pretend it's Forever (Sophia & Carson)

Book 6: Wish it Were You (Flynn & Luna)

Book 7: Only Half Without You (James & Emery)

Book 8: Time Stands Still (Theo & Nina)

Next in the Cage Family Series:
Things get interesting with Flynn & Luna:
Wish it Were You

And if you'd like to read a bonus scene you can find it HERE!
I love this scene so much!

If you'd like to read the next Generation with the Montgomery Ink Legacy Series:
Bittersweet Promises

In the mood for more small town romance? Check out the Ashford Creek series with LEGACY. Or as I like to call it "The Small Town of Single Dads".

If you want to make sure you know what's coming next

from me, you can sign up for my newsletter at www.CarrieAnnRyan.com; follow me on twitter at @CarrieAnnRyan, or like my Facebook page. I also have a Facebook Fan Club where we have trivia, chats, and other goodies. You guys are the reason I get to do what I do and I thank you.

Make sure you're signed up for my MAILING LIST so you can know when the next releases are available as well as find giveaways and FREE READS.

Happy Reading!

Also from Carrie Ann Ryan

The Montgomery Ink Legacy Series:

Book 1: Bittersweet Promises (Leif & Brooke)

Book 2: At First Meet (Nick & Lake)

Book 2.5: Happily Ever Never (May & Leo)

Book 3: Longtime Crush (Sebastian & Raven)

Book 4: Best Friend Temptation (Noah, Ford, and Greer)

Book 4.5: Happily Ever Maybe (Jennifer & Gus)

Book 5: Last First Kiss (Daisy & Hugh)

Book 6: His Second Chance (Kane & Phoebe)

Book 7: One Night with You (Kingston & Claire)

Book 8: Accidentally Forever (Crew & Aria)

Book 9: Last Chance Seduction (Lexington & Mercy)

Book 10: Kiss Me Forever (Brooklyn & Reece)

Book 11: His Guilty Pleasure (Dash & Aly)

Book 12: Maybe it's You (Riley & Gage)

Book 13: Kiss Me in the Morning

The Cage Family

Book 1: The Forever Rule (Aston & Blakely)

Book 2: An Unexpected Everything (Isabella & Weston)

Book 3: If You Were Mine (Dorian & Harper)

Book 4: One Quick Obsession (Hudson & Scarlett)

Book 5: Pretend it's Forever (Sophia & Carson)

Book 6: Wish it Were You (Flynn & Luna)

Book 7: Only Half Without You (James & Emery)

Book 8: Time Stands Still (Theo & Nina)

Ashford Creek

Book 1: Legacy (Callum & Felicity)

Book 2: Crossroads (Bodhi & Kiera)

Book 3: Westward (Atlas & Elizabeth)

Book 4: Patience (Teagan & Rush)

Book 5: Watershed

Book 6: Expanse

Clover Lake

Book 1: Always a Fake Bridesmaid (Livvy & Ewan)

Book 2: Accidental Runaway Groom (Jamie & Sharp)

Book 3: His Practically Fake Proposal (Galen & Addy)

The Wilder Brothers Series:

Book 1: One Way Back to Me (Eli & Alexis)

Book 2: Always the One for Me (Evan & Kendall)

Book 3: The Path to You (Everett & Bethany)

Book 4: Coming Home for Us (Elijah & Maddie)

Book 5: Stay Here With Me (East & Lark)

Book 6: Finding the Road to Us (Elliot, Trace, and Sidney)

Book 7: Moments for You (Ridge & Aurora)

Book 7.5: A Wilder Wedding (Amos & Naomi)

Book 8: Forever For Us (Wyatt & Ava)

Book 9: Pieces of Me (Gabriel & Briar)

Book 10: Endlessly Yours (Brooks & Rory)

The Falling for the Cassidy Brothers Series:

(Formerly the First Time Series)

Book 1: Good Time Boyfriend (Heath & Devney)

Book 2: Last Minute Fiancé (Luca & Addison)

Book 3: Second Chance Husband (August & Paisley)

Montgomery Ink Denver:

Book 0.5: Ink Inspired (Shep & Shea)

Book 0.6: Ink Reunited (Sassy, Rare, and Ian)

Book 1: Delicate Ink (Austin & Sierra)

Book 1.5: Forever Ink (Callie & Morgan)

Book 2: Tempting Boundaries (Decker and Miranda)

Book 3: Harder than Words (Meghan & Luc)

Book 3.5: Finally Found You (Mason & Presley)

Book 4: Written in Ink (Griffin & Autumn)

Book 4.5: Hidden Ink (Hailey & Sloane)

Book 5: Ink Enduring (Maya, Jake, and Border)

Book 6: Ink Exposed (Alex & Tabby)

Book 6.5: Adoring Ink (Holly & Brody)

Book 6.6: Love, Honor, & Ink (Arianna & Harper)

Book 7: Inked Expressions (Storm & Everly)

Book 7.3: Dropout (Grayson & Kate)

Book 7.5: Executive Ink (Jax & Ashlynn)

Book 8: Inked Memories (Wes & Jillian)

Book 8.5: Inked Nights (Derek & Olivia)

Book 8.7: Second Chance Ink (Brandon & Lauren)

Book 8.5: Montgomery Midnight Kisses (Alex & Tabby Bonus(

Bonus: Inked Kingdom (Stone & Sarina)

Montgomery Ink: Colorado Springs

Book 1: Fallen Ink (Adrienne & Mace)

Book 2: Restless Ink (Thea & Dimitri)

Book 2.5: Ashes to Ink (Abby & Ryan)

Book 3: Jagged Ink (Roxie & Carter)

Book 3.5: Ink by Numbers (Landon & Kaylee)

The Montgomery Ink: Boulder Series:

Book 1: Wrapped in Ink (Liam & Arden)

Book 2: Sated in Ink (Ethan, Lincoln, and Holland)

Book 3: Embraced in Ink (Bristol & Marcus)
Book 3: Moments in Ink (Zia & Meredith)
Book 4: Seduced in Ink (Aaron & Madison)
Book 4.5: Captured in Ink (Julia, Ronin, & Kincaid)
Book 4.7: Inked Fantasy (Secret ??)
Book 4.8: A Very Montgomery Christmas (The Entire Boulder Family)

The Montgomery Ink: Fort Collins Series:

Book 1: Inked Persuasion (Jacob & Annabelle)
Book 2: Inked Obsession (Beckett & Eliza)
Book 3: Inked Devotion (Benjamin & Brenna)
Book 3.5: Nothing But Ink (Clay & Riggs)
Book 4: Inked Craving (Lee & Paige)
Book 5: Inked Temptation (Archer & Killian)

The Promise Me Series:

Book 1: Forever Only Once (Cross & Hazel)
Book 2: From That Moment (Prior & Paris)
Book 3: Far From Destined (Macon & Dakota)
Book 4: From Our First (Nate & Myra)

The Whiskey and Lies Series:

Book 1: Whiskey Secrets (Dare & Kenzie)
Book 2: Whiskey Reveals (Fox & Melody)
Book 3: Whiskey Undone (Loch & Ainsley)

The Gallagher Brothers Series:

Book 1: Love Restored (Graham & Blake)

Book 2: Passion Restored (Owen & Liz)

Book 3: Hope Restored (Murphy & Tessa)

The Carr Family Series:

(Formerly the Less Than Series)

Book 1: Breathless With Her (Devin & Erin)

Book 2: Reckless With You (Tucker & Amelia)

Book 3: Shameless With Him (Caleb & Zoey)

The Fractured Connections Series:

Book 1: Breaking Without You (Cameron & Violet)

Book 2: Shouldn't Have You (Brendon & Harmony)

Book 3: Falling With You (Aiden & Sienna)

Book 4: Taken With You (Beckham & Meadow)

The Campus Roommates Series:

(Formerly the On My Own Series)

Book 0.5: My First Glance

Book 1: My One Night (Dillon & Elise)

Book 2: My Rebound (Pacey & Mackenzie)

Book 3: My Next Play (Miles & Nessa)

Book 4: My Bad Decisions (Tanner & Natalie)

The Ravenwood Coven Series:

Book 1: Dawn Unearthed

Book 2: Dusk Unveiled
Book 3: Evernight Unleashed

The Aspen Pack Series:

Book 1: Etched in Honor
Book 2: Hunted in Darkness
Book 3: Mated in Chaos
Book 4: Harbored in Silence
Book 5: Marked in Flames

The Talon Pack:

Book 1: Tattered Loyalties
Book 2: An Alpha's Choice
Book 3: Mated in Mist
Book 4: Wolf Betrayed
Book 5: Fractured Silence
Book 6: Destiny Disgraced
Book 7: Eternal Mourning
Book 8: Strength Enduring
Book 9: Forever Broken
Book 10: Mated in Darkness
Book 11: Fated in Winter

Redwood Pack Series:

Book 0.5: An Alpha's Path
Book 1: A Taste for a Mate
Book 2: Trinity Bound

Book 2.5: A Night Away
Book 3: Enforcer's Redemption
Book 3.5: Blurred Expectations
Book 3.7: Forgiveness
Book 4: Shattered Emotions
Book 5: Hidden Destiny
Book 5.5: A Beta's Haven
Book 6: Fighting Fate
Book 6.5: Loving the Omega
Book 6.7: The Hunted Heart
Book 7: Wicked Wolf

The Elements of Five Series:

Book 1: From Breath and Ruin
Book 2: From Flame and Ash
Book 3: From Spirit and Binding
Book 4: From Shadow and Silence

Dante's Circle Series:

Book 1: Dust of My Wings
Book 2: Her Warriors' Three Wishes
Book 3: An Unlucky Moon
Book 3.5: His Choice
Book 4: Tangled Innocence
Book 5: Fierce Enchantment
Book 6: An Immortal's Song
Book 7: Prowled Darkness

Book 8: Dante's Circle Reborn

Holiday, Montana Series:

Book 1: Charmed Spirits
Book 2: Santa's Executive
Book 3: Finding Abigail
Book 4: Her Lucky Love
Book 5: Dreams of Ivory

The Branded Pack Series:
(Written with Alexandra Ivy)

Book 1: Stolen and Forgiven
Book 2: Abandoned and Unseen
Book 3: Buried and Shadowed

From One Way Back to Me

ELI

When my morning begins with me standing ankle-deep in a basement full of water, I know I probably should have stayed in bed. Only, I was the boss, and I didn't get that choice.

"Hold on. I'm looking for it." East cursed underneath his breath as my younger brother bent down around the pipe, trying his best to turn off the valve. I sighed, waded through the muck in my work boots, and moved to help him. "I said I've got it," East snapped, but I ignored him.

I narrowed my eyes at the evil pipe. "It's old and rusted, and even though it passed an inspection over a year ago, we knew this was going to be a problem."

"And I'm the fucking handyman of this company. I've got this."

"And as a handyman, you need a hand."

"You're hilarious. Seriously. I don't know how I could ever manage without your wit and humor." The dryness in his tone made my lips twitch even as I did my best to ignore the smell of whatever water we stood in.

"Fuck you," I growled.

"No thanks. I'm a little too busy for that."

With a grunt, East shut off the water, and we both stood back, hands on our hips as we stared at the mess of this basement.

East let out a sigh. "I'm not going to have to turn the water off for the whole property, but I'm glad that we don't have tenants in this particular cabin."

I nodded tightly and held back a sigh. "This is probably why there aren't basements in Texas. Because everything seems to go wrong in these things."

"I'm pretty sure this is a storm shelter, or at least a tornado one. Not quite sure as it's one of the only basements in the area."

"It was probably the only one that they had the energy to make back in the day. Considering this whole place is built over clay and limestone."

East nodded, looked around. "I'll start the cleanup with this water, and we'll look to see what we can do with the pipes."

I pinched the bridge of my nose. "I don't want to have to replace the plumbing for this whole place."

"At least it's not the villa itself, or the farmhouse, or the winery. Just a single cabin."

I glared at my younger brother, then reached out and knocked on a wooden pillar. "Shut your mouth. Don't say things like that to me. We are just now getting our feet under us."

East shrugged. "It's the truth, though. However much you weigh it, it could have been worse."

I pinched the bridge of my nose. "Jesus Christ. You were in the military for how long? A Wilder your entire life, and you say things like that? When the hell did you lose that superstition bone?"

"About the time that my Humvee was blown up, and when Evan's was, Everett's too. Hell, about the time that you almost fell out of the sky in your plane. Or when Elliot was nearly shot to death trying to help one of his men. So, yes, I pretty much lost all superstition when trying to toe the line ended up in near death and maiming."

I met my brother's gaze, that familiar pang thinking about all that we had lost and almost lost over the past few years.

East muttered under his breath, shaking his head. "And I sound more and more like Evan these days rather than myself."

I squeezed his shoulder and let out a breath, thinking of our brother who grunted more than spoke these days. "It's okay. We've been through a lot. But we're here."

Somehow, we were here. I wasn't quite sure if we had made the right decision about two years ago when we had formed this plan, or rather *I* had formed this plan, but there was no going back. We were in it, and we were going to have to find a way to make it work, flooded former tornado shelters and all.

East sighed. "I'll work on this now. Then I'll head on over to the main house. I have a few things to work on there."

"You know, we can hire you help. I know we had all the contractors and everything to work with us for some of the rebuilds and rehabs, but we can hire someone else for you on a day-to-day basis."

My brother shook his head. "We may be able to afford it, but I'd rather save that for a rainy day. Because when it rains, it pours here, and flash flooding is a major threat in this part of Texas." He winked as he said it, mixing his metaphors, and I just shook my head.

"You just let me know if you need it."

"You're the CEO, brother of mine, not the CFO. That's Everett."

"True, but we did talk about it so we can work on it." I paused, thinking about what other expenses might show up. "And what do you need to do with the villa?"

The villa was the main house where most things

happened on the property. It contained the lobby, library, and atrium. My apartment was also on the top floor, so I could be there for emergencies. Our innkeeper lived on the other side of the house, but I was in the main loft because this was my project, my baby.

My other brothers, all five of them, lived in cabins on the property. We lived together, worked together, ate together, and fought together. We were the Wilder brothers. It was what we did.

I had left to join the Air Force at seventeen, having graduated early, leaving behind my kid brothers and sister. After nearly twenty years of doing what we needed to in order to survive, we hadn't spent as much time with one another as I would have liked. We hadn't been stationed together, so we hadn't seen one another for longer than holidays or in passing.

But now we were together. At least most of us. So I was going to make this work, even if it killed me.

East finally answered my question. "I just have to fix a door that's a little too squeaky in one of the guestrooms. Not a big deal."

I raised a brow. "That's it?"

"It's one of the many things on my list. Thankfully, this place is big enough that I always have something to do. It's an unending list. And that the winery has its own team to work on all of that shit, because I'm not in the mood to learn to deal with any of the complicated machinery that comes with that world."

I snorted. "Honestly, same. I'm glad there are people that know what the fuck they're doing when it comes to wine making so that didn't have to be the two of us."

I left my brother to this job, knowing he liked time on his own, just like the rest of us did, and went to dry my boots. I was working by myself for most of the day, in interviews and other "boss business," as Elliot called it, so I had to focus and get clean.

I wasn't in the mood to deal with interviews, but it was part of my job. We had to fill positions that hadn't been working out over the past year, some more than others.

Wilder Retreat was a place that hadn't been even a spark in my mind my entire life. No, I had been too busy being a career military man—getting in my twenty, moving up the ranks, and ending up as a Lieutenant Colonel before I got out. I had been a commander of a squadron, and yet, it felt like I didn't know how to command where I was now.

When my sister Eliza had lost her husband when he was on deployment, it had been the last domino to fall in the Wilder brothers' military career. I had been ready to get out with twenty years in, knowing I needed a career outside of being a Lieutenant Colonel. I wasn't even forty yet, and the term retirement was a misnomer, but that's what happened when it came to my former job.

East had been getting out around that time for reasons of his own, and then Evan had been forced to. I rubbed my hand over my chest, that familiar pain, remembering the phone call from one of Evan's commanders when Evan had been hurt.

I thought I'd lost my baby brother then, and we nearly had. Everett had gotten hurt too, and Elijah and Elliot had needed out for their own reasons. Losing our baby sister's husband had just pushed us forward.

Finding out that Eliza's husband had been a cheating asshole had just cemented the fact that we needed to spend more time together as a family so we could be there for one another.

In retrospect, it would have been nice if Eliza would have been able to come down to Texas with us, to our suburb outside of San Antonio. Only, she had fallen in love again, with a man with a big family and a good heart up in Fort Collins, Colorado. She was still up there and traveled down enough that we actually got to get to know our sister again.

It was weird to think that, after so many years of always seeing each other in passing or through video calls, most of us were here, opening up a business. And all because I had been losing my mind.

Wilder Retreat and Winery was a villa and wedding

venue outside of San Antonio. We were in hill country, at least what passed for hill country in South Texas, and the place had been owned by a former Air Force General who had wanted to retire and sell the place, since his kid didn't want it.

It was a large spread that used to be a ranch back in the day, nearly one hundred acres that the original owners had taken from a working ranch, and instead of making it a dude ranch or something similar, like others did around here, they'd added a winery using local help. We were close enough to Fredericksburg that it made sense in terms of the soil and weather. They had been able to add on additions, so it wasn't just the winery. Someone could come for the day for a winery tour or even a retreat tour, but most people came for the weekend or for a whole week. There were cabins and a farmhouse where we held weddings, dances, or other events. We had some chickens and ducks that gave us eggs, and goats that seemed to have a mind of their own and provided milk for cheese. Then there was the main annex, which housed all the equipment for the retreat villa.

The winery had its own section of buildings, and it was far bigger than anything I would have ever thought that we could handle. But, between the six of us, we did.

And the only reason we could even afford it, because one didn't afford something like this on a military salary, even with a decent retirement plan, was because of our uncles.

Our uncles, Edward and Edmond Wilder, had owned Wilder Wines down in Napa, California, for years. They had done well for themselves, and when we had been kids, we had gone out to visit. Evan had been the one that had clung to it and had been interested in wine making before he had changed his mind and gone into the military like the rest of us.

That was why Evan was in charge of the winery itself now. Because he knew what he was doing, even if he'd growled and said he didn't. Either way though, the place was huge, had multiple working parts at all times, and we had a staff that needed us. But when the uncles had died, they had left the money from the sale of the winery to us in equal parts. Eliza had taken hers to invest for her future children, and the rest of us had pooled our money together to buy this place and make it ours. A lot of the staff from the old owner had stayed, but some had left as well. Because they didn't want new owners who had no idea what they were doing, or they just retired. Either way, we were over a year in and doing okay.

Except for two positions that made me want to groan.

I had an interview with who would be our third wedding planner since we started this. The main component of the retreat was to have an actual wedding venue. To be able to host parties, and not just wine tours. Elliot was our major event planner that helped with our yearly and seasonal minute details, but he didn't want anything to do with the actual weddings. That was a whole other skill set, and so we wanted a wedding planner. We had gone through two wedding planners now, and we needed to hire a third. The first one had lied on her résumé, had given references that were her friends who had lied and had even created websites that were all fabrication, all so she could get into the business. Which, I understood, getting into the business is one thing. However, lying was another. Plus, we needed someone with actual experience because we didn't have any ourselves. We were going out on a limb here with this whole retreat business, and it was all because I had the harebrained idea of getting our family to work together, get along, and get to know one another. I wanted us to have a future, to be our own bosses.

And it was so far over my head that I knew that if I didn't get reliable help, we were going to fail.

Later, I had a meeting with that potential wedding planner. But first, I had to see what the fuck that smell was coming from the main kitchen in the villa.

The second wedding planner we hired was a guy with great and *true* references, one who was good at his job but hated everything to do with my brothers and me. He had hated the idea of the retreat and how rustic it was, even though we were in fucking South Texas. Yes, the buildings look slightly European because that was the theme that the original owners had gone for. Still, the guy had hated us, hadn't listened to us, and had called us white trash before he had walked away, jumped into his convertible, and sped off down the road, leaving us without help. He had been rude to our guests, and now Elliot was the one having to plan weddings for the past three weeks. My brother was going to strangle me soon if we didn't hire someone. And this person was going to be our last hope. As soon as she showed up, that was.

I looked down on my watch and tried to plan the rest of my day. I had thirty minutes to figure out what the hell was going on in the kitchen, and then I had to go to the meeting.

I nodded at a few guests who were sipping wine and eating a cheese plate and then at our innkeeper, Naomi. Naomi's honey-brown hair was cut in an angled bob that lit her face, and she grinned at me.

"Hello there, Boss Man," she whispered. "You might need to go to the kitchen."

"Do I want to know?" I asked with a grumble.

"I'm not sure. But I am going to go check in our next guest, and then Elliott needs to meet with the Henderson couple."

"He'll be there." I didn't say that Elliot would rather chew off his own arm rather than deal with this, considering we had a family event coming in, one that Elliot was on target with planning. The wedding for next year was an important one, so we needed to work on it.

Naomi was a fantastic innkeeper, far more organized than any of us—and that was saying something since my brothers and I knew our way around schedules, to-do lists, and spreadsheets. Naomi was personable, smiled, and kept us on our toes.

Without her, I knew we wouldn't be able to do this. Hell, without Amos, our vineyard manager, I knew that Evan and Elijah wouldn't be able to handle the winery as they did. Naomi and Amos had come with the place when we had bought it, and I would be forever grateful that they had decided to stay on.

I gave Naomi another nod, then headed back to the kitchen and nearly walked right back out.

Tony stood there, a scowl on his face and his hands on his hips. "I don't understand what the fuck is wrong with this oven."

"What's going on?" I asked as Everett stood by Tony. Everett was my quiet brother with usually a small smile on his face, only right then it looked like he was ready to scream.

I didn't know why Everett was even there since he was part responsible for the financials side of the company and usually worked with Elliot these days. Maybe he had come to the kitchen after the smell of burning as I had after Naomi's prodding.

Tony threw his hands in the air. "What's going on? This stove is a piece of shit. All of it is a piece of shit. I'm tired of this rustic place. I thought I would be coming to a Michelin star restaurant. To be my own chef. Instead, I have to make English breakfasts and pancakes with bananas. I might as well be at a bed and breakfast."

I pinched the bridge of my nose. "We're an inn, not a bed and breakfast."

"But I serve breakfast. That's all I do these days. That and cheese platters. Nobody comes for dinner. Nobody comes for lunch."

That was a lie. Tony worked for the winery and the retreat itself and served all the meals. But Tony wanted to go crazy with the menu, to try new and fantastical items that just weren't going to work here.

And I had a feeling I was going to throw up if I wasn't careful.

"I quit," Tony snapped, and I knew right then, it was done for. I was done.

"You can't quit," I growled while Everett held back a sigh.

"Yes, I can. I'm done. I'm done with you and this ranch. You're not cowboys. You're not even Texans. You're just people moving in on our territory." And with that, Tony stomped away, throwing his chef's apron on the ground.

I was thankful that the kitchen was on the other side

of the library and front area, where most of the guests were if they weren't out on one of the tours of the area and city that Elliott had arranged for them. That was the whole point of this retreat. They could come visit, and could relax, or we could set them up on a tour of downtown San Antonio, or Canyon Lake, or any of the other places that were nearby.

And yet, Tony had just thrown a wrench into all of that. I didn't know what was worse, the smell of burning, Tony leaving, the water in the basement that wasn't truly a basement, or the fact that I was going to smell like charred food and wet jeans when I went to go meet this wedding planner.

"You're going to need to hire a new cook," Everett whispered.

I looked at my brother, at the man who did his best to make sure we didn't go bankrupt, and I wanted to just grumble. "I figured."

"I can help for now, but you know I'm only part-time. I can't stay away from my twins for too long," Sandy said as she came forward to take the pan off the stove. "I wish I could do full time, but this is all I can do for now."

Sandy had come back from maternity leave after we had already opened the retreat. She had been on with the former owners and was brilliant. But she had a right to be a mom and not want to work full time. I understood that, and I knew that Sandy didn't want to handle a whole kitchen by herself. She liked her position as a sous chef.

I was going to have to figure out what to do. Again.

"I'll get it done," I said while rubbing my temples.

"You know what we need to do," Everett whispered, and I shook my head.

"He'll kill us."

"Maybe, but it'll be worth it in the end. And speaking of, don't you have that interview soon? Or do you want me to take it?" His gaze tracked to my jeans.

I shook my head. "No, help Sandy."

Everett winced. "Just because I know how to slice an onion, it doesn't mean I'm good at cooking."

"I'm sorry, did you just say you could slice an onion? Get to it," Sandy put in with a smile, pointing at the sink. "Wash those hands."

"I cannot believe I just said that out loud. I just stepped right into it," Everett said with a sigh. "Go to the interview. You know what to ask."

"I do. And I hope we don't get screwed this time."

"You know, if we're lucky, we'll get someone as good as Roy's wedding planner, or at least that woman that we met. You know who she is." Everett grinned like a cat with the canary.

I narrowed my eyes. "Don't bring her up."

"Oh, I can't help it. A single dance, and you were drawn to her."

"What dance? You know what? No, I don't have time. We have to work on lunch and dinner. Tell me while you work," Sandy added with a wink.

Everett leaned toward her as he washed his hands. "Well, you see, there was this dance, and he met the perfect woman, and then she got engaged."

Sandy's eyes widened. "Engaged? How did that happen? She was dating someone else?" she asked as she looked at me.

I pinched the bridge of my nose. "It was at Roy's place when we were looking at the venue to see if we wanted to buy the retreat here." I sighed, I knew if I just let it all out, she would move on from this conversation, and I would never have to deal with it again. "Somehow, I ended up at a wedding there, caught the garter. This woman caught the bouquet, and she happened to be the wedding planner. We danced, we laughed, and as she walked away, her boyfriend got down on one knee and proposed."

"No way!" She leaned forward with a fierce look on her face, her eyes bright. "What did she say?"

"I have no clue. I left." I ignored whatever feeling might want to show up at that thought. Everett gave me a glance, and I shook my head. "Enough of that. Yes, the wedding that she did was great, but I honestly have no idea who she is, and she has a job. She doesn't need to work here." And I didn't know what I would do if I saw her again or had to work with her. There had been such an intense connection that I knew it would be awkward as hell. But thankfully, she had her own business and wasn't going to come to the Wilder Retreat for a job.

I left Sandy and Everett on their own, knowing that they were capable, at least for now. And I knew who we would have to hire if she said yes, and if my other brother didn't kill me first.

I washed my hands in the sink on the way out, grateful that at least I looked somewhat decent, if not a little disheveled, and made my way out front, hoping that the wedding planner who came in through the doors would be the one that would stick. Because we needed some good luck. After the day we've had, we needed some good luck.

I turned the corner and nearly tripped over my feet.

Because, of course, fate was this way.

It was her.

Of all the wedding planners from all the wedding venues, it was her.

In the mood to read another family saga? Meet the Wilder Brothers in One Way Back to Me!

From Bittersweet Promises

LEIF

"NOT ONLY DID YOU CONVINCE ME TO SOMEHOW go on a blind date, it became a double date. How on earth did you work this magic on me, cousin?" I asked Lake as she leaned against the pillar just inside the restaurant.

Lake grinned at me, her dark hair pulled away from her face. She had on this swingy black dress and looked as if she were excited, anxious, nervous, and happy all at the same time. Considering she was bouncing on her toes when usually Lake was calm, cool, and collected, was saying something. "I asked, and you said yes. Because you love me."

"I might love you because we're family, but I still think we're making a mistake." I shook my head and pulled at my shirt sleeves. Lake had somehow convinced me to wear a button-up shirt tucked into gray pants, I even had on shiny shoes. I looked like a damn banker. But if that's what Lake wanted, that's what I would do.

Lake might technically be my cousin, even though we weren't blood-related, but we were more like brother and sister than any of my other cousins.

I had siblings, as did Lake, but with the generational gap, we were at least a decade older than all of our other cousins. That meant, despite the fact that we had lived over an hour apart for most of our lives, we'd grown up more like siblings.

I loved my three younger siblings and talked to them daily. Unlike some blended families, they *were* my brothers and sister and not like strangers or distant family members. I didn't feel a disconnect from the three of them, but Lake was still closer to me.

Probably because we were either heading into our thirties or already there, where most of our other cousins were either just now in their early twenties or still teenagers in high school. With how big we Montgomerys were as a family, it made sense that there would be such a widespread age group. That meant that Lake and I were best friends, cousins, practically siblings, and sometimes the banes of each other's existences.

We were also business owners and partners and saw each other too often these days. That was probably why she convinced me to go on a blind double date. But she had been out with Zach before. I, however, had never met

May. Lake had some connection with her that I wasn't sure about, and for some reason Lake's date had said yes to this double date.

And, in the complicated way of family, I had agreed to it. I must have been tired. Or perhaps I'd had too many beers. Because I didn't do blind dates, and recently, I didn't do dates at all.

Lake scanned her phone, then looked up at me, all innocence in her smart gaze. "You shouldn't have told me you wanted to settle down in your old age."

I narrowed my eyes. "I'm still in my early thirties, jerk. Stop calling me old."

"I shouldn't call you old since you're only a few years older than me." She fluttered her eyelashes and I flipped her off, ignoring the stare from the older woman next to me. Though I was a tattoo artist, I didn't have many visible tattoos. Most of mine were on my back and legs, hidden from the world unless I wanted to show them. I hadn't figured out what I wanted on my arms beyond a few small pieces on my wrists and upper shoulders. And since tattoos were permanent, I was taking my time. If a client needed to see my skin with ink to feel comfortable, I'd show them my back. My body was a canvas, so I did what I could to set people at ease.

But I still had the eyebrow piercing and had recently taken out my nose ring. I didn't look too scary for most people. But apparently, flipping off a woman, growling, and cursing a time or two in front of strangers probably made me appear too close to the dark side.

"Yes, I want to settle down, but this will be awkward, won't it? Where the two of us are strangers, and the two of you aren't?" I wanted a life, a future, and yeah, one day to settle down with someone. I just didn't know why I'd mentioned it to Lake in the first place.

"If it helps, May doesn't know Zach, either. So it's a group of strangers, except I know everybody." She clapped her hands together and did her version of an evil laugh, and I just shook my head.

"Considering what you do for a living and how you like to manipulate things in your way, this makes sense. Are you going to be adding a matchmaking company to your conglomerate?"

Lake just fluttered her eyelashes again and laughed. Lake owned a small tech company that made a shit ton of money over the past couple of years. And because she was brilliant at what she did, innovative, and liked pushing money towards women-owned businesses, she owned more than one company at this point and was an investor in mine. I wouldn't be surprised if she found a way to open up a women-owned matchmaking company right here in town.

"It might be fun. I can call it Montgomery Links." Her eyes went wide. "Oh, my God. I have to write that down." She pulled out her phone, began to take notes, and I pinched the bridge of my nose.

"You know I trust you with my actual life, but I don't know if I trust you with my dating life."

Lake tossed her hair behind her shoulder as she continued to type. "Shut up. You love me. And once I finish setting you up, the rest of the family's next."

"Oh, really? You're going to get Daisy and Noah next?" I asked, speaking of two more of our cousins.

"Maybe. Of course, Sebastian's the only one of the younger group that seems to have a serious girlfriend."

I nodded, speaking of our other familial business partner. Sebastian was still a teenager, though in college. He had wanted to open up Montgomery Ink Legacy with me, the full title of our company. There was a legacy to it, and Sebastian had wanted in. So, though he didn't work there full-time, he was putting his future towards us. And in the ways of young love, he and his girlfriend had been together since middle school. The fact that my younger cousin was better at relationships than I was didn't make me feel great. But I was going to ignore that.

"You're not going to start up a matchmaking service, are you? Or maybe an app?"

"Dating apps are ridiculous these days, they practically want you to invest in coins to bid on dates, and that's not something I'm in the mood for. But maybe there's something I can try. I'll add it to my list."

Lake's list of inventions and tech was notorious, and knowing the brilliance of my cousin, she would one day rule the world and might eventually cross everything off that list.

"Oh, here's Zach." Lake's face brightened immediately, and she smiled up at a man with dark hair, piercing gray eyes, and an actual dimple on his cheek.

Tonight was not only about my blind date, but me getting the lay of the land when it came to Zach. I was the first step into meeting the family. Oh, if Zach passed my gauntlet, he would meet the rest of the Montgomerys, and we were mighty. All one hundred of us.

"Zach, you're here." Lake's voice went soft, and she went on her tiptoes even in her high heels as Zach pressed a soft kiss to her lips.

"Of course, I'm here. And you're early, as usual."

Lake blushed and ducked her head. "Well, you know me. I like to be early because being on time is late," she said at the same time I did, mumbling under my breath. It was a familiar refrain when it came to us.

"Zach, good to meet you," I said, holding out my hand.

The other man gripped it firmly and shook. "Nice to meet you too, Leif. I know you might be the one on a blind date soon, but I'm nervous."

I chuckled, shaking my head. "Yeah, I'm pretty

nervous too. Though I'm grateful that Lake's trying to look out for me."

My cousin laughed softly. "You totally were not saying that a few minutes ago, but be suave and sophisticated now. Or just be yourself, May's on her way."

I met Zach's gaze and we both rolled our eyes. When I turned toward the door, I saw a woman of average height, with black straight hair, green eyes, and a sweet smile. I didn't know much about May, other than Lake knew her and liked her. If I was going to start dating again after taking time off to get the rest of my life together, I might as well start with someone that one of my best friends liked.

"May, I'm so glad that you're here," Lake said as she hugged the other woman tightly.

As Lake began to bounce on her heels, I realized that my cousin's cool, calm, and collected exterior was only for work. She was bouncing and happy when it came to her friends or when she was nervous. I knew that, of course, but I had forgotten how she had turned into the mogul that she was. It was good to see her relaxed and happy.

Now I just needed to figure out how to do that for myself.

May stood in front of me, and I felt like I was starting middle school all over again. A new school, a new life, and a past that didn't make much sense to anyone else.

I swallowed hard and nodded, not putting out my

hand to shake, thinking that would be weird, but I also didn't want to hug her. I didn't even know this woman. Why was everything so awkward? Instead, I lifted my chin. "Hello, May. It's nice to meet you. Lake says only good things."

There, smooth. Not really. Zach began to move out of frame, with Lake at his side as the two went to speak to the hostess, leaving May and me alone.

This wasn't going to be awkward at all.

The woman just smiled at me, her eyes wide. "It's nice to meet you, too. And Lake does speak highly of you. Also, this is very awkward, so I'm so sorry if I say something stupid. I know that your cousin said that I should be set up with you which is great but I'm not great at blind dates and apparently this is a double date and now I'm going to stop talking." She said the words so quickly they all ran into one breath.

I shook my head and laughed. "We're on the same page there."

"Okay, good. It's nice to meet you, Leif Montgomery."

"And it's nice to meet you too, May."

We made our way to Lake and Zach, who had gotten our table, and we all sat down, talking about work and other things. May was in child life development, taught online classes, and was also a nanny.

"I'm actually about to start with a new family soon.

I'm excited. I know that being a nanny isn't something that most people strive for, or at least that's what they tell you, but I love being able to work with children and be the person that is there when a single parent or even both parents are out in the workforce, trying to do everything."

I nodded, taking a sip of my beer. "I get you completely. With how my parents worked, I was lucky that they were able to get childcare within the buildings. Since they each owned their own businesses, they made it work. But my family worked long hours, and that's why I ended up being the babysitter a lot of the times when childcare wasn't an option." I cleared my throat. "I'm a lot older than a lot of my cousins," I added.

"Both of us are, but I'm glad that you only said yourself," Lake said, grinning. She leaned into Zach as she spoke, the four of us in a horseshoe-shaped booth. That gave May and me space since this was a first date and still awkward as hell, and so Lake and Zach could cuddle. Not that that was something I needed to be a part of.

"Oh, I'm glad that you didn't judge. The last few dates that I've been on they always gave me weird looks because I think they expected a nanny to be this old crone or someone that's looking for a different job." She shrugged and continued. "When I eventually get married and maybe even start a family, I want to continue my job. I like being there to help another family achieve their goals. And I can't believe I just said start a family on my first date.

And that I mentioned that I've been on a few other dates." She let out a breath. "I'm notoriously bad at dating. Like, the worst. Just warning you."

I laughed, shaking my head. "I'm rusty at it, so don't worry." And even though I said that, I had a feeling that May felt no spark towards me, and I didn't feel anything towards her. She was nice and pleasant, and I could probably consider her a friend one day. But there wasn't any spark. May's eyes weren't dancing. She wasn't leaning forward, trying to touch my hand across the table. We were just sitting there casually, enjoying a really good steak, as Lake and Zach enjoyed their date.

By the end of dinner, I didn't want dessert, and neither did May, so we said goodbye to the other couple, who decided to stay. I walked May to her car, ignoring Lake's warning look, but I didn't know what exactly she was warning me about.

"Thanks for dinner," May said. "I could have paid. I know this is a blind date and all that, but you didn't have to pay."

I shook my head. "I paid for the four of us because I wanted to be nice. I'll make Lake pay next time."

May beamed. "Yes, I like that. You guys are a good family."

"Anyway," I said, clearing my throat as I stuck my hands in my pockets. "I guess I'll see you around."

May just looked at me, threw her head back, and laughed. "You're right. You are rusty at this."

"Sorry." Heat flushed my skin, and I resisted the urge to tug on my eyebrow ring.

"It's okay. No spark. I'm used to it. I don't spark well."

"May, I'm sorry." I cringed. "It's not you."

"Oh, God, please don't say that. 'It's not you. It's me. You're working on yourself. You're just so busy with work.' I've heard it all."

"Seriously?" I asked. May was hot. Nice, but there just wasn't a spark.

She shrugged. "It's okay. I'll probably see you around sometime because I am friends with Lake. However, I am perfectly fine having this be our one and only. You'll find your person. It's okay that it's not me." And with that, she got in the car and left, leaving me standing there.

Well then. Tonight wasn't horrible, but it wasn't great. I got in my car, and instead of heading home where I'd be alone, watching something on some streaming service while I drank a beer and pretended that I knew what I was doing with my life, I headed into Montgomery Ink Legacy.

We were the third branch of the company and the first owned by our generation. Montgomery Ink was the tattoo shop in downtown Denver. While there were open spots for some walk-ins and special circumstances, my father, aunt, and their team had years' worth of waiting lists.

They worked their asses off and made sure to get in everybody that they could, but people wanted Austin Montgomery's art. Same with my aunt, Maya.

There was another tattoo shop down in Colorado Springs, owned by my parents' cousins, who I just called aunt and uncle because we were close enough that using real titles for everybody got confusing. Montgomery Ink Too was thriving down there, and they had waiting lists as well. My family could have opened more shops and gone nationwide, even global if they wanted to, but they liked keeping it how it was, in the family and those connected.

We were a branch, but our own in the making. I had gone into business with Lake, of course, and Sebastian, when he was ready, as well as Nick. Nick was my best friend. I had known him for ages, and he had wanted to be part of something as well. He might not be a Montgomery by name, but he had eaten over at my family's house enough times throughout the years that he was practically a Montgomery. And he had invested in the company as well, and so now we were nearly a year into owning the shop and trying not to fail.

I pulled into the parking lot, grateful it was still open since we didn't close until nine most nights, and greeted Nick, who was still working.

Sebastian was in the back, going over sketches with a client, and I nodded at him. He might be eighteen, but he was still in training, an apprentice, and was working his ass off to learn.

"Date sucked then?" Sebastian asked, and Nick just rolled his eyes and went back to work on a client's wrist.

"I don't want to talk about it," I groaned.

The rest of the staff was off since Nick would close up on his own. Sebastian was just there since he didn't have homework or a date with Marley.

"Was she hot at least?" Sebastian asked, and the client, a woman in her sixties, bopped him on the head with her bag gently.

"Sebastian Montgomery. Be nice."

Sebastian blushed. "Sorry, Mrs. Anderson."

I looked over at the woman and grinned. "Hi, Mrs. Anderson. It's nice to see you out of the classroom."

She narrowed her eyes at me, even though they filled with laughter. "I needed my next Jane Austen tattoo, thank you very much," the older woman said as she went back to working with Sebastian. She had been my and then Sebastian's English teacher. The fact that she was on her fifth tattoo with some literary quote told me that I had been damn lucky in most of my teachers growing up.

She was kick-ass, and I had a feeling that she would let Sebastian do the tattoo for her rather than just have him work on the design with me as we did for most of the people who came in. He had learned under my father and was working under me now. It was strange to think that he wasn't a little kid anymore. But he was in a long-term relationship, kicking ass in college, and knew what he wanted to do with his life.

I might know what I want to do with my work life, but everything else seemed a little off.

"So it didn't work out?" Nick asked as he walked up to the front desk with the clients after going over aftercare.

"Not really," I said, looking down at my phone.

The client, a woman in her mid-twenties with bright pink hair, a lip ring, and kind eyes, leaned over the desk to look at me.

"You'll find someone, Leif. Don't worry."

I looked at our regular and shook my head. "Thanks, Kim. Too bad that you don't swing this way."

I winked as I said it, a familiar refrain from both of us.

Kim was married to a woman named Sonya, and the two of them were happy and working on in vitro with donated sperm for their first kid.

"Hey, I'm sorry too that I'm a lesbian. I'll never know what it means to have Leif Montgomery. Or any Montgomery, since I found my love far too quickly. I mean, what am I ever going to do not knowing the love of a Montgomery?"

Mrs. Anderson chuckled from her chair, Sebastian held back a snort, and I just looked at Nick, who rolled his eyes and helped Kim out of the place.

I was tired, but it was okay. The date wasn't all bad. May was nice. But it felt like I didn't have much right then.

And then Nick sat in front of me, scowled, and I realized that I did have something. I had my friends and my family. I didn't need much more.

"So, you and May didn't work out?"

I raised a brow. "You knew her name? Did I tell you that?"

Nick shook his head. "Lake did."

That made sense, considering the two of them spoke as much as we did. "So, was it your idea to set me up on a blind date?"

"Fuck no. That was all Lake. I just do what she says. Like we all do."

I sighed and went through my appointments for the next day. "We're busy for the next month. That's good, right?" I asked.

"You're the business genius here. I just play with ink. But yes, that's good. Now, don't let your cousin set you up any more dates. Find them for yourself. You know what you're doing."

"So says the man who dates less than me."

"That's what you think. I'm more private about it. As it should be." I flipped him off as he stood up, then he gestured towards a stack of bills in the corner. "You have a few personal things that made their way here.

Don't want you to miss out on them before you head home."

"Thanks, bro."

"No problem. I'm going to help Sebastian with his consult, and then I'll clean up. You should head home. Though you're doing it alone, so I feel sorry for you."

"Fuck you," I called out.

"Fuck you, too."

"Boys," Mrs. Anderson said, in that familiar English teacher refrain, and both Nick and I cringed before saying, "Sorry," simultaneously.

Sebastian snickered, then went back to work, and I headed towards the edge of the counter, picking up the stack of papers. Most were bills, some were random papers that needed to be filed or looked over. Some were just junk mail. But there was one letter, written in block print that didn't look familiar. Chills went up my spine and I opened it, wondering what the fuck this was. Maybe it was someone asking to buy my house. I got a lot of handwritten letters for that, but I didn't think this was going to be that. I swallowed hard, slid open the paper, and froze.

"I'll find you, boy. Oops. Looks like I already did. Be waiting. I know you miss me."

I let the paper hit the top of the counter and swallowed hard, trying to remain cool so I didn't worry anyone else.

I didn't know exactly who that was from, but I had a horrible feeling that they wouldn't wait long to tell me.

Read the rest in Bittersweet Promises! OUT NOW!

About the Author

Carrie Ann Ryan is the New York Times and USA Today bestselling author of contemporary, paranormal, and young adult romance. Her works include the Montgomery Ink, Redwood Pack, Fractured Connections, and Elements of Five series, which have sold over 3.0 million books worldwide. She started writing while in graduate school for her advanced degree in chemistry and hasn't stopped since. Carrie Ann has written over seventy-five novels and novellas with more in the works. When she's not losing herself in her emotional and action-packed worlds, she's reading as much as she can while wrangling her clowder of cats who have more followers than she does.

www.CarrieAnnRyan.com

www.ingramcontent.com/pod-product-compliance
Lightning Source LLC
Chambersburg PA
CBHW010545110826
49663CB00039B/582
9781636957203